I0766073

The
Lost

Their Champion Companion Novel

K.A. Knight

The Lost (Their Champion Companion Novel)

Copyright © 2020 K.A. Knight, all rights reserved: Written by K.A. Knight

This is a work of fiction. Any resemblance to places, events or real people are entirely coincidental.

All rights reserved.

No part of this book may be reproduced in any form or by any electronic or mechanical means, including information storage and retrieval systems, without written permission from the author, except for the use of brief quotations in a book review.

Edited By Jess from Elemental Editing and Proofreading.

Formatted by The Nutty Formatter.

Art by Dily Iola Designs

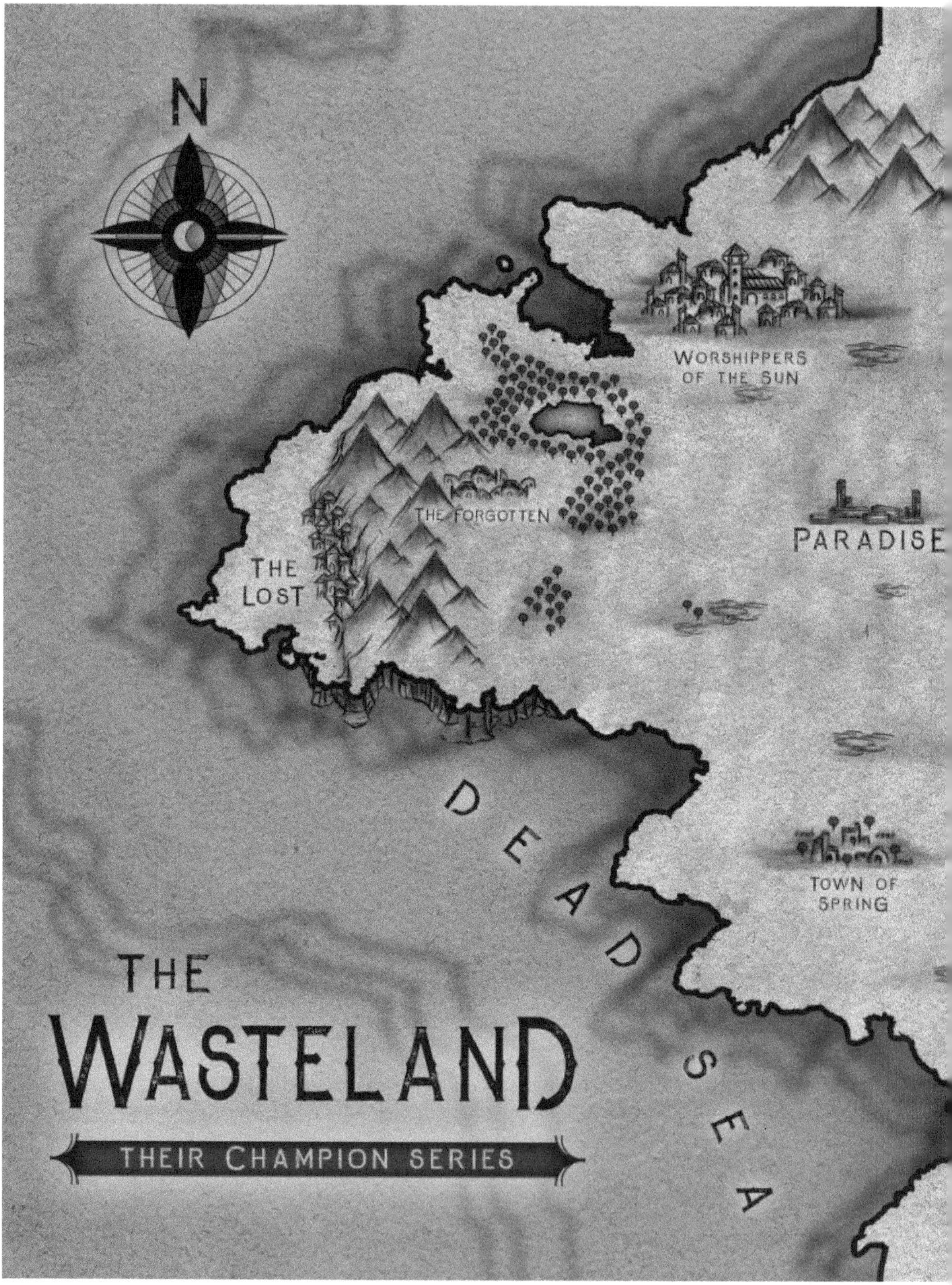

N

WORSHIPPERS
OF THE SUN

THE FORGOTTEN

THE
LOST

PARADISE

D E A D   S E A

TOWN OF
SPRING

THE
WASTELAND

THEIR CHAMPION SERIES

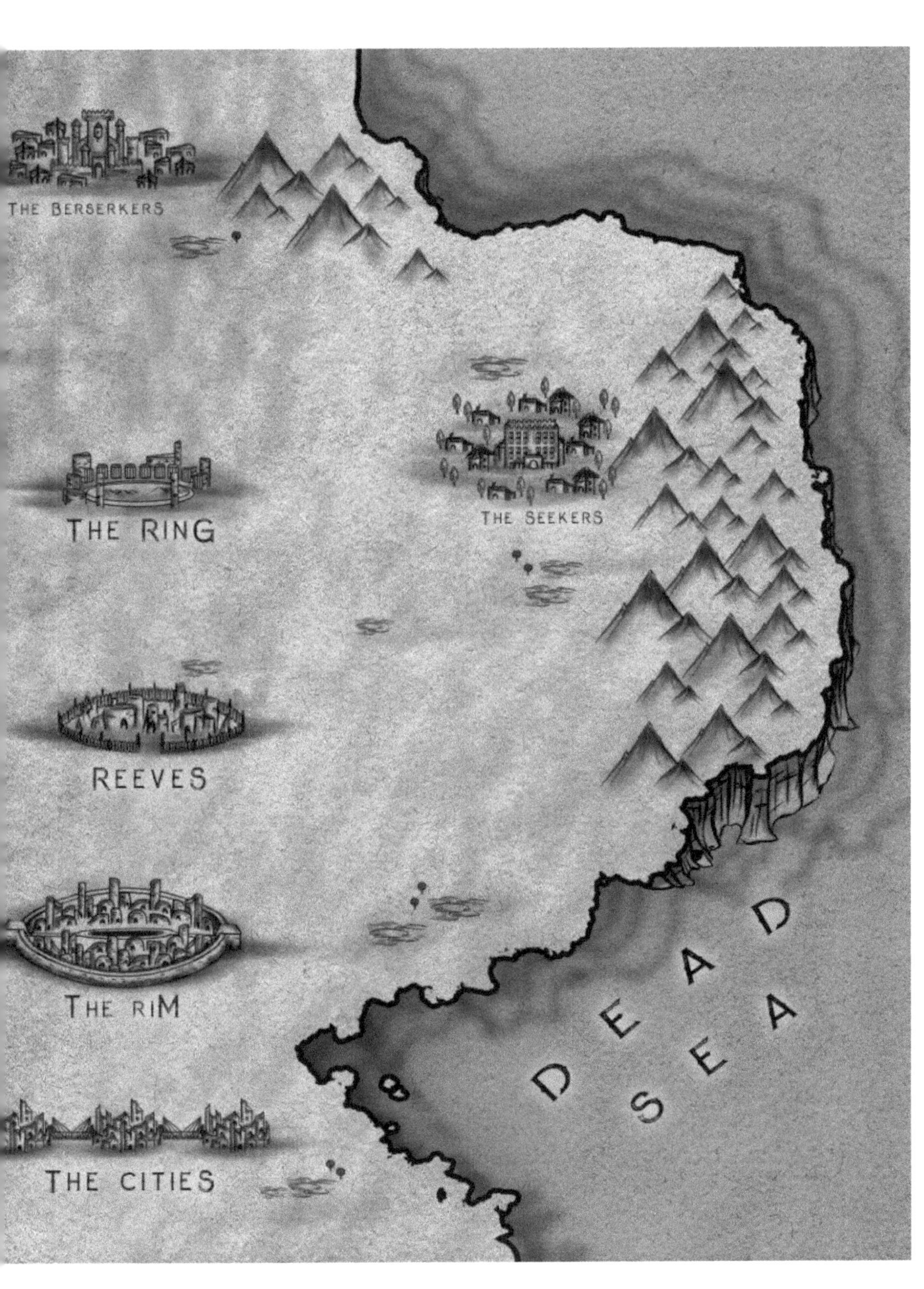

THE BERSERKERS
THE RING
THE SEEKERS
REEVES
THE RIM
THE CITIES
DEAD SEA

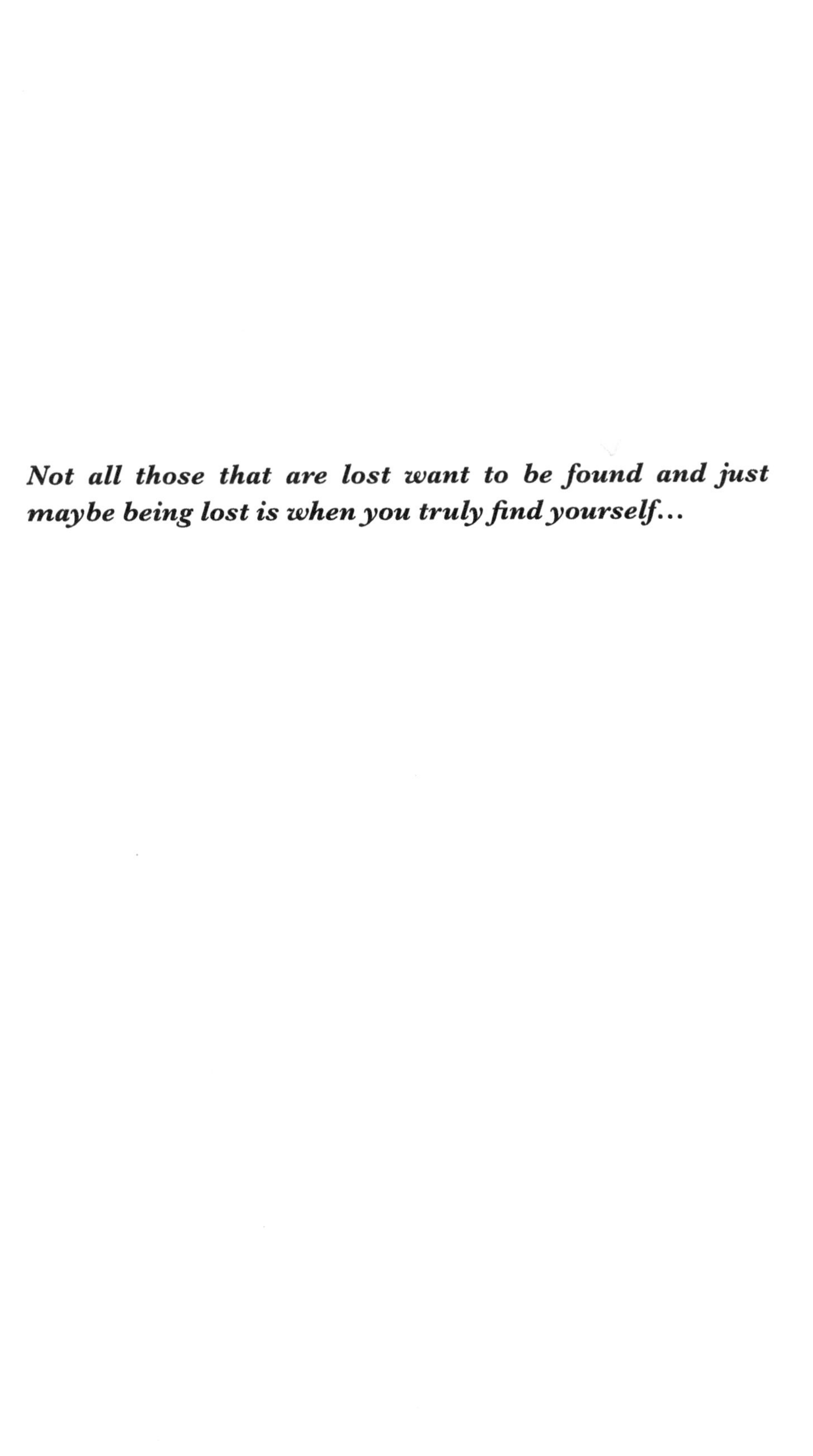

Not all those that are lost want to be found and just maybe being lost is when you truly find yourself...

Chapter 1
Lady Boner

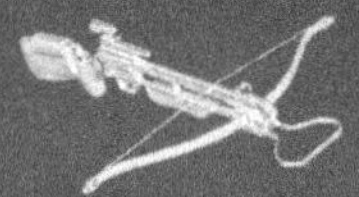

"Silence!" Trev screams, as the gathered Forgotten start to talk over the tribesman who is still bent over, recovering after delivering his message about Paradise falling.

I look at Trev. "We need quiet. I say just you and me talk to the tribesman, find out what has happened," I suggest and he nods.

"Everyone, listen up, you have your orders. This changes nothing! Simon, Piper, and—" He looks over at Jago, who steps closer to me.

"I go where she goes," he growls and Trev smiles, throwing me an amused look.

"And Jago with me and the scout. We will find out everything and decide on a course of action. Until then, back to work!" he yells, and the gathered tribesman finally break away, but they look angry and confused. I know the feeling.

Paradise has fallen.

That's what he said...Evan. God, Evan, please be okay.

We head back to the tent we just left, Jago sticking close to me until we get seated back inside. The scout stands in the middle of the room, guzzling water and breathing heavily as he gazes around at us.

"Go ahead, son, tell us everything," Trev encourages. We are all waiting, though not patiently.

"I was scouting far out, on the three-day food run, when we heard about it. It was a messenger, a clan member. He was racing to somewhere else to tell them that Paradise had fallen, it had been attacked by Berserkers."

Berserkers? I remember Archel telling me about them. This can't be good.

"Anything else? Any other survivors?" I ask, leaning forward, Ev's face flashing in my mind as my heart squeezes.

"I don't know, that's all I heard, the attack couldn't have happened long before the messenger left," he explains, swallowing and watching us.

"Thank you, dismissed, go get some food and a seat," Trev tells him, and the man nods, scurrying out of the tent as we turn to look at each other.

"What do we do?" I ask.

"I don't know, we just agreed to secure our home and train our people. If we leave now, and head into an attack no less, we are putting this place in danger. What are your thoughts, Piper? You were there last."

I glance at the floor, trying to sort through my thoughts, but all I keep seeing is Evan. "I don't know." Looking up, I meet his eyes. "You're right, I think. Archel told me about the Berserkers, they are fighters, the best...we have no hope against them if they are still there, but what if they aren't and people need our help?"

"Did they help us?" Trev counters, not harshly, but just querying.

I look away then. He's right and I have more to think about now than just me. These people look to me, listen to me, and that is a heavy responsibility. I can't run off into danger...I'm not a child anymore. "I think we should continue with the plan and send out more scouts, see what they find, that way it's only a few lives in danger instead of many, and in that time, we train and secure. Only then do we make a decision," I suggest, looking between Trev and Jago.

"That's a good plan, Brawler." Jago nods and I glance at Trev.

"I agree, we will send more scouts and stick to our plan. We will not cause panic in our people, not for this." He nods, smiling brightly at me. "You are starting to act like a real leader." He stands then and I do the same.

"Thank you," is all I can say, my attention split between here and Evan.

"I will leave you to settle in and..." He looks at Jago. "Get reacquainted."

He winks at us and leaves us alone in the tent. I look at Jago, both of us just staring at each other again. It's been a rush since he got here and we haven't had much time alone, running from one thing to the next, never stopping, never breathing.

I missed this man so much. I never thought I would see him again, and he's here before me. He knows what happened, he never stopped fighting or looking for me, and he's here.

Right now.

"I spy with my little eye something beginning with b," I tease, and he frowns in confusion, those fire eyes alight as he stares at me.

He's just as big as I remember, maybe even bigger. His clothes are clean and his face is no longer covered in blood, but that doesn't make him any less rugged, and it has my lady bits perking up and taking notice. Like the first time I saw him, I have a giant lady boner.

"Brawler," he growls, stepping closer. "Beast," I counter with a grin.

He groans, rolling his eyes, but I spot his lips twitching and I can't help it. "It was the boobs that brought you back, right? Had to search the world for these handfuls of happiness?" I taunt, unable to help myself. Strangely, it feels right. After everything happened, I didn't think I would smile again, but this, with Jago, feels right. I always loved teasing him and it seems we are falling into our old ways...this time with just more scars and pain between us, and a distance which he is currently covering.

He stops when we are almost touching, his head tilting down to see me, and I hate that he hesitated. Does he think differently of me? Is he scared of touching me? I can't voice my questions, but my eyes must do it for me because he grabs my ass and hoists me into the air until our faces are level.

Grinning, I wrap my legs around his waist, holding on as he stares into my eyes, his gaze on fire. "Brawler," is all he says, as I lean down and kiss him, softly at first, just a featherlight touch, but then he deepens it. His tongue sweeps in and tangles with mine as I dig my nails into his shoulders, trying to drag him closer.

My pussy is wet...and pulsing. Holy shit.

Two times now I have reacted to men, it's real, my lady place is back in business. Lady boner, here we come.

"Jago," I whisper as I pull back, flickering my eyes open to see him. "I honestly didn't think I would see you again."

"Like you can get rid of me," he murmurs, smiling then, that special one just for me. "It seems I can't go on patrol without my partner."

"Knew it! My crazy ass warrior skills are handy."

He laughs, leaning his forehead against mine, as my whole world narrows down to his face. "Looks like I'm back in the training business. Let's hope none of my students are as naughty as you."

"You loved it, big man, using that excuse to feel me up," I tease, kissing him again before I hop down. He grabs my hips to keep me steady.

"True, why don't you show me around?" he suggests, his eyes searching the tent, always on alert.

"Sure, does that mean you're staying?" I inquire, walking backwards out of the tent.

"I meant what I said, Brawler—where you go, I go. If this is your home now, then it's mine too, if you'll have me?"

I stop then, tilting my head, and running my eyes purposely over his body before ending on his face. "You'll do. Are you house trained? Because you don't look like you are. You're not going to drag dead people in as presents, are you?"

He rolls his eyes to the sky. "Brawler," he grumbles, and then looks back at me. "Forget what I said about missing that fucking mouth of yours."

"Really? Well then, I guess you two don't need a reunion," I purr, intentionally looking at his cock before I turn and saunter away.

He groans behind me before I hear his boots stomping after me. I can't seem to stop grinning, even with the news hanging over our heads.

Evan, Jago, Archel...am I just collecting men now? Maybe I should get them name tags.

Chapter 2
Big Spoon

I show Jago around the forgotten camp. He analyses every weakness and points out where we need to improve security, which I relay to Simon who says he will get on it. It's handy having Jago around, since he's a security expert. I spot some of the tribe members looking at him warily, but when all he does is follow after me, they seem to relax a little.

He doesn't let me far out of his sight, like he is scared I will disappear again or something will happen to me...it's comforting, but it could get suffocating, so I'm hoping it won't last forever. I started healing, getting better, and he needs to help me with that, which means letting me be independent and building up my confidence regarding being alone again. Though Archel does have a point, I do tend to get into trouble when someone isn't here. Maybe I need three men to keep up with me.

Wait, three? Am I still counting Evan?

When night falls, I head back to my hut with Jago on my heels, and I strip off, hesitating when I realise I won't be able to sleep with Archel's shirt without explaining why. I put it on, sniffing the material which is losing his scent...I miss him.

I hear Jago moving about behind me, so I slip into bed, scoot toward the wall, and watch him as he undresses, throwing his stuff on the chair before he adds a knife under his pillow and a sword under the bed. He looks at me, freezing. "Are you okay with me sharing your bed?"

I sigh, I can't help it. "Jago, I'm fine, honestly, you don't have to treat me with kid gloves, like I'm going to break. I just need you to be normal, okay? Plus, I think we can share a bed, you have had your penis inside me after all...unless you're worried you can't control yourself. Too long without my fun bags...too long—oh God, the horror! You have turned into a pussy craved man, haven't you?" I say dramatically, my eyes wide as I flutter my hand to the base of my throat.

"You're right," he deadpans, and then lifts his arms theatri- cally. "Must eat pussy," he teases, prowling towards me and making a startled laugh burst from my lips as I watch and he smiles, leaning over the bed to kiss my forehead.

"I just want to hold you, Brawler. I thought I had lost you. I need to feel you in my arms, wake up with you there, knowing you are safe and we are together again," he murmurs, looking down at me, and I grin.

"Well, if you insist, but I get to be big spoon though!" I call, making him laugh and shake his head as he slips into the bed. He opens his arms and I slide into them, resting my head against his chest, the sound of his racing heart soothing me as I close my eyes and listen.

"I was so scared, Brawler, thought I'd lost you forever," he whispers into my hair, making me shiver and hold on to him tighter. "There's nothing else in this world worth living for without you, Brawler. It's crazy but true. I was existing until you came along with your jokes, smart mouth, and crazy ass plans. You threw it all out of whack, chaos wherever we went, and I missed that. I missed your brand of crazy," he admits, and I raise my head, meeting his searching gaze. "I love you, Brawler, so fucking much, don't ever leave me again.

I couldn't bear it. Promise me that whatever we do now, we do it together. Whether it be Paradise falling, wars, clans, whatever, we do it together."

I think those are the most words I've ever heard him say voluntarily. He must have been really scared...he really loves me. "I love you too," I tell him, but I don't want to promise some- thing I can't keep, and there is Archel...and even Evan. "I promise we will do everything together," I vow, not letting on that the others might be there too. "I have to admit, I missed having you around."

"Yeah?"

"Oh yeah, your muscles and cock..." I grin and he groans, and then I turn serious. "I missed you. I missed the feeling of safety and how happy we were. I wished you were there when it happened, so much."

He closes his eyes in pain. "Me too. I'm so sorry I wasn't there, Brawler. I will never forgive myself."

"Well, I do, so you have to. It was going to happen no matter what. If you were there they would have tried to kill you. What happened, happened. It's in the past, we have to keep moving. We will find our new happy. Down there, we knew what would happen every day, but up here we don't. You going to embrace that chaos?" I smile.

"If it comes with you?" he whispers, stroking my face. "Always."

"Knew you liked me," I tease.

"Shut up, Brawler, for once," he grumbles, and I go to protest, but he kisses me, hard. The one he always gave me before, so uncontrolled and wild, like the man himself.

I groan into his mouth, moving closer until I'm plastered across his body, his hands massaging my lower back. We don't go further, just happy to be together again, and when we pull back we are both panting.

"Goodnight, Beast," I whisper, leaning my head against his chest.

"Night, Brawler," he grunts, kissing my head as he wraps his arms around me and holds me tight.

I shut my eyes, my smile remaining as I let his heartbeat lull me to sleep.

I wake up first, which is strange for us, and just watch him sleep. He looks so peaceful with his arms still wrapped around me and his legs twisted with mine to trap me against him, even in sleep. When I move slightly, his eyes twitch, showing he's always on, even now. Grinning, I trail a finger across his lips and they open, letting me slip it inside, and when he starts to suck, I look up to see his eyes open and wide awake, watching me.

I pull my finger from his mouth. "Morning," I mumble. "Morning," he replies softly. "We better get up for training." "Oh God, you haven't changed," I pretend whine, rolling over onto my back, my arm thrown over my eyes as he laughs. "Come on, Brawler, time to get up and show me what you learned. I'm going to whoop your ass back into shape."

"I'd rather you whoop it another way," I retort, but blink open my eyes and peek around my arm at him to see him staring, pressed up on his elbow. "Fineeeee, I'm getting up." I huff.

He climbs from the bed, stretching when he stands, and I let my eyes run down his body, appreciating the fine specimen of a man. He's eye candy and brawn—what more could a girl want? He catches me watching and his lips twitch as he tosses my clothes at me. "Get dressed, Brawler, you can't distract me."

"Sure I can. I bet if I flashed you my fun bags, I could have a minute head start to run away."

His eyebrow rises then as he leans over the bed, stopping when his face is almost touching mine. "I'd catch you, I'll always catch you," he murmurs, before kissing my nose and getting back up, dressing quickly, and strapping on all his weapons as I watch, my mouth dry and my pussy wet...ain't that strange how it works?

Why does your pussy get wet and your mouth dry? Does that moisture go below like men's blood does?

"Brawler," he warns, and I blink, brought out of my thoughts.

"Does the moisture from my mouth go to my pussy when I'm turned on like the blood does to your cock?" I ask him, and he just stares at me, bewildered.

"You would have thought I would be used to this by now," is all he says, shaking his head as he turns away to put his boots on.

"You would have thought so, after all, I am a delight," I chirp happily as I get dressed, adding both katanas and grabbing my crossbow from the side of the door. I fold Archel's shirt, placing it under my pillow to keep safe, kissing it and him goodbye. Jago doesn't notice or question it, thank God, as we head out of the door. The sun barely hovers over the mountains behind us, the top of the peaks hidden under cloud cover and the rays already beginning to heat up the land.

I take a moment, just drinking in the air and camp before me. The fires are low, as people are either still asleep or the early morning risers are just getting up, starting the fires, and getting food cooking for breakfast. I spot patrols in the woods and wave as I lead Jago down to grab a drink of water before heading to the clearing to practice. It feels weird, like I shouldn't be bringing him here, this is mine and Archel's spot.

So I stay closer to camp, not wanting to tread on other memories as we set up. I place my crossbow just on the edge of our circle, and rest my katanas there as well, as we warm up, stretch, and then jog the perimeter for at least thirty minutes, side by side, and it's like old times.

It feels right.

"Spar first, let me see what we are working with," he suggests once we stop, and I nod, swiping the sweat from my brow. I think I've gotten better and I have been practicing, so I am weirdly looking forward to him kicking my ass.

We stand opposite each other and I raise my fists, making his lips twitch as he takes in my stance. "Easy. What does the winner get?" I inquire, and he groans, but then seems to perk up.

"You mean what do I get? Well, the winner should get to be big spoon all the time," he teases, and I roll my eyes.

"You liked it and you know it. Now, are we fighting or flirting, big guy?" I taunt.

He winks at me then before jumping into action, coming at me fast. For a moment, I have a flash of another man, another time, coming at me, and fear flows through my veins, but I grit my teeth and push it away. I can't afford to let flashbacks control me and I know Jago would never hurt me. He either doesn't notice or doesn't comment, but it does mean I'm too slow to avoid his leg sweep. I go down hard, but then roll to the side to avoid his punch and jump back to my feet behind him, kicking at the back of his legs. They bow and he stumbles, letting me leap onto his back and encircle my arm around his thick neck.

I wrap my legs around him to hold on as he tries to throw me off, and rain kisses on his neck and face, making him huff with laughter. "Brawler," he warns, so I hop down and circle to face him, grinning as he rolls his eyes at me, but his lips are turned up in a smile.

He comes at me again, a whirlwind of fists, and I duck and weave, using the environment. I dance behind trees and he almost punches one. I slip around the side, kicking out at his waist, and he gasps and hunches for a moment before straight- ening and coming at me again.

We spar for a long time, but I tire faster than he does, and not too long after he has me pinned to the ground, my hands above my head as he grins down at me. "I. Win."

But it's not his face I am seeing.

My chest aches as I stop breathing, my heart racing as my whole body goes cold like I am retreating inside myself. I can't see him, his face swimming and replaced with those of my attackers. Until I feel them pulling at my clothes, their hands and rancid breath wafting over me.

"Brawler?" I hear him call, worried, but it sounds far away.

I can't move, I can't fight, I'm trapped until his hand squeezes mine, and it's like a switch is flipped. I start clawing and kicking, and tears race down my face unchecked as I fight the ghosts of my past. There is not much logic happening, I know they are dead, but I can feel them...see them.

Oh God, not again. I can't, not again.

"Brawler, look at me." The voice is stronger now, closer, and a smell hits me, a familiar scent, causing me to freeze again. I stop fighting and blink, my eyes swimming into focus to see Jago. When he notices I'm back, he lets go of my hands and sits up so he isn't holding me down.

Swallowing, I lie there for a moment, embarrassed and in pain, until I can't take it anymore. I sit up and meet his eyes. I don't know who moves first, but suddenly I'm in his arms and he is holding me, whispering in my ear as I cry into his chest, just getting it all out.

A while later, when I have no more tears, he places gentle kiss after gentle kiss on my head.

"I'm sorry, next time I'll know, okay? You can do this, Brawler, you're so strong." I pull back and he cups my face. "So strong, you hear me? And when you aren't feeling strong, I will be right here for you to lean on."

I close my eyes. "Thank you. I love you," I whisper. "I love you too."

"It's weird that we are sitting here crying on the ground, want to go back to fighting?" I tease, but it falls flat.

"Brawler, we don't have to if you need a minute," he assures me, stroking my face, so I open my eyes.

"No, I need to, I need to keep moving. I broke, but I'm back up. Let's keep going," I insist and get to my feet, offering him my hand. He takes it and stands up, squeezing it before letting go.

"If you're sure, let's go." He nods and steps away.

I blow out a breath, focusing on the here and now—the way the sun is heating my skin, the smell of him, the sight of him— until I feel normal. He helps bring me back, and we spar for a while until we hear people begin to head our way, ready for train- ing, then we stop and take a drink. "You lead, I'll help."

"These are your people," he tells me, watching me over his water.

"But you are the teacher, we will work together. I want these people to be able to protect themselves."

"Together." He nods as they break into our training area. I turn to face them, happy with how many turned up. "Pick a spot and stretch! We are going to work you hard!" I call and they groan, but do as they are told.

Who knows, maybe this teacher shit will be fun. I definitely enjoyed my lessons, though that probably has to do with the hotness of my teacher and the reward system involving orgasms.

Chapter 3
Cinderella Guy

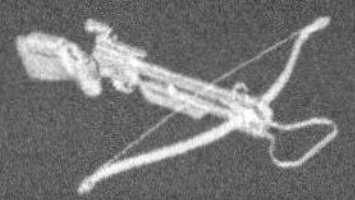

Trev comes over as they are warming up and stands between us. "We have sent scouts, they will be back tomorrow," he tells me, and I nod, watching as a woman is barely able to bend over, never mind touch her toes. "How's it going?"

"We just started, I feel like we need a soundtrack or something to get these people going," I mutter. I had watched an old kids' film once, where the main woman was disguised as a man and she sung a song as she was training. Would that be weird to do it right now? I would guess probably, so instead I hum it, and Jago looks over at me with his eyebrow raised. "Mulan, really?"

My mouth flops open as I point dramatically at him. "Oh dear God, you are a secret Disney nerd!" He frowns at me. "You watched them all, didn't you? You know the words...oh dear God...do you know the dances?"

"Brawler," he warns, as Trev huffs a laugh. "They were always playing during the early morning in the cinema, is all, and I couldn't sleep."

"Uh, sure thing, nerd." I grin and his eyes narrow on me as he steps closer.

"Say it again," he challenges.

"Now, big question, who is your favourite princess? I bet you're a Cinderella guy, right?"

"Run," he orders, as I laugh and duck around Trev when he tries to grab me.

"You totally used to touch yourself over Disney princesses, didn't you? I bet if I sing, you will get all horny!" I tease, and then duck again as he tries to grab me once more.

The people have stopped stretching now and are watching us, laughing and smiling as he chases me around the clearing. All the while, I am screaming Disney lyrics to him. He eventually catches me and throws me over his shoulder as he strides to the front of the class. He slaps my ass and then ignores me, leaving me hanging there.

"Now, first things first, I need to know how much you know. We are going to test you and then pair you with someone on your level. We are going to work on hand-to-hand and weapons, so you will need to get your stamina and strength up in your own time," he instructs, pacing in front of them, like he isn't holding me hostage over his shoulder.

"Big guy," I whine and lift my head, but he spanks me again. "Shush, I'm trying to teach," he snaps, and then raises his voice again. "Youngest first, line up!"

I look at a grinning Trev, the blood rushing to my head. "Help me?"

"Nope." He shakes his head and I snort, blowing my hair from my face.

Fuck it, ninja mode initiated.

I wiggle on his shoulder and when his hand loosens, I throw myself forward, rolling last minute and ending up on my feet. I turn, grinning to see him watching me. "Ninja Piper at your service!"

"Well, ninja Piper can go first then, show them what to expect." His lips twitch and I groan.

"You enjoy my misery way too much for a man who watches

Disney. Oh my God, you liked the villains best, didn't you?" I shiver in fake horror and he groans.

"Line up, Brawler!"

"Sir, yes sir!" I salute, winking at Trev as I slip past, and I whisper to Jago as I go, "I can call you that later if you like, or maybe sing you a song, whatever floats your boat." I spank him, making him jerk at my touch.

He groans as I stand at the front of the line, his fire eyes blazing as he turns to face me and the rest of the able-bodied fighters. "We are going to spar, this way I will see how fast you are, how quick your reflexes are, and what weaknesses you have. Be prepared, I won't go easy on you, you might get hurt, but out there? They won't go easy either, they will try to kill you whether you are ready or not. It's better it happens now so you know how to react to the pain than when you are facing down a sword or a gun." Murmurs go through the crowd. They look uneasy, so I step away and face them, turning serious.

"He's right, I went out there thinking it was easy, that it has to be exaggerated, that I could handle myself. I was wrong, I soon learned that. This man has saved my life and if you let him, he will save yours too. We need to be ready, even if no one attacks you here or we decide to stay hidden, you never know what will happen. Just the other week we were attacked by eaters, in our very homes, and next time we may not get as lucky. We can't stand idly by, we need to be prepared. It will be hard work, he will make you want to quit at least three times in the next hour and wonder if you are crazy, but the outcome? The hard work pays off, and when you get into a fight, which will happen, and you know how to defend yourself and the ones you love? You will be thankful for this then. I know he is a stranger to you, an outsider, but so was I. I need you to trust me, to trust him. If you do, he will give you everything you need to protect you and yours." My speech seems to rally them and they nod, still nervous and unsure, but trusting me, hearing me. I turn to Jago then to see a proud look on his face. "I will demonstrate first so you know what to expect, watch how we move, what we do."

I step up to him and he dips his chin in thanks, facing off with me. "Pulled blows, no bloodshed," he instructs, and I nod, blowing out a breath and centering my body. I watch him for hints he is going to move, but he gives me none, just comes at me like a wild animal, all speed and strength. Only my training keeps me out of his clutches. Having sparred with him before, I never really won and I always got hurt, but each time I got hurt a little less. The pain and bruises are worth it, and one day I will be able to keep up with him.

I duck and weave, trying to think ahead like he taught me, but his movements are so unpredictable that I just have to roll with it, relying on my instincts. I barely duck a punch aimed at the side of my head, the air whizzing as his fist flies past, and while he is unprotected, I sucker punch him in the side and kick his legs before dancing back, grinning when he smiles at me, proud of my moves.

He comes at me again, and this time I meet him, we trade blows, forgetting about our audience, and they gasp and clap. He manages to kick my legs and I roll, groaning at the instant pain, knowing I will have a bruise there later. He comes after me, his feet fast for his size. I turn to the side and then leap up, making a weird noise as I thrust my fist at him, not expecting it to connect, but it does.

Right into his face.

We both freeze, my fist still touching him, his eyes wide, and then suddenly he starts laughing, even as he reaches up and prods at his nose, trying to see if it's broken. I pull my fist back and wave it off like I meant to do it all along, my hand on my hip.

"Ninja Piper," I state seriously.

"Lucky Piper, more like. You left your side open though, watch that next time, but that wasn't bad," he concedes, and I grin, pride filling me at his words. His approval means a lot to me, and when he steps back and looks at the crowd who is staring at me in shock, I almost beam, filled with excitement at landing such a hit.

That wouldn't have been possible two months ago, now look at me.

I meet Trev's eyes and see the respect there, and I am almost jittering as I look away. Healing, yes, I'm healing, and it seems Jago is part of that journey as well, because today, these last few days, I found something I had forgotten.

A piece of me I thought they had taken.

Me. I found the old childish part of myself, and I know I'll never be that girl again who used to joke and tease with everyone and I have to work at it, but it's coming back and that makes me happy. I don't want to change all of myself, so this bit coming back, this piece fitting into place makes me feel more whole, and I hold myself straighter as he directs the next person forward who edges towards him nervously. She is an older woman, skinny and lithe, one of our scouts, I believe. Her brown hair with greying streaks is tied back tight, her face pale as she watches Jago.

"Just relax, react," I advise her, circling her as she stands tightly, her body restricted by her panic. "Breathe in and out, let it out, you can do this. Don't fear the pain, don't close your eyes or jerk away, don't let your fear conquer you, conquer it. Remember who you are," I encourage, and when she nods, her arms loosening by her sides, I know she is ready so I step back.

"Go," I instruct.

She lasts thirty seconds before he knocks her down, but she gets back up and I see a confidence there now she did not have before.

"Next!" I shout, and a young man steps up, looking cocky until he is knocked out with one punch from Jago who isn't even trying.

"Next!" I call.

We go through the line until everyone has been evaluated and faced Jago. Though banged and bruised, they all seem grimmer but more alive...more energised. Like they finally understand, understand what we are trying to teach them. I help Jago pair them up and then we stand at the front again, using each other to display moves for women and men, what will work best, and demonstrating and making them practice as we prowl through their midst, correcting their forms or helping them get the move right.

A couple of hours later, we call it a day. "Well done, get some water and head back to your jobs, you did really well today. We will meet again tomorrow!" I call, and as they disperse, I see some of the men and women talking to Jago, laughing and joking with him, and that makes me smile, knowing they are slowly accepting him.

Trev joins me as we watch him. "He is one hell of a teacher."

"The best," I reply with a grin, remembering everything he

taught me.

"Piper," Trev starts, turning to me. "What will you do when the scouts get back?"

I sigh, I have been thinking about this very thing myself. "Go, go back," I whisper, and then strengthen my voice. "I have to see for myself, and if it's safe enough, I will go. I have someone I have to look for, a promise to keep."

"Promise?" he asks.

"To an old friend. I promised I would always come back to him when we were kids with no other family. I can't forget, though, I have to know what happened to him," I explain, and Trev nods as we watch Jago once again.

"I hope you know your home is here now, but I understand, I won't ask for such a promise, but I hope you stay safe and find your way back here," he tells me, placing his hand on my shoul- der. I flinch at first, but suck in a breath and the panic recedes.

I go to speak when an explosion rocks the earth, the ground actu- ally moving, and my head snaps up, meeting Jago's eyes as he races towards me. He takes me to the ground, his body covering mine, and only when it stops does he release me, both of us grab- bing our weapons and ready to fight, but when we look to the sky, we see a plume of smoke coming from the other side of the mountain...

The mountain behind The Forgotten, the one I thought held no one or nothing...so who just blew something up?

Chapter 4
Precious

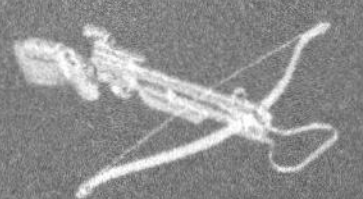

"What the fuck was that?" I ask Trev, who holds his hands up and addresses the crowd.

"Back to work, nothing to worry about," he calls, and they break up, used to this. This has happened before...they expect this.

Who the fuck is hiding out there? "Trev," I snap, and he looks at me.

"Just a border precaution," he tells me, but I know he's lying when he glances away. "I will see if the scouts are back yet. Please wash up and get something to eat, Piper."

And then he is gone, the lie sitting uneasily with me as my eyes go back to the mountain. Are there people living there? If so, why is Trev hiding them, protecting them? I'll get the truth out of him, but he's right, I'm hungry and need to wash now that I've made my mind up about going to Paradise.

"He's lying," Jago tells me, as we both watch him walk away. "I know, it will be for a reason, though, so we trust him for

now." I sigh and look at him. "Jago, I'm going to Paradise." "I know."

I blink and he grins down at me. "Really, Brawler? I know you too well, I knew you would, when do we leave?"

I leap at him and he catches me with a laugh, turning as he starts walking, his hands spanning my ass and holding me in the air. "We will wait for the scouts to return. We need to wash first though, you stink, big guy."

He huffs. "So do you." "Charming, aren't you?" I tease.

"I never said you smell bad, maybe you smell good enough to eat," he taunts, his fire eyes looking down at me.

"Is that an offer?" I wink and gasp when my back presses against a tree. "Sneaky."

"It's always an offer with you, Brawler, you know I am yours. Whatever you need, even if it's to kill someone or to fuck," he growls, lowering his head. "You're a bad influence. I was in control until I met you, now I'm constantly hard at inappropriate times."

"Like when you are peeing? Is that hard to do when you have wood?" I inquire, and he groans, pressing his face to my shoulder as he shakes with laughter. "Hey, I'm curious, Evan would never answer me." I huff and he rolls his eyes up to see me.

"Yes, it's not easy," he deadpans.

"Huh, I think I would like to have a cock just for a day, you know? To try it out."

"Piper," he mumbles, shaking his head as he effortlessly pins me to the tree. I expect to freak out, but maybe because I can see who is holding me and I know Jago will never hurt me, I don't.

"Okay, okay, I'll stop talking about cock."

"Please stop saying cock." He groans, his eyes pinching in pain.

"Is me saying cock making your cock wish I was talking about it? Also, we should stop calling it cock, I still think I need to name him. What about Beast Jr.?"

He shuts me up by kissing me, making me moan into his mouth as he sweeps his tongue inside and tangles it with mine, switching my attention from his cock to his hands and mouth. His fingers dig into my hips, holding me up with one hand as the other roves up my chest and grips my chin, clutching me to him as we clash.

My hands go to his hair, tangling in the long locks and scratching his scalp, making him jerk between my legs and break free, both of us panting as we stare at each other. "Princess Beast?" I offer breathlessly, and he starts laughing, shaking against me again, his cock still pressing against my leg.

"Brawler, my life was dull before you," he says softly, his chuckles dying off. "Come on, let's get you washed so we can feed you."

"Will you wash my back? And that isn't slang for sex....it could be though." I wiggle my eyebrows at him and he stumbles as he laughs.

"Dear God, has that fighting riled you up or something?" he deadpans.

"It could, you know how wet I used to get when we fought. It was like trying to fight with a shower between my legs," I tell him. "The gushing." I shake my head. "Truly, no one ever tells you how hard it is to fight when your vagina is demanding attention."

"Please stop," he begs, and I snap my mouth shut with a grin. "Missed you," I say instead, as he carries me to the lake.

He drops me to my feet and I kick off my shoes and shimmy out of my jeans and top, wearing my panties and bra. I don't bother with modesty and when I see his eyes running over my body. I wink at him and dive into the shallow pool, popping back up and slicking my hair away from my face.

"Come on in, big guy, I promise not to touch Princess. I'll be good."

"Wish you wouldn't." He sniffs, but strips off as well, and I whistle, checking him out because hey, I missed his body. I definitely missed him more...okay, no, I missed his body more. Those thighs...that ass...that cock. Dear God, cocks aren't pretty, but if they had a beauty competition, I think his would win. I would give it first place, my vagina as its prize.

"Stop staring at my cock," he grumbles, and slips into the water. He swims my way and grabs me, hoisting me up. I wrap my legs around him. He isn't the only one who has missed this, missed touching him, like if I let go he might disappear.

"I was thinking about making a ribbon for him if you must know." I huff.

"I'm not even going to ask, Brawler." He sighs, wrapping his arms around me as I lean into him, the water warm and washing over us.

We float there for a bit before washing each other and getting dried and dressed. Once we are, we head back to see others sitting around eating. I grab some nuts and berries for us both while Jago grabs drinks and we head to the tent. I want to see if the patrols are back yet and if they have heard anything.

"I think that one's even scarier than the last shadow you had," Maria jokes as we pass, and I giggle and wave, ignoring Jago's questioning look. I'm not ready to talk about Archel yet. I haven't heard anything from him in a while, and to be honest, I'm scared something has happened.

Archel can look after himself, but everyone can make mistakes. So instead, I distract myself by nibbling at the food as we duck into the tent to see Trev talking to Simon in hushed whispers. They silenced when they spot us, but welcomed us in with a friendly smile. "Hey, heard you were whooping people into shape and I missed it," he calls.

"Yeah, we missed you there, were you out on patrol?" He nods and Trev gestures towards the seats, so we all take one as I lean forward. "What did you learn?"

"Whatever happened at Paradise, it is still there, quiet as well for now. We couldn't see much from where we were, which is normal, but there was no blood or bodies like usual with an attack."

I frown. "So what are we thinking?"

"I think if there was an attack, it's over and they have moved on. The rest of the Paradise people probably took cover inside and rode it out."

I nod then, staring at the nuts in my hand, and I feel them

watching me, so I blow out a breath and sit back. "Then it's settled, I'm going to see for myself."

"Piper," Simon starts, but Trev holds his hands up, his eyes on me.

"Are you sure?" he asks calmly.

"I need to know," I whisper, and then clear my throat. "First sign of trouble, I will get out of there, but it's better we know what happened. If people are being attacked, we need to know why and how so we can prepare."

"Then we support you," he tells me, reaching across and laying his hand on mine. "Be safe, say goodbye before you go, and I will make sure they keep sparring like you did today. The precautions we outlined are already in place, so don't worry about us."

"Good, stay safe here. Make sure to keep the fires low at night, increase patrols, and have the sniper out on the mountain to give you a long enough warning, okay?" I advise him, worried about leaving. Not that I can do much when I'm here, but I feel responsible for these people now. They are my tribe.

"We will," he agrees with a grin, pride shining on this face. "If you are leaving today, you are better going at night, less people to see where you are coming from and going to, but beware of hunting parties."

I nod and we stand as I look at Jago. "We better get packed and I need to let some people know we are leaving."

"I'll join you, I need to check out your leg before you go," Simon interjects, standing with a stretch.

I nod once again at Trev, but his voice stops me. "Show them who they messed with," he calls, and I laugh as we duck back out.

Jago takes my hand and I squeeze his. This feels like the right decision. I need to know for sure what happened and to ask about Evvie before I can ever think about moving on with my life and starting a future here with my people.

We head back to my hut and I begin to pack up, making sure to take my weapons and some extra clothes the tribe's people gave me. I also stick Archel's shirt in the back, unable to help myself. I find my tin of coffee on the side and pick it up with a smile.

Don't come back while I'm gone, I think. He will panic, even if he says he won't.

Maybe he's right, I do get into trouble when he's gone, because I'm heading directly into trouble right now and I'm choosing to.

"What's that?" Jago queries behind me, packing his own stuff, not that he really unpacked in the first place.

"Just a present," I tell him, and then put it back before turning to him. "You sure about coming with me?"

He looks up. "Brawler," he warns, and I smile.

"Okay, okay, looks like J and P are back together again," I joke and he chuckles, coming up and wrapping his arms around me.

"I guess so. He's right, we will leave tonight. I have a bike stored before the tunnel entrance."

"Tunnel?" I echo, and he raises his eyebrows. "I've never left." I shrug. "And I was passed out when I was brought here."

He sucks in a breath and squeezes me tighter. "You'll see, until then, let's get some food and you should try to get some sleep."

"Yeah, you're right. Wanna nap? I'll let you be big spoon, no forking though, I'm afraid."

He grins down at me. "You can be big spoon, get in." He jerks his head at the bed, and I kick off my boots and crawl in, slipping under the quilt. Jago follows me, facing the door as I wiggle until my front is to his back with my arm over his middle.

"Does this make you feel like a girl?" I laugh.

"Actually, it makes me hard and feel precious all at the same time, I can feel your entire body pressed against me."

"Precious," I repeat, choking on laughter. "It makes you feel precious."

He huffs and my laughter tumbles out as I bury my head in his back. "Go to sleep," he rumbles.

"Sure, sure, will do, precious."

"You aren't going to let that go, are you?" he grumbles. "Nope, just like I plan to find out which princess really makes

you hard."

"Sleep, Brawler," he orders, as I snigger into his skin. "Night, precious."

—❦—

When I can stop giggling, I eventually fall asleep, only waking up when I hear the chatter and laughter of the tribe, the smell of cooking meat hitting me and making my stomach roar.

"Fucking hell, what a wakeup call." Jago huffs, turning over and pulling me closer, all with his eyes closed.

"Go back to sleep and I'll touch Princess to wake you up." I snicker, blinking open my eyes.

"Stop calling my penis Princess or you won't get to climb his tower anymore," he grumbles, his arms tight around me, his legs entwined with mine.

"Aww, won't he let me play with his crown?"

"Fucking hell, woman." He puffs, rolling on to his back, and I laugh when I spot his cock begging for attention. It sends a pulse through my pussy too, and soon my laughter cuts off as I watch his profile.

I want him.

I realise it all of a sudden.

Not in the future, not in general, but right now, right here.

I want him to touch me, to fuck me and love me, and to replace any lasting feelings I have from those...

I can't even think of the word.

I know he is trying to look after me and protect me, and probably doesn't think I'm ready, but that's my decision and maybe I will freak out, maybe it won't work out well, but I want to try.

I trust him implicitly.

I know unless I make the first move, he never will again, despite how much he wants me. Letting my natural instincts—or crazy radar, as Evvie used to call it—guide me, I slip closer before flinging my leg over his lap and straddling him.

He grunts, grabbing my hips and then stilling as he looks up at me. His hair is spread across the pillow, his fire eyes low and simmering, but heating up as he watches me.

"Piper."

The way he says my name, like a caress, like a plea, undoes me like nothing else.

"I need you," I confess.

He searches my gaze, obviously noting my resolve. "Are you sure?" he asks, not judging. After all, I know my own body.

"Never been more sure in my life. I love you, I don't want to spend another moment apart. I still crave you, ache for your touch, and lying next to you without it is killing me," I admit, and his hands clench along my waist and his lips part.

"Do I need to sing to get you in the mood?" I tease, and he groans, his eyes closing for a moment.

"I know you're joking, but you know I'm always in the mood for you. It's like walking around with a tent pole in my pants."

"You know how to make a girl wet." I laugh and then gasp when he drags me forward, pressing his cock to my pussy through my pants, the pressure amazing.

"You were saying?" he purrs, cocky as hell. "Because from where I'm sitting, I think if I touched your pussy right now, you would be drenched."

"Oooh, dirty talk," I taunt, "but not a lot of action."

His hands skate up my sides and cup my breasts through my shirt, his eyes watching me the whole time as he rolls my nipples between his fingers. Gasping, I rock against him, my head falling back as he plays with them, and then suddenly, he is ripping the shirt over my head. I lift my arms to help, the cool air hitting my chest and tightening my nipples as he leans up and sucks one into his mouth. I groan again, my hands digging into his hair, holding him to me as he catches his teeth on the bud before swapping to the next and giving it the same treatment. Like shots of pure, unfiltered lust, the sensations shoot from my nipples to my pussy with each suck. Each rasp of his lips and chin across my skin, his touch—God, I feel starved for it.

My whole body trembles from his hands, from the simplicity of it, it feels right. It feels good, and that last barrier breaks down inside me, the one that thought I would never be able to do this again, that thought every touch would bring imaginary pain, would make me curl up in a ball and wish I was the way I was before, but it doesn't...it feels good. So good.

"Don't stop," I beg, my head tilting back as he kisses across my chest and up my neck, open-mouthed and wet. Again and again, my rocking picks up speed with each touch of his lips, almost unable to take it, it's too much.

My eyes shut of their own accord and a flash of mocking laughter floats through my brain. Swallowing, I push it away and anchor myself in his hair again, but it comes again, phantom hands following this time, and I freeze.

"Stay with me," he orders, his voice rough and demanding, pulling me back from the brink until all I see is him, all I feel is him.

No one else is allowed here, this is for us. They had my past, he gets my future.

I open my eyes and look down at him, getting lost in those fiery depths. "Feel me, taste me, it's me, only me. No one else will ever touch you, I will never hurt you," he whispers against my skin, placing a gentle kiss on my racing heart. "You are in charge, see?" He lies back then, taking the heat and his mouth with him.

I fall forward, catching myself with my palms against his chest as he looks up at me, his hands held above his head, his eyes watching me hungrily but patiently, his body rock-hard and almost rolling beneath mine.

"I want to be able to—fuck, why is this so hard?" I whisper, looking away as tears fill my eyes.

"Look at me," he says strongly, and I shake my head.

"Look at me," he demands, his voice harsh, and my head snaps around. "It isn't hard. It's just you and me, that's all that matters, we can take as long as you need. I'd wait forever for you, Brawler, and if I never get to touch you again, that's fine with me, this is enough, being with you. Seeing you every day, knowing you are safe and by my side, I can take it. What I can't take is being away from you. What I can't fucking stand is that regret and pain in your eyes. You are so fucking strong, stronger than you even know. You can beat this, you can beat whatever this world throws at you, and I will be at your back the whole time. You aren't alone, never alone. You don't need me, Piper, not to fight with you. You don't need me like I need you, but you aren't getting rid of me. So when you're ready, or if you never are, know that it doesn't matter to me. I'm yours. No dead men, scars, or ghosts will stop that. Yours." He nods, each word hammering into my heart and helping seal up the cracks as I swallow hard, a tear rolling down my cheek. He leans in and captures it, kissing it away. "I will always catch you when you fall, you and me against the world, Piper. We can make it, we can do it. You lean on me and I'll lean on you, that's all we need."

He cups my face then. "Say it."

"Us," I whisper, my eyes closing. "You'll always be there." "Not even the fucking dead themselves could tear me away from you, so stop being so goddamn scared that whatever you say, whatever you do, will push me away. I want to know when it hurts. I want to know when you need to scream and fight and rage against the world because this planet isn't fair, baby, and it kills the best of us, but it won't kill you. You are Piper mother- fucking Smith, you take the hits and you get back up with that goddamn smile on your face and a smart ass comment."

"Knew you liked my ass," I tease, unable to help myself. "Mask it with humour, I don't care. I see your pain, Piper, and I promise I will make it mine, we will fight those ghosts together."

Licking my lips, I roll my hips again, making him gasp, and that fire comes back. Steady, slow almost, like a frog in a hot pan. Until they don't realise they are boiling. "Together." I nod.

Leaning down, I seal that promise with a kiss, losing myself in his mouth and taste. Letting him wash it all away, letting him catch me as I lose myself in his touch...

Gasping, I pull back slightly, his hands on my hips now, digging in, anchoring me to this world and keeping me with him so I don't float back to the past. I don't know if it's his words or the fact that I'm on top and in charge, but suddenly, all I can think about is riding him, fucking him, showing him how much I love him. Not just for him, but to prove to myself that I can. That I can be with the man I love, because he's right, he will wait, I know that. But I won't.

I'm a greedy fucking bitch, I want his everything, even as my heart cries for two others, I want all of his.

"I want you so badly," I admit, and he groans, low and deep, almost thrusting upwards to meet me.

"Brawler, please don't tease me," he whispers.

"I'm not teasing, I'm not that cruel...only did you remember the wet wipes this time?"

He rolls his eyes and tickles my side, making me laugh as I jerk on top of him, then we both gasp. "Fucccck," he moans.

He closes his eyes, breathing heavily, and I watch him, watch the utter need and devotion on his face, so I lean up and yank my panties off, settling back over his trousers, and when they open, I'm naked before him.

"Well, you just going to lie there? How lazy," I whisper, as I trace my hands up my chest and cup my breasts while he watches.

His eyes narrow and he pushes my hands away, replacing them with his, covering my breasts completely and squeezing. "I want to watch you come," he growls, his voice rough.

"Then you better make me, Beast." I grin, rocking against his hard cock as he pinches and squeezes my nipples, making me gasp and roll my hips.

"Come here," he orders, and I tilt my head in confusion, the haze of lust clouding my mind until I can barely think. "I can't reach your pussy there, Brawler, and I want a taste, want to feel you come on my tongue."

He grabs my hips again and lifts me, his muscles bulging with the movements as he raises me clear off him, his abs rolling with the movements as he drags me across his pecs until my knees fall to the pillow on either side of his head, my pussy pressed to his face.

I moan, the feel of his lips, his beard, and chin pressed to me so intimately while I'm still in control...my fucking Beast Man always looking after me.

"Please," I beg, rocking against his mouth, unable to help myself, my thighs drenched from my need.

He groans and I feel the warm, wetness of his tongue as he laps at me, cleaning my thighs as he works his way up to my pussy. With the first touch of his tongue, I am lost.

"Missed how you taste," he whispers, muffled. God, this man.

The tip of his tongue touches my clit and I nearly come away from his face, but his hands hold me to him as I rock against him, fucking myself on his mouth, his chin pressed to my pussy as he laps at my clit in teasing strokes, which have me moaning his name. My hands are lost on where to go, so I grip my breasts, rolling my nipples as he dips a finger inside me, giving my pussy something to clamp down on.

"Scream my name," he mutters. "I want them to know, everyone to hear."

My head drops back, it's too fucking much, yet I can't move away. My breathing comes out in pants, pleasure pulling from every limb as he demands it, his tongue lashing my clit again and again, harder now as his finger curls inside me.

"You taste like heaven, like home."

"Jago," I gasp, my movements speeding up until he catches his teeth on my clit as he sucks it into his mouth, adding another finger at the same time, and I fall apart.

I scream his name like he asked, my whole body seizing from the force of my release until I go limp and fall backwards, my eyes darkening. "Fucking—" Gasp. "Hell."

He laughs beneath me, and I lift my head to see him smirk- ing, his mouth and chin sparkling with my cream, his lips almost bruised from the force of me, but I've never seen him look so happy. "You ready for the next one, Brawler? Or are you getting slow in your old age?"

"Old age?" I yell. "I'll give you old fucking age." I crawl up his body, unable to lift myself more than that, my legs too weak to hold me up, the pleasure leaving me boneless. It's been so long, my body is unused to it, the shock of it rather than the pain, leaving me almost crying.

Once my face is even with his, my eyes on his fiery orbs, I lick his lips, tasting myself on him as I reach between us and yank down his pants, wrapping my hand around his hard length. He groans, thrusting into my hand as I center myself over him and rub the head of his cock back and forth over my pussy, moaning myself when it bumps my oversensitive clit.

"Brawler," he moans, but I swallow it with a kiss. I want him to feel how I feel, I need him inside of me so badly.

Finding my strength, the one he spoke of, I sit back, resting my knees on either side of his hips, and line him up at my entrance. Grinning down at him, I lift myself and slide down his cock.

He groans, his head thrown back as I work his hard, long length inside me until my pussy rests on his skin, then I start to move, raising myself and dropping, twisting my hips, chasing another release, his cock stretching me. There's no pain, fuck, there's nothing but pleasure, and I crack, I lose it. Control, it's all his, he can have everything.

His hands grip me and help, guiding me to move faster, keeping his eyes on mine as I moan and writhe, his hardness stretching me, filling me so completely, I don't know where I start and he ends.

The slap of our skin is loud, our heavy breathing the only other sound in the room, his name like a prayer on my lips. One he answers by thrusting up harder, meeting my every move and giving me more, giving me everything.

"Fuck, baby, I'm so close," he groans. "I can't take it, you're so tight, too fucking tight and wet." His hips lose their rhythm, as do I, throwing myself back and forth, chasing my own release until suddenly, it's there, hitting me like a truck, and I scream wordlessly as my pussy clamps down on him like a vice, pulsing with it as I shake.

He groans my name and stills beneath me, filling me with his own release as I collapse on top of him. My heart racing in time with his as we both gasp for air, our bodies covered in sweat. He wraps his arms around my back, his cock still buried inside me, connecting us, and a smile curls up at my lips.

I'm not broken, just darker, that's all. Stronger, fiercer, and ready to fight for what is mine.

"Seriously, wet wipes?" I joke and he groans, jiggling me, and we both freeze as I whimper at the feeling.

"Kill. Me. Now," he grumbles, and I laugh as I kiss over his heart like he did to me.

"I promise to protect it, never break it," I whisper, and flutter my eyes up to his. The fire is muted now, not a raging storm...but a slow burning, one that I know will always be there for me.

"Good, but I want yours in return, Brawler."

Chapter 5
Hole of My Ass

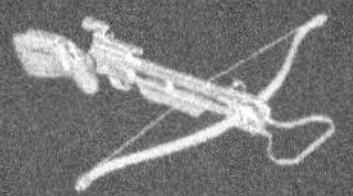

"We need to pack," I mumble, but make no move to push away from his warm embrace, his arms comforting and not restraining. Another win for me that this isn't freaking me out or bringing back memories, but maybe he fucked all that out of me for a minute—hell, he can keep doing that if he wants. I am too chilled to care about anything right now.

"Soon," he grumbles, his arms tightening around me and yanking me farther up his chest as I laugh, and bring my face into his neck, smelling the fire scent that he always seems to carry.

"We can't stay in here forever," I tease.

"Sure we can," he counters, and then sighs. "But you are like a child and can't sit still, so maybe not, you might drive me crazy."

I lift my head and rest it on his chest as I grin up at him. "Might? Babe, you're already there. You totally went to crazy town when you went to pound town."

"Pound town?" he says slowly, then shakes his head. "I did create a monster, should have left you to Evan's care. I swear that boy was a saint for managing not to touch you for so long."

"What?" I ask dumbly.

"Brawler, seriously, you are so smart, but sometimes you are a real idiot. That boy wanted you so badly. I don't know how he resisted, it didn't take long for you to wear down my restraint. I blame it on those tight little shorts you wore. Drove me batshit inside and when you started training and I had to touch you..." He groans. "Torture, having you pressed against me like that. I had to take so many cold showers."

"Huh, is that what the old ones call it? Cold showers?" I taunt.

"I remember us taking a shower," he recollects, and we both groan as he gets hard again.

"So...showers, huh? I can add that to the list along with princesses, all things that make Beast Man a walking erection."

"Woman," he groans, his eyes shuttering. "What were you saying about packing? Let's do that, anything to keep your mind off my cock, otherwise I'm going to look like a pervert following you around with a hard-on."

"Don't you always?" I laugh. "I'm like the piper but for penis- es." He stares up at me, lost for words. "Oh my God, get it? Piper the Penis Caller? No, wait, the Piper of Cocks."

He leans up and covers my mouth with his hand. "Please, stop," he begs.

I nod and he replaces his hand with his mouth, kissing me softly. "Time to pack, Brawler, you ready to get back on the road?"

"Always."

Our bags are fastened to the bike, weapons strapped to our bodies, and food and water ready to go. We are all dressed and facing down the tribe members. Trev is standing at the front, with Simon at his side. I step away from Jago and the bike and move towards him. "We will be back, look after him for me, won't you?" I tease, jerking my head towards Trev, and Simon laughs.

"I'll try, look after yourself out there." He opens his arms and sweeps me into a hug. I laugh and pat his back before moving away to face Trev. He grabs my hands and holds them.

"Be safe. I hope you find what you need out there and come home," he whispers, leaning down and kissing my hands. I step back with a nod and look at the amassed people.

"I'll be back, until then keep training, keep vigilant, and most of all, look after each other," I call loudly. There is a chorus of agreement and goodbyes, and I wave before turning and climbing on the bike behind Jago. I wrap my arms around him and grin.

"Let's go, Beast Man."

He fires up the bike, revving it, and I look over my shoulder as we speed away, my new home getting smaller and smaller until we turn the corner and I can't see them anymore. But I know this is right, one way or another, I need to know what happened and so do the people of The Forgotten. If Paradise is truly gone, no one is safe.

Evan.

Like a whisper on the wind, the name comes to me like always. I owe him that. I owe him to see what is going on. We didn't end on the best of terms, but he was always my family. Families have arguments, they fight. I can see now he wanted the best for me, even if he was being an asshole about it.

Before this trip is through, I'll have my answers, and then Jago and I can start our life here...hopefully with Archel, if he ever turns up again. That will be fun to explain, but one day at a time. That's how I'll take it, it's all you can do in a world like this.

One thing I know for sure is that I'm not losing Jago again.

Whatever we find, whatever we face, we do it together.

We twist through bends and roads until even I am lost. No wonder no one just stumbles into this place, and it makes me wonder how long Jago was out here trying to find me and how he eventually did.

"Tunnel," he yells over the wind, and I perk up to see what he was talking about earlier. I need to memorise this in case I am driving next time or have to give directions.

An old tunnel sits ahead, graffiti covering nearly every inch in faded colours, names, dates, and words that I can't understand decorating the dark brown brick. An old-style sign still hangs over the top, but it's covered in sand and dirt, so I am unable to see what it says. The inside is dark, almost black as we speed towards it, and when we are inside, Jago flicks on the light, illuminating the interior. Sand is piled and trampled, but as we go further in it fades to cement, the curving walls dripping water from some- where. We whizz by an old door on the left with a yellow light barely lit up above it.

It only takes a few minutes, but I'm on alert for those few moments until we break out of the other side, the sun blinding us after the dark, the world coming back into focus. The road crunches under the bike, the sun heating us up, and on either side of the tunnel and stretched before us is sand. When I look back, I realise why no one spots it or tries to find it. Above the tunnel stands an old, half destroyed building. Rubble falls down one side, the windows smashed long ago, leaving nothing but dark- ened holes. It's tall, probably an old apartment building, with debris blocking the left and right of the tunnel—strategically placed? But it's not that which would stop people...but the sign.

Bright red, dripping like the old graffiti, the new one declares this eater territory with a skull painted next to it. You would have to be stupid or insane to ignore that and keep going...yet Jago did.

To find me.

He went into the dark, not knowing what he would find, but hoping it would lead to me. Ready to fight eaters for me, anything. Fuck, I love this man. I turn back to the front and wrap my arms tighter around him as he guns it into the open desert before us.

We don't spot anything for at least an hour—no buildings, no people, nothing. Just some old roads, signs, and the usual broken- down cars and trucks littered here and there, and of course sand. Yet another reason we have never been found, it's in the middle of nowhere. You would only get so far and turn back, realising there is nothing out here but death and more sand. The Forgot- ten, Trev planned this well.

The mountains are behind us, but Jago seems to know where we are going, so I close my eyes, grimacing at the crusty feeling as sand blows into them, making it hard to see, and I rest my cheek on his back. Letting the rhythmic sensation of his chest rising and falling soothe me as we eat away at the miles, the bike purring beneath us.

I missed this.

As much as I love my new home, I love exploring, I love the never knowing. It was what pulled me out here to begin with, what drew me from the safety of the bunker and into the sands. And that burning passion, that call, is still there, like a fine wire linked tightly from me and further out into the Wastelands than I have ever been. A density, a calling, but I ignore it. We have things to do. People to find. Maybe after, once the people have been trained, Jago and I could start scouting, going farther and farther. I still want to see everything this world has to offer, even if it's covered in sand and blood.

This world is the only one we have, I would have to be stupid not to want to know everything it has to offer.

The sun is starting to set, lower and almost blinding as it dips down below the horizon and the stars take its place, the night only marginally cooler, but Jago doesn't put his light on—prob- ably not wanting to give away our position—and we keeping driving for another hour. We pass an abandoned gas stop and a burned down town before we suddenly stop, yanking me from my musings.

The bike turns off, the abrupt silence deafening. "What is it?" I ask, my voice overly loud after becoming used to shouting over the purr of the engine.

"Lights," he growls, and I follow his pointed finger to see he is right. Up ahead is what looks like bike lights and a fire, really bright, like a beacon in the night.

"Can we go around?" I inquire.

"We can, but it will mean another day added to our journey," he grumbles, hitting the bike handles.

"Then we sneak past, drive as close as we dare, and then push the bike and slip through in the night. We don't know who it is, but I'm betting they aren't expecting visitors this late and all the way out here," I ponder out loud.

"Maybe, but I don't like it." He sighs.

"Jago, you can't protect me from everything, you wouldn't have hesitated before, so don't now. We can do this, partners, remember? Plus, I'm badass now. Worst case we fight our way through," I tease.

"Badass," he quips.

"You know it, baby," I purr, leaning forward and licking his earlobe, making him shiver against me. "You in?"

"Let's do it, Brawler, stay low and quiet. Stick close," he mutters, and I nod, wrapping myself around him as he starts the bike again. He only drives ten minutes farther until we can see the outline of buildings, two sheltering whoever is there, with a fire between them, lights on either side, and laughter floating to us on the wind, as does… music. Well, shit. Makes it easier for us.

After that he cuts the engine and we swing off. I bite back my groan and stretch my sore legs and body. Palming my crossbow, I nod at him. "Got your back," I whisper quietly, knowing he will have to push the bike.

He nods, and I am almost unable to see him in the dark if not for the moon. He places a knife in his hand as he holds the handlebars and starts to push the bike. It's hard at first because of the sand and it's slow going, my eyes darting everywhere as I stay close. I am almost straining into the dark to see if anyone is sneaking up on us, my body on alert and strung tight until Jago's training kicks in and I breathe slowly, loosening up, and getting ready in case there is an attack.

Moving sluggishly, I feel sweat dripping down my face from my concentration as we try to stay quiet. The music and voices get louder as we draw nearer, and Jago cuts a wide berth around the side so that they don't see us. Even if they happen to look out into the night, all they will see is sand.

Until something catches my eye. We are directly opposite the building now, but the hairs on the back of my neck rise, so I grab his arm and stop him, tilting my head and pointing forward. He nods and looks that way too, both of us straining until it comes again, the noise. A dragging, like a chain slithering through the sand.

Blinking my eyes, which are finally clear enough to see, I cover my mouth to stifle my gasp. What the fuck?

There, on chains, spiked into the sand next to the building, are four ferals. Feral pets, snapping and pulling, fighting each other to get free, until one stops and raises his muzzle to the air, sniffing, no doubt smelling us. Jago quickly backpedals and I follow after him, keeping low, my eyes on the ferals. No wonder they have music going and lights, they have a fucking alarm system on either side in case people try to get by. Who the fuck is crazy enough to catch and try to muzzle those people eaters though? I'm surprised they even managed it without getting seri- ously hurt.

When we are far enough away again, Jago kicks out the stand on the bike and we duck behind it, our heads bent close together. "What do we do?" I hiss.

He shakes his head, looking back over the bike with a calculating expression. "Stay here, I'm going to check the other side and see how many people there are. Remain close to the bike, and if I'm not back in thirty minutes, take off in the other direction," he orders, ducking back down and then kissing me swiftly like he can feel my protest. "Trusting you to do this, Brawler," he whispers against my lips, and then he is gone, fading into the darkness. I strain my eyes again until I see his fast-moving form, low to the sand, like a creature of the night himself. I struggle to keep up with his progress until he is too far away for me to see.

Fuck.

Fuckity McFuck.

Such an asshole move, splitting up. I swear, I will get him back for this, but for now I need to watch his back and mine. It's the first time I've been alone in the sands out here and it's bringing back memories —the grit brushing along my skin, the howls of the ferals.

Swallowing, I move closer to the bike, feeling the metal pressing into my arm as I fight off the flashbacks. I need to be strong, I have an important job to do. If he comes back and I have been attacked, he will get hurt, or worse, so I need to the lady the fuck up.

'Cause, girls, let's face it, we are stronger than any man...I wonder why people say man the fuck up? They might be physi- cally stronger, but with just one quick hit to the balls, they are left scream- ing. Whereas our vaginas take a pounding, like it, and come out stronger. Oh yeah, I'm going to lady the fuck up.

Gripping my crossbow, I blow out air and go back to scan- ning the sand on either side of us, ready to fight if need be. I'm stronger than last time, smarter too, and a whole lot less trusting. I won't let those sick fucks ruin my life or this world for me.

The time stretches on slowly, my neck crawling with aware- ness as I wait for him to come back.

Suddenly, I feel the air move, and I roll forward, bringing up my crossbow with my finger on the trigger as he freezes, his hands up. "Brawler."

Pulling my finger away, I drop the crossbow and he edges closer. "Four of them, that's it, ferals on the other side too. We are going to have to fight our way through. The issue is they will spot us before we even get close, they could get a shot off," he snaps. "I don't like it, fuck, let's take the detour, an extra day won't matter."

"It will," I hiss. "What if that day is the difference between the life and death of someone? We fight, we just need a distrac- tion," I argue, and then I hear him groan. "I have it!"

"Oh God, I'm not going to like it, am I?" he growls.

"Nope, but it's happening. I'll distract them while you sneak in from behind, then we go all ninja and kill them. Plan?"

"It's a shitty plan," he grumbles.

"Don't worry, Beast Man, my plans always work," I tease. "They never work," he reminds me, but I ignore him.

"Trust me," I retort, as I strip off my jacket and crossbow, and drape it over the bike. "Keep those safe," I mutter, and hide my katanas at my back. I rough up my hair and slap myself in the face, the skin hitting skin sound ringing it out.

"What the fuck?" Jago growls, but I am already moving over the sand. I run fast and hear him swearing, but he quickly goes quiet, no doubt trying to get around the feral and to the back of them so he can use the building. I wait five minutes before the reach of the light, and then stand up and stumble into it.

He was right, four men, big, burly men with bellies and thick arms. Older too, some with grey hair or grey beards. Four bikes are stationed near the building on the left, with a fire in the middle of the cracked street, and an old-style radio still working next to it, blaring music as they sit and stand around it, drinking and laughing. I take in the scene quickly, noting only two of them are armed, one with a gun —he needs to go first—and one with a hammer. I spot two more gun holsters hanging over their bikes, they weren't expecting trouble, thinking the ferals would scare anyone off.

Well, I'm crazy enough to stumble into them.

It takes them a while to see me, and I almost debate moaning dramatically. "What the fuck!" one of them yells, and jumps to his feet, alerting the others as I move closer, almost touching the fire before I stop. They all freeze, staring at me open-mouthed, the one with the gun has his hand on it, but he hasn't pulled it out yet, most likely thinking I'm a weak woman.

*Er, now would be a good time for an idea, Piper...*except I lied. I was just going to distract them, I didn't think of how. The silence stretches on as they share a look and move closer to me. *Anytime now, Piper,* I scold myself, racking my brain.

"Oh God, please help," I cry theatrically.

"What's wrong, little lady?" the one with the gun asks, drop- ping his hand away from it as two of them move closer.

Erm, what's wrong. Good question. Think, think, think...

I panic, I didn't think this far ahead. "It's my ass," I blurt. "Asshole, the hole of my ass, erm, it hurts, I think I wiped with the wrong plant." Oh God, what am I saying?

It throws them long enough for me to grab my sword. "Fuck it," I mutter, and leap forward, impaling one's head on the end of my blade. "My plan totally worked," I brag, as I yank the sword out and spin to see Jago wrestling with the man with the gun, Jago on top of him on the ground. The other two are coming at me. I dodge a punch and outstretched hands and dance near the fire, another plan forming.

"My ass, you totally fell for it." I smirk, and one of them gets mad and rushes forward. I move at the last second, his hands almost touching my hair before he falls into the fire. He screams and rushes out, dropping to the sand and rolling as flames race up his legs. It gives me time to take out the other as he is staring in shock at his friend.

"Never underestimate a girl, motherfucker," I cry, before slashing across his neck. Blood spurts out, hitting me in the face and neck as his hands reach up and try and cover the wound, but it's no use, it's too deep. He falls to the ground and then to his side.

A shot goes off, ringing through the night, and I jerk around, fear filling me, but Jago has the gun and it's pointed right at the head of the man he was fighting for it. He turns it quickly and shoots the screaming man, still rolling, and then gets to his feet and glares at me. "Your ass? That was your plan? Help me, I hurt my ass?"

"Worked, didn't it?" I grin, sauntering up to him. "Shiny, can I have it?" I nod at the gun and his eyes narrow further, dangerously, not that I care.

"Brawler," he warns.

"Ah, come on, you can't be too mad, it got us through, didn't it? Let's keep going." I lean on my tiptoes, drop a kiss on his mouth, and while he is still shocked, I slip the gun from his grip, place it at the base of my spine, and turn away, but then he grabs me, his hand on my arm, and when I look back, his face is hard, eyes alight. He pulls me to him, yanking me across the distance, and covers my mouth with his.

I groan, our tongues tangling as his hands grip my ass. As soon as it started, it's over, and I'm the one left gobsmacked.

"Wait here, I'll get the bike. See if they had anything useful, won't you?" he rumbles, before striding away, the night swal- lowing him up.

What a man. One day, I'm going to wife him the fuck up...as long as Archel and him don't kill each other first...women can have two husbands, right? One for when the other is being annoying? That's what I'm going with anyway, not like the laws of old matter much anyway now.

I do as I am told for once, and ignoring the bodies, I head to their saddlebags on an old cement block, their belongings strewn wherever they last used them. I find some stray bullets for the gun and add them to my pockets. I also find some water bottles and some bits of meat, but I leave them, knowing we have our own supplies. They don't have much else until I dig through the last bag and find an old porno magazine. Grinning, I grab one of their spare shirts and wrap it up just as I hear Jago and the bike pull up.

"Got anything?" he asks, as he hops off and heads my way. "Not much, but I did get you a present." I thrust the badly wrapped magazine at him and he frowns as he takes it. "Now, it's not princesses, but..." I trail off as he opens it and stares down at the tits on the front page in shock.

His eyes slowly come up to meet mine. "You are giving me a stolen porno?"

"I know, you are so lucky." I sigh and pat his chest as I wander towards the bike. "You can ride bitch now."

"Wait, what?" I hear him sputter behind me.

Chapter 6
Divine Self

I can hear him grumbling to himself as he wraps his arms around my waist. Laughing, I gun it, and he grips on tighter as we leave the bodies and ferals behind, and head back into the Wastes. We will need somewhere to stop soon, as I am having a hard time seeing, but we don't want to be anywhere near those damn pets.

We travel for another half hour, but I have to slow down since it's getting really hard to see, and when I can't anymore, I pull over. Luckily, we found an old building not too far back, so I circle around and we hide the bike behind the structure and move around the front. Only then does our location click—it's a fucking church.

The cross from the top is gone, the stained glass windows are broken, and the old brick is still standing somehow, the double doors shut. It's a bit small, but it's still a fucking church.

Jago opens the door and I stop him with a hand, staring at him in horror. "What if I burst into flames when I step inside?" I whisper, and he chuckles.

"Really?"

I nod. "Really, God ain't no joke. He used to smite mother- fuckers. Let's face it, if one of us is going up in flames, it's going to be me, I have bad luck like that."

He peers down at me, obviously lost for words, then suddenly I am over his shoulder as he steps across the threshold and then puts me down, grinning at me. "See? No flames."

I nod solemnly. "Yet, maybe he's waiting, being sneaky-like, you don't know."

He shakes his head and strolls down the middle of the pews, some of which are tossed to the side and broken, others barely standing. This place looks like it has been ransacked and forgotten a long time ago, so I'm not surprised we don't find anyone. It's one giant room with an altar at the front, the cross, silver, and gold gone. We did find some candles in a small side room, which has a sofa and a chair, so we board up the front door to keep anyone out and give us some warning then head there.

Jago lights the wicks and places the tapers around the room, the firelight dancing off the old stone. If anything, it seems colder in here than outside. There is an old fireplace in the corner, but we ignore it and I pat down the sofa, brushing away as much dust and sand as I can before dropping my bag on it and throwing myself down on the cushions.

I watch as he inspects the room, ensuring everything is secure before he looks over at me. "We are sharing that, don't get comfortable," he teases.

"Ugh, is it not enough I give you my fun bags and sausage wallet? You really need to share my sofa too?" I groan dramati- cally, and he stumbles with a snort.

"Sausage wallet?" he repeats, his eyes wide with suppressed laughter.

"Lady garden?" I suggest, and when he stays silent, I carry on, "Muff ? Meat sleeve? Snatch? Penis fly trap?"

He strides over and covers my mouth with his hand. "God, please stop."

My eyes widen and I bite his hand, making him remove it. "Shhh, he can hear you." I raise my voice. "Sorry! He didn't mean it, carry on with your divine self."

"Just when I think you can't get weirder," he mutters, but leans down and kisses me. "You hungry, Brawler?"

"Starving, are we talking hungry for you or actual food, because I could go for either."

He laughs and grabs his bag, passing me some meat we stored and water. He sits on the floor as we share, and once we are finished eating, a yawn splits my face. I grab my bag and drop it on the floor before stretching out on the sofa and patting the spot next to me.

"One second," he murmurs, then he places the chair under the door, another warning, before heading my way. "We need an early start, so let's get a few hours of sleep."

The reminder of where we will be tomorrow dampens my spirits and he obviously sees it, because he climbs on next to me and pulls me into his arms. "Whatever we find, we find it together."

"I know." I sigh, burying my face into his chest. I don't know if I'm hoping Evan is there or not, or what I will say to him if I see him at all.

"You did amazing today," he admits begrudgingly, and I lift my head with a triumphant smile. "You can keep the gun."

"What gun?" I ask with wide eyes, and he grins down at me, his eyes alight.

"You are not sneaky at all," he mumbles, and lowers his head, kissing me gently. "It's a good job you're funny."

"I knew it!" I cry out, and laugh as he groans. "I shall remind you of that every time you forget."

"Looking forward to it," he murmurs, stroking my side, his rough fingers catching on my skin and leaving goosebumps in their wake.

Time seems to stand still as we both look at each other, and then suddenly it's restarted, my mouth smashing to his. He groans, grabs my thigh, and yanks it over his legs, holding me tightly to him as he dominates my mouth, leaving me at his mercy. Rolling, he lands on his back with me on top, our mouths still locked, our teeth clashing from the force as his hands drop to my ass and pull me closer, right over the hard bulge in his jeans.

I have to turn my head away to breathe, sucking in air as he strokes up my back, pulling my shirt with him. Sitting up, he helps me pull the top off and then he tosses it onto our bags. My bra goes next, his mouth closing around my nipple straightaway as I shiver from the cool air hitting my skin.

Moaning, I grip his head, running my fingers through his long hair as he licks and sucks my hard nipple before moving to the other, giving it the same treatment. My head falls back as I rock over his hardness, my pussy pulsing, urgent need racing through me.

"Jago," I whisper, and my nipple pops from his mouth as he grins up at me.

"Thought you were worried about being set on fire?" he teases, his hands spanning my waist and stroking just below my belly button.

"Fuck it, he can set me on fire as long as I get to come first," I declare, pulling at his shirt. He grabs the back of it and tugs it over his head, tossing it aside as I run my hands down his wash- board abs to his jeans.

He watches me with fiery eyes as I flick open the button and jerk down the zipper, the sound loud in the high-ceilinged room. He isn't wearing any underwear, so I promptly meet skin, licking my lips as I grab his hard length and pull it free, stroking as I go. He falls back, groaning as he thrusts into my hand.

Letting go, I stand up quickly and yank off my pants and panties, sand falling out of them as I step free of the fabric. When I'm naked, I stare down at him, his hand around his cock as he watches me, his mouth parted and chest heaving. He makes me feel so powerful, so fucking beautiful. His eyes are begging for me, his body waiting for whatever I'll do to him. All that power he has, all that strength, yet I can bring him to his knees, erm, back...it's addictive.

Stroking my hands up my belly to cup my breasts, I watch him as I touch myself until he narrows his eyes, darts his hands out, and grabs me, yanking me down to him. I laugh at his urgency, the sound soon turning into a groan as his clever fingers brush my pussy.

"You want to tease me?" he growls, dipping a finger inside me before rubbing my clit and flicking it, again and again, until I am moaning and dripping, needing more.

"Jago," I groan, my hands catching on his chest as I try to ride his finger, but he pulls it free, leaving me whimpering. "Dude, either fuck me or let me fuck myself."

"So impatient," he mutters, and then thrusts two fingers inside me, stretching me as my eyes close in bliss.

"Yess," I hiss, lifting myself as he holds still, riding them, but it's still not enough. I don't want teasing and fingers, I want his cock, so I pull free and grasp his hard length, squeezing him and lining him up, bumping my clit with the swollen head, making us both moan.

"Yes, Brawler," he tells me, grabbing my hips and lifting me as I slowly start to sink down onto his cock. Only when our skin meets do I stop, my heart thundering as I stare down into his blazing eyes, which are almost too bright, like the fire from the candles.

Then we start to move together, in sync, as he helps raise and drop me while he thrusts up, his cock stretching me, the angle making me pant and moan wantonly, the sound off flesh hitting flesh loud in the church.

Looking down at this man, I nearly come from the sight alone. His muscles bulge as he holds me effortlessly, his pecs rippling, abs rolling as he fucks me. Sweat dripping down his torso, his long hair spread around him, his fire eyes bright, his lips so plump and parted for me.

He's beautiful. His hands bring me pleasure as easily as they bring pain and death.

He flips us and I gasp as I fall to my side, his cock still inside me. He grabs my leg and throws it over his as he pulls me closer, his lips fumbling until he finds mine.

Kissing as he holds me close, both of us on our sides as he drives into me again and again, I come with a scream. He swal- lows the sound of my pleasure, and when I bite down on his lower lip, he grunts, stilling as he finds his own release.

✹

"Well, God certainly got a show." I laugh.

He groans and kisses me again. "He did."

I cuddle into his chest, not bothering to get dressed since I don't want sweaty clothes stuck to me, and I am warm enough with Jago's arms wrapped around my body.

"Night, big guy," I whisper, kissing the skin right over his heart.

"Night, my love," he whispers, kissing my head as I fall asleep in his arms.

✹

"Brawler," comes a call.

I turn my face away, and I hear someone laugh as kisses are dotted on my head. "Come on, beautiful, we need to get going."

"Nooo, five more minutes," I whine, not even opening my eyes until I am flipped onto my back. I blink them open to see a grinning Jago staring down at me. "You are way too happy for an early morning. What are you, a demon? It's 'cause you got the sausage wallet, isn't it?" I groan, throwing my arm over my eyes and trying to go back to sleep.

"Either you get up or I am going to start tickling you," he warns.

"I'm not ticklish." I sniff, yawning, and it goes quiet. "Last warning, Brawler," he threatens, his voice deadly. "Lick me," I retort.

He goes silent again, and I grin triumphantly, starting to fall back to sleep when suddenly, hands wrap around my thighs and yank them open. I blink stupidly, pulling my arm away. "What are—"

I gasp as he licks a long line across my pussy and grins up at me. "You offered," he rumbles.

"This brings a whole new meaning to breakfast," I grumble, and then gasp again as he lashes my clit in punishment, and laps at my pussy before looking up at me.

"Are you awake yet?" he asks with a smirk.

"Er, no, not yet, ooh look, my eyes are closing...so tired... must carry on," I taunt theatrically, shutting my eyes.

He sucks my clit into his mouth, and I almost come away from the sofa. Moaning, I grab his head and pull him closer, pressing my pussy against his face as he licks and teases me before dipping two fingers inside and curling them.

Lightning rolls through me from his talented tongue. I release his head, and with one hand, I cup my breast and roll my nipple between my fingers as I ride his face. He rumbles, "Delicious," and I groan, the vibration sending me higher and higher as he fucks me with his fingers and tongue.

When he dips the latter inside my pussy, tasting me, I gasp, my legs shaking as he yanks an orgasm out of me and licks me through it, careful not to touch my oversensitive clit too hard, brushing it with his tongue as he pulls his fingers free and replaces them with his tongue, wiggling it inside me.

My eyes won't open, my body lax, letting him do whatever he wants to me. He teases me, the aftershocks still racing through my veins, but my eyes fly open when he touches his finger to my other hole, just pressing it there, the pressure killing me.

I push towards him and he slips one inside me up to the knuckle, just staying there as he fucks me with his tongue, his finger in my ass. Unable to help myself, I start to move again, rolling my hips as he slowly drags another orgasm from me. Before I know it, I'm screaming with release, my pussy clamping down on his tongue and my ass on his finger.

I drop back to the sofa, breathing heavily, unable to move. My legs are wide open, my pussy wet and quivering as he pulls out, drops a kiss on my clit, and sits up, his chin and mouth covered in my release.

"Best breakfast I've had in a long time." He smirks. "Now get your ass up."

Then he's striding away, and I'm left gasping, my legs like jelly and my heart racing. That man is way too deadly for my heart...okay, vagina, but still. I wonder, if I fake sleep, will he start again? Probably not, I best not push it.

Evan.

The thought brings me back down to earth, and with a sigh, I get up, cringing at the sticky feeling between my thighs. Oh yeah, that's hot. Grabbing a towel I brought and a bottle of water, I clean myself. When I look up, I spot Jago watching me. "What? This isn't the movies, buddy, the cum just doesn't disappear." I huff and he laughs and throws my shirt and pants at me.

"Get dressed, Brawler," he orders, shaking his head as he turns and grabs our bags. "Bloody woman is going to turn me into a sex pest," I hear him mumble, as he unblocks the door and heads out into the rest of the church.

I get my clothes on, grab the water bottle, and go after him. I find him outside loading up the bikes. The sun is just rising, the heat slowly increasing, making me sweat already. It couldn't have been an ice age, could it? No, it had to be heat and sand. God, I can already feel it in my asscrack, and let me tell you, sand gets stuck everywhere. I mean everywhere, and it's a bitch to get out, you don't half get a chafing rash with it.

"You know you're speaking out loud, right?" He sniggers, leaning against his bike, and I blink, coming back to myself and staring at him.

"All I'm saying is, you can't tell me you don't get sand in your balls and it's a bitch. It ain't like no face scrub, it's annoying as hell."

"Face scrub," he mutters, shaking his head and climbing on the bike. "I'm not even going to dignify that with an answer. Get on," he orders.

"You totally get ballsack sand rash, don't you? I wonder if they have a cream for that," I muse, as I swing my leg over, scoot up, and wrap my arms around his back. "Jago?" I whisper when he can't see me, and he sighs, squeezing my hands which are resting over his stomach.

"I know, Brawler, whatever we find, remember, we have each other. Now that's enough delaying, it will only get worse the longer we wait." I nod and bury my face in is back, protecting it from the sand that kicks up when we start the bike, blanketed in the harsh granules overnight as we slept.

We pull away and begin the last leg of our journey to Paradise. I wish I knew what we were going to find when we got there. Anxiety is winding through me from having to see those people again, the people who ordered my death and suffering...but if they are dead... that means Evan probably is too.

I'd take facing them again if it meant he was alive and well. I'd confront a hundred bastards like them if it meant seeing those piercing blue eyes again and that snarky smile he used to give me.

Evvie, you better be alive, or I am going to kick your ass like I did when we were younger.

The miles pass by in a blur, my mind locked in the past, the fear of not seeing him alive again making me look beyond our last argument and to the love we had before it all went wrong.

"Evvie," I whisper, standing over his bed, clutching the bear he gave me. It dangles from one hand as I dart a look around the darkened room, the other beds empty since we are the only orphans down here.

"Evvie," I whisper again, shaking his shoulder.

He flips over, cracking open one eye when he spots me, then he frowns and opens the other. "You okay, Pip?" he murmurs, his voice cracking from sleep, his face finally losing that baby fat as he grows up. There are only a few years between us, but he seems so much older recently.

"Nightmare," I confess quietly, looking away in embarrassment.

He scoots back on the single bed and pulls up the covers for me, so I slip in and turn my back to him. He drapes the blankets over me and wraps his arm around my waist, spooning me as we share the pillow, his breath wafting over my ear. "I'll protect you from them, Pip, I always will, now get some sleep, and if you have any more you close your eyes and you tell them that they have to deal with me," he tells me. I smile and giggle and shuffle closer.

"Thanks Evvie, night." I yawn and close my eyes, happy now.

"Night, Pip, love you." His voice floated with me into my night-mare-less dreams.

Licking my lips, I move closer to Jago as we speed through the Wastes, my heart locked in pain as I try to fight off the memories. They are too painful, too much when I don't know where or how he is, but they don't care, they keep coming after being locked away for so long from my anger, which is dissipating with each mile we cover and being replaced with fear...fear I will never see my best friend again.

"Your office is huge!" I laugh, turning with my arms spread wide as he stands at the door, beaming. It was assigned to him this morning, the youngest doctor on staff. I grin at him and he opens his arms.

I rush into them and he lifts me into the air, spinning me around as we laugh before he puts me back on the floor and moves a wisp of hair out of my face, his eyes filled with happiness, his smile still stretched across the face I love so much.

"I couldn't do it without you, Pip," he whispers, and for a moment our eyes catch, and he loses his smile. His tongue darts out, he licks his lips, and starts to lower his head.

Oh God, is he going to kiss me?

The door bangs and we leap away like guilty children as he answers it, his face red. I turn away and busy myself by looking around the office, disap- pointment filling me. I always thought Evvie and I were meant to be together, fated, but maybe I was wrong. Maybe he doesn't see me like that, but the way he just looked at me has me all confused. This crush is getting out of hand, that's for sure.

He shuts the door and I turn to face him, leaning against the counter as he shuffles awkwardly, so I take pity on him. "So, how are we celebrating? What trouble can we get into?" I wiggle my eyebrows and he laughs, relief filling his face.

"I'm a doctor now, I'm supposed to behave." He grins.

"Nah, that's definitely not a rule, who wants a boring doctor?" I shake my head. "Nope, you only get one life, Evvie, why would you want to spend it conforming to rules? I'd rather have fun."

"You always do." He laughs. "One day, you will understand why rules are so important, they keep us safe and alive, Pip."

I smile but it's false now as hurt races through me. He's started to do this recently. Talk down to me like I'm a child. "I know that, Evvie, doesn't mean you can't have fun though, the world is shitty and fucked up as it is, why not make the most of it?"

"I wish I could, Pip." He sighs.

"About another hour," Jago yells over the wind and the sound of the engine. I nod to show him I understand and stretch my fingers before holding on again, turning my head so I can look out into the Wastes with the sun burning down on the sand, heating the grit and everything else left behind. I wish Evvie could have seen the world the way I did, something to explore, something to love and have fun with. Instead, he was always worried about everything. I just hope that worry hasn't killed him.

"What did you do now, Piper?" He frowns, as I hop up onto the table and swing my legs back and forth.

He slides his chair over to me as I lift my hand. "You hit some-one?" he asks, eyebrows raised.

"Technically, she ran into my fist...repeatedly...and my foot." I grin and he shakes his head with a smile.

"Pip, what am I going to do with you?" He sighs and grabs the stuff he needs to clean out the cuts on my hand.

"Call me pretty and get me coffee?" I tease, as he leans over and cleans the wounds, making me hiss from the sting of the cleaner.

"What did she do?" he questions, too busy prodding the cuts to notice me wince as I rack my brain for a believable lie...not the truth that she was bad-mouthing him.

"Er, I didn't like her face, it scared me, and I was always taught to punch what scares me." I nod, proud of myself.

He looks up then, smiling. "Liar, you always crinkle your nose when you lie," he says, leaning back. "What happened?"

"Dude, how did you even see me do that?" I moan and glance away, but he moves closer and tilts my chin so I'm forced to look at him. "Piper, we promised to always tell each other the truth."

"I hate when you bring logic to the party," I mutter and sigh. "She was saying shit about you."

"Like what?" he presses, blinking.

"Just that you don't deserve this role, orphaned bastard and shit." I shrug, not willing to tell him everything. It had been bad, and although he wouldn't let it show, it would hurt him to hear it. He worked hard for this position, he doesn't need some precious princess ruining it.

"I see," he mutters, looking down, and then gazes back up at me. "So you were defending my honour?" he teases.

"Don't make it weird, Evvie," I grumble, but he smiles brightly and leans over, kissing my forehead.

"Thank you, Pip, I love you too," he whispers, and then pulls back. "Next time, punch better though. Come on, let's fix this fist so you can get back to causing chaos."

"You know it, Doc. Let's fix me up so I can kick some basic bitch ass."

He wasn't perfect, but he was always there for me, more than anyone will ever know. He was the one who looked after me, held me all night every night even when he couldn't sleep himself. He dried my tears and pulled my broken heart together. It was him and me, always. We were family and I left. He was hurt, scared for me, and I left.

I'm not saying he was right, in fact he fucked up big in the way he went about things, but his heart was behind it. He only did it to protect me and keep me safe like he always did, like I always did for him.

If I thought he was in danger, I would have done anything to stop it and protect him. So maybe I can't be too mad at him, maybe we just need to fight it out...as long as he is alive.

"We are almost there," he shouts, so I lift my head and stare into the distance where I can see buildings.

"Get ready," he warns me, and I nod. We don't know what we will find there, after all. We locate the gap in the fence—used to it from when we did patrols—and I realise it doesn't feel like old times. We head straight to the bunker door and idle there, frowning when it doesn't open.

"Maybe they can't see us?" I suggest, looking around. They only open it for patrols, but they should recognise us...

A whistle cuts through the air and we both jerk around, trying to pinpoint the noise. My eyes widen when I spot people, lots of people, waiting by the side of the building next door. Someone at the front waves their hand, the sun blurring them.

"What do we do?" I query, and he hesitates.

"It's up to you, Brawler," he hedges, obviously as unhappy with this as I am.

I bite my lip and debate my options. "If they wanted to kill us, they could have already. We better go see, they will know what happened," I tell him, and he revs.

"You sure, Brawler? I can outride them," he cautions.

"No, let's go, I need to know." I sigh and wrap my arms tightly around him as he pushes us backwards, and then turns us to face the people, and starts to slowly head their way.

As we get closer, I can make them out. They definitely aren't from Paradise. They look like scav parties we'd meet outside, they are too hard to live down there. The woman at the front draws my eyes, though, as we stop feet away. Jago keeps the engine going, but I hop off and stand next to her, staring at her.

Jesus Christ, what a woman.

She is covered from head to toe in weapons, a sword peeking over her shoulders, and her clothes skintight, showcasing her athletic build. Her arms are muscular and strong, her face blank and scary, but oh so beautiful. Her hair is braided and messy, much like the men around her, and her eyes are calculating and very intelligent. She is terrifying in a holy shit she's hot kind of way.

"Piper," comes a strangled whisper, floating to me on the air. My head jerks around, but another voice catches my attention, a familiar one, one I worried I would never hear again.

"Pip?" someone yells, and I turn to see Evan rushing towards me, only to be held back by an equally scary and scarred man who is half naked and looks like an ad for weapons-r-us. Who are these people?

I turn again to see Archel stepping forward, his mouth open and eyes worried, but I grin at him, I can't help it.

"Brawler?" Jago prompts, shutting off the engine, but I swing glances between Evan and Archel who are both staring at me.

Tits on a dick, all three men are here...now this is going to get awkward.

Chapter 7
Reunion

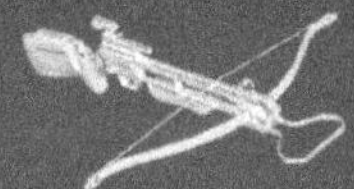

"Okay, someone better tell me what the fuck is going on before I start kicking ass and taking names...or Jago does and I cheer from the side." I huff, propping my hands on my hips and staring at Archel. What is my shadow doing here? Why is Evan? Who is this woman and the army behind her? Seriously, what is going on? "Should have figured you would be here if there was trouble," I scoff and then grin, unable to help myself. I made him promise to come back alive, but it seems I got bored and found him first. I mean, he has been gone a long time.

"Missed you, Shadow. Wait until you see what I can do with a dagger now." I wiggle my eyebrows as he grins at me, and then I suck in a breath and turn to Evan.

I don't know what to say, but the silence is awkward, so I do what I do best, talk. "Hi, Evvie, long time no see. Loving the whole hobo chic look you are going for." I force my mouth shut as he gapes at me and then gasps in pain, sagging in the scarred man's arms.

"Pip, fucking hell. Pip, they told me you were dead!" he screams, the sound of my nickname on his tongue like a dagger to my heart. The entire way here, I was wondering if I could forgive him, what I would do when I found him, but it didn't prepare me for this. I'm lost, staring into those blue eyes I used to know better than my own, only they are filled with ghosts and pain now, so different from when I knew him...and I realise we have both changed...grown up...we are different.

Do we even know each other anymore?

I wince as tears gather in those eyes and the woman's voice drags my gaze to her. "Let's take this inside, we have a lot to discuss." She whistles, waving her fingers in the air in a circle before looking at the scarred man. It's strange watching as all the big, scary men jump to do what she orders. "Let him go. Bern, get the patrol back on it. Henry, work with the dwellers. I want to know what the fuck is going on down there. Everybody else, I want no fucking bodies, fight, fuck, I don't care, but no deaths!"

Damn, she swears more than me, maybe I could take lessons from her? Also, why am I weirdly wanting to cheer her on right now? She looks at me then, her eyes boring into me like she sees everything, and I find myself standing up taller. This woman is clearly no one to be trifled with, if the fear, adoration, and worship on the gathered men's faces are anything to go by. "Follow me."

She turns and starts to walk away, the scarred man falling into step behind her as they rush to do her bidding. I lean into Jago and lower my voice. "Who is she? She is badass as hell, total girl crush material. Think she would let me touch her sword? What? Don't look at me like that, I meant an actual sword, not cock, jeez."

"Brawler," Jago groans, looking pained as he shakes his head. "What? Not saying I would swing that way, ha, but damn, that is one scary fine woman, like I bet she even fucks scary hot, you know?"

"Pip," Evan calls, moving closer, but Archel steps in front of him and grins at me.

"Hey, Princess, couldn't stay away, could you?" he teases and laughs, grabbing me into a hug before releasing me when Jago growls. Yep, awkward.

"Er, woman, orders," I sputter, and push past them, leaving them all staring at me as I rush after the woman, anything to get away from the awkward tension before they all kill each other.

I weave through the impromptu camp they have set up, where more big men in leather, covered in scars, tattoos, and weapons, watch as I move through their midst and into the tent where the woman and the scarred man just ducked into. I follow and stop at the doorway as Jago, Archel, Evan, and a few others file in behind me.

I let them move past me and then gaze around, as the scarred man sprawls on the bed on the floor to the left, his eyes half shut like he couldn't give a fuck if we are here or not. His lean, muscled body stretches like a purring cat's. Evan moves past me to stand near the woman, which sends a pang of pain through me, but I hide it, avoiding his gaze, which hasn't left me.

Archel moves to my right, so close I can feel his arm brushing mine as Jago stands to my left, staring down everything and everyone.

"Feeling needy, assassin? Why don't I let your girl know how you lost to me last night?" the woman calls, and I glance between them, more pain flowing through my veins—wait, is this why he left? To go to her?

I'm so confused. Who is she? Is she wanting Evan or Archel or the scarred man? Archel laughs and I move away from him slightly, the pain constant though I don't let it show. "I'm calling a rematch once the whole war thing is out of the way," he fires back, waving his hand.

War thing?

What the fuck have I missed? I've had enough of this, so I cross my arms and stare at them all, trying to imitate them and look as scary as Jago. "Okay, seriously, what the hell is going on?"

Looking at the woman, since she is clearly in charge here, and I wait, knowing if I'm to get any answers, they will be from her.

"I'm Worth," she says instead.

"Berserker Queen," a big guy adds from the floor.

"The Champion of the Wastes," a good-looking man inserts. "Soulmate!" the scarred man interjects with a smirk, making the woman roll her eyes. Damn, this woman has a lot of names, think I could get some like that?

Piper, the kicker of asses.

Piper, sexy fun bags, lover of men, killer of assholes?

I'll keep working on it for sure, 'cause that group of names is awesome.

"Or just Worth, ignore them," she replies, her face softening as she looks around at the gathered men.

I really don't know whether to be turned on or scared by this woman...it's very confusing to my body, which wants to run and also throw myself at her to learn her ways.

"More like pain in the ass," Evan mumbles, so I look at him and he swallows hard, his eyes telling me things I can't handle right now. But hearing him call her that, it shows he cares about her.

"Why don't you tell us why you are here?" Worth demands, drawing my gaze once more to her, breaking Evan's and my staring contest.

"Why don't you?" Jago counters, sounding fierce, prowling closer to me. He doesn't like strangers, being unprepared, and not knowing what is happening, but he doesn't move too far away, making me smile.

Worth takes him in with a quirk of her lips, like she knows something I don't. "I'm not your enemy. My father used to run Paradise. I met him this last year, but I didn't even know he was alive. I was heading back here after...a pit stop, shall we say, to get some information. While we were here, however, they were attacked." She rubs her head then, the only sign of weakness I have seen from her, and then crosses her arms. "We helped protect it. Now, the guards and captain are locked down there, sweeping the place for explosives and survivors. Why are you here?"

Captain.

The name sends a shiver of fear and pain through me, but I try to mask it, not wanting to give away how much one word can hurt me and knock me back down. I look to Archel, asking if I should trust her, and he nods, so I blow out a breath.

"A messenger came, told me Paradise was attacked, it was gone, so we came straightaway. I wanted to make sure...you were okay," I finish, looking to Evan.

"Came to where?" Worth asks. Damn, she is good.

I don't answer, I won't betray the people who took me in when I had no one else. Even if Archel trusts her, I don't know her well enough.

"We are going to have to trust each other. Like it or not, there are bigger threats out here than me right now. I trust Archel and even Evan, and they are vouching for you, so you should extend the same courtesy. We are not enemies. In fact, I think we might just be allies right now," she tells me, her eyes serious. I catch on the 'right now' part. I knew she was deadly, but is this what Archel was talking about? War? Is that why they were here? Is that why Paradise was attacked?

"What clan?" Jago questions.

"Was a slave for a while to Berserkers, then a fighter at The Ring, then a bounty hunter. I recently killed Ivar the Mad and took his throne, so I now rule the Berserkers and have peace ties with all clans. Which clan?" she fires back, holy shit. She's a queen? Of those animals Archel told me about? No wonder she is scary as hell, but I feel a kinship, I saw the pain flash in her eyes at the word 'slave'...a woman recognises that in another. She has been through the same as me, and a lot more, yet she is still here. I can respect that.

"None, not yet," he answers.

"This is getting us nowhere. I have information, you have information, we need to work together." Worth shrugs. "Other- wise, feel free to leave, we have shit to deal with and a war to win."

"I've heard that twice now. What war?" I inquire, excitement coursing through me as well as worry. Worth looks at Archel with a smile and he returns it, a message passing between them.

"Huh, picked a fighter, did you? Can she kick your ass or do I need to teach her?" She laughs and I like her even more then.

He groans. "Fuck no, don't teach her your dirty tricks." Damn, if she took down Archel, she has more than my fucking respect, that man is unstoppable.

"What donkey dick war?" I ask louder, since they are ignoring me, and Jago groans.

"Really, Brawler, donkey dick?" he questions.

Worth gets serious then, giving me a considering look. "The Cities came north, took some of our people, and they want Paradise. I plan to stop them, want to join?" she queries, and I blink at the blunt question, but the answer is obvious. War, protecting people...that sounds like one hell of an adventure.

"Shit, yeah." I nod, ignoring Jago who groans and Archel who laughs.

"Why don't we discuss exactly what is happening?" Worth suggests, as she leans back against the scarred man, using him as a chair. The tension is broken with one move, so I drop myself to the floor and cross my legs and face Worth.

"I was from Paradise," I start, knowing I need to share to earn her trust and get the same back, but even that hurts me, so I close my eyes for a moment and gather my strength.

"Piper," she calls, and I look up at her, my eyes no doubt swimming with the pain I can't seem to hide. "Everything you have been through, I can tell you I have been through the same. You aren't a slave for years without seeing the worst of the world.

My body is covered in scars, brands, their torture, and pain. Ivar, the king I killed, was my master. I was his favourite, and he tried for years to break me again and again. He raped me, his men raped me." The man behind her flinches, and Jago growls as Archel steps closer to me, both of them knowing what that word will do to me. Strange that one word can be so hurtful, so fucking devastating even after surviving the act. "They tortured me, they killed the boy I loved, they killed the man I loved, and they took me from my family. I don't say this to diminish your pain, I say it to be frank. Whatever happened, here, there is no judgement. How could there be when most of us have been through the same? You were from Paradise, correct? Evan told me you disap- peared, that he was told you were dead, but he searched anyway. What happened? You do not have to share every-thing," she adds, smiling at me with understanding.

I sit up straighter, her pain calling to mine, echoing my own ghosts and past and I know, whatever this woman faces, wherever she goes...I would follow her. She told me her pain, her story, so the least I can offer her is mine. I stare at no one but her as I open my mouth.

"I was usually on patrol with Jago, they changed that, and on patrol that night they attacked, raped, and tried to kill me. Ferals got to them, and Archel saved me. He took me to a place, The Forgotten, and the people there were once from Paradise as well. They learned of the corruption and left."

"Who, what corruption?" she asks, leaning forward, my words catching her attention.

I suck in a breath. If she is asking, it's important, and saying the words do not give them power. They can't do anything else to me they haven't already. "The captain, he ordered it, he warned me. The people, my people, told me this was done often, nearly all the time, and anyone digging too deeply was killed. Paradise, it's corrupt, you said the captain is here? Let me be the one to kill him," I beg, the idea coming out of nowhere, but when I say it out loud it settles inside me and I know, I know it's what I need to do, I know it's one of the reasons I came here without even realising it.

"He's yours," she agrees instantly. "Sands below, I knew some-thing was off here." The scarred man reaches out and rubs her back, and she leans into him more, seeking comfort without even realising it. "Okay, you know anything about the Cities?"

I shake my head. I have never heard anything about them until a couple of minutes ago, but then Jago interrupts, shocking me. "I do."

Worth narrows her eyes on him. "Tell me," she demands, making him growl, so I lay a hand on his arm, calming him.

"I trust her, Jago, and I trust Archel and Evan," I assure him, looking into those fire eyes. He sighs, curling his hand around mine, and looks back at Worth.

"I've been there once, was sent to map it," he admits, and I stare at him in shock. Why didn't he ever tell me this? If I know him, it's probably because he thought it wasn't important enough to, not that he was hiding it from me.

"Let us start from the beginning. Bern, grab us some water and food and get Erik and my father," she orders, as the big guy lumbers from the tent on her command.

I swing my head back to her. What a woman. I can't help it, my mouth opens. "Will you marry me?" I blurt, and she just stares at me in shock. I don't think many people shock her. "Sorry, but damn, that whole power, in control thing is hot as hell." I shrug as I smile at her.

"When she's marrying anyone, it's me," the scarred man behind her pipes up, and Worth turns to him with a glare. "What? I said when," he teases.

"Does that mean I get to be best man?" Archel asks, and I blink as it clicks into place. That man must be his best friend, the one he told me about...Drat? Dax? Dray! That's it. Gotta admit that makes me feel better...but I still have to know, so when Worth looks at me, I wince.

"Sorry, awkward, so I gotta know. Girl to girl, you slept with him?" I jerk my head at Archel. It won't change anything...really. I don't know who I would be jealous of, him or her. Jago jerks under my touch, but I don't look at him.

She laughs, it tumbles out of her. "I like my heart in my chest, not on his knife, thank you."

"Plus, I'd kill him," Dray adds.

I nod, grateful. "Okay, what about Evan?" I might as well ask about them all, but I don't look at him, not wanting to see his reaction.

"Nope, sorry, not my type." She grins at me and I return it. "Huh, figured. You like the big warrior kind, right? I bet they throw you around and you get all kinky—sorry, I'll stop now." I roll my lips to physically stop myself from talking as she just blinks at me, the awkward silence stretching on as I try not to break it, but nope, no can do.

"I like what you've done with the place, very minimalistic," I comment, looking around the tent.

Just then the tent flap opens behind me as the big guy from before pushes in, followed by a few others. "Let's get started, shall we?" she suggests, clearly wanting to move on from my awkward questions and rambling. "Jago, tell us everything."

I feel him bristle at the command, but I tighten my hand and he starts to talk. "I was born out here, came to Paradise as a kid, and when I made guard, they wanted maps of everything. I prefer it out here, so I volunteered. One day, they said they knew of a city down south, they wanted it mapped just in case, so I snuck in..." I listen closely, adding it to what I already know of Jago. Sometimes, I feel like I know nothing, sometimes I feel like I know more than anyone. He holds my hand the entire time, and as the discussion goes on, I lean into him, tired from the drive and last few days as I listen.

After a few hours, I think everyone is overloaded, so we decide to take a break. When Worth announces it, though, she rushes out of the tent with her men, leaving Jago, Evan, Archel, and me...

Oh shit, this should be fun...Dr. Phil, anyone?

❧

"Soo...circle time, anyone?" I inquire, sitting up from Jago as all eyes go to me. "We go around and introduce ourselves, names...sexual kinks...no..." I trail off. "Awkward," I mutter, making Archel laugh and even Evan's lips twitch.

"Princess." Archel shakes his head. "I can't believe you are here, thought you were waiting back home."

"I got tired of waiting." I grin. "No one to spar with, plus I needed to know, Trev understood."

"Pip," Evan starts but stops, licking his lips, looking between us and then sighing. "I'm glad you're alive."

I sag at that, disappointed that's all he had to say. "Yeah, you too." I nod as Jago wraps his arm around my shoulders and pulls me closer, knowing how hard this must be for me and offering me comfort. Archel watches the movement with sharp eyes, narrowing them slightly as he strokes a knife at his side. I warn him with my gaze not to start anything.

How do you broach the subject that you have a boyfriend... with your...Archel?

It goes quiet again and Jago drops a kiss on my head, his every movement watched by both Evan and Archel. "I'm going to grab us some drinks, why don't you all catch up?" he tells me, and gets to his feet, waiting for me to nod before he leaves.

One man down, two to go.

Archel glances between us and then back to me. "I'm going to... go," he offers, stopping before me and crouching down.

"Catch you in a bit, Princess," he murmurs with a wink, and then lowers his voice. "Are you okay if I leave?"

I lick my lips, feeling nervous, but this conversation needs to happen. "Yeah, see you in a bit?" I ask, needing to talk to him alone as well.

"Don't worry, Princess, I'm not going anywhere without you again." He grins and leans closer, his back blocking us from Evan as he drops a kiss on my lips, wearing a grin as he leans back. "Wanted to do that since I saw you ride in. Go easy on him, he's missed you like crazy."

I nod and he stands, looking back over at Evan. "Be gentle with her, she has been through hell and back just to be here today. You fuck that up, you be a bastard to her, and I will slit your throat in your sleep," he warns, and then slides from the tent, whistling to himself, leaving me alone with Evan.

We just stare at each other, both not knowing what to say. There's too much history...too many bad words and fights between us.

But I was given another chance at life, even if we are never as close as we once were, we deserve to give us a chance. We were family before, best friends, and if I've learned anything from my suffering, it's that you can lose someone in an instant, life isn't guaranteed.

"Evvie—"

"Pip."

We say at the same time and then laugh, the tension broken. He strides closer and drops to his knees before me, like he can't stand to be farther away anymore, like he needs to see I'm here for himself, I'm alive. I feel the same way, even after everything, I still love this man.

My heart pounds and tears fill my eyes, I see them reflected back in his.

"I'm so sorry, Pip, for everything. God, I was such an asshole. I don't deserve your forgiveness, but I'm asking for it. I realised when you left, when you disappeared, that all that mattered was you. The rules, my life, being a doctor. I did everything for you, and without you...it was worthless. I should have supported you, I should have been there, but I was so scared, Pip." He sniffs, tears rolling down his cheeks. "So scared that you would get hurt and then...you were good, really good, and I saw you pulling away, saw you with him and it hurt. It hurt so fucking much, the idea you could replace me...it's always been my deepest fears. I always knew you were amazing, Piper, and would do great things, and I was terrified you would outgrow me and leave me behind."

Tears roll down my face then, unchecked. "Eva—"

"But that isn't an excuse, my fears shouldn't have come out in such a vile way. It wasn't your fault, you aren't to blame for my anger or darkest secrets. I shouldn't have taken them out on you. You aren't responsible for my emotions, I am, and I was stupid. I should have fought harder for you...for us, Pip, and I will regret it every day for as long as I live, which to be honest, might not be long with this war thing."

He laughs and I laugh too, the sound choked and tear filled. "I know we can't go back to the way we used to be, and that's okay, but if you'll let me, I'd love to get to know the new you, to be part of your life in whatever way you'll let me. I'll try to control my asshole tendencies and not throw my shit all over you."

I wipe my face and he laughs, helping me, brushing away my tears. "That's all I ever wanted to hear...I'd like that. As long as you haven't gotten boring, then I'm afraid you're screwed."

"I'm sure you will ensure I'm not." He grins, wiping his face on his arm. "God, I missed you, Pip, so fucking much, I didn't even know it was possible to miss someone this much," he sobs, ugly crying now. As he smashes his fist into his heart, he contin- ues, "You took this when you left. I didn't even know it was yours, but it is, it always has been. I'm not asking you to give me yours back...I've seen you with him and that's okay, I'll be happy for you if you're happy, if he's what you want. I just needed you to know."

"Jago's amazing," I answer, and he flinched but nods. "But I always loved you, Evvie, since we were kids. My heart is his, that's true, I love him. I'm sorry, I know that hurts."

"No, don't be sorry, it's my own fault. I wasted the chance I had." He sniffs, looking away, so I lean over and turn his face to mine, just like he used to do to me so many times before.

"But you are always in here, I think you always will be. No matter how much you hurt me or pushed me away, I couldn't help it, because it didn't belong to me. It belonged to you. I gave what was left to Jago, but you still have a piece. I'm not saying I—" I swallow then. "I'm not saying I can jump in with you, because I don't want to hurt Jago and yes, even Archel. But if you want to be a part of my life, Evan, you need to accept them. If you came searching for that same girl, she's not here anymore. I've grown up, so if you are hoping for that ghost, then you need to leave before you hurt me again, because I've had my heart broken by you too many times."

"Pip, you have to learn to trust me. I know, I'm sorry, but if you trust me with your heart again, I won't break it. If you let me, I'll mend it, I promise," he whispers.

"Can you? Can you accept that I love you...but I love them too?" I murmur, and he sits back.

"I don't know, I hope I can, but I don't know," he tells me. "Least you were honest." I snort, wiping my face again.

"Shouldn't be surprised that others realised how amazing and sexy I am, though, can you blame me?" I tease, trying to lighten the mood.

"No," he chuckles, "I can't. I'm going to try, can you let me try?"

"I can do that." I nod, wiping my cheeks, which are probably splotchy, my eyes red. Just then, the tent opens and we both turn to see Archel and Jago who take one look at me and growl, both of them moving in sync.

Jago grabs me and pushes me behind him as Archel clutches Evan and holds him in the air. "What the fuck did you do?" Jago yells as Archel snaps, "I told you what would happen."

"Guys," I call, giggling, "let him go."

They ignore me as Evan's face turns purple from Archel cutting off his air, so I leap to my feet. "Let him down right fucking now!" I yell, and they all turn to me in shock. Archel drops him and he falls to the floor, wheezing.

I cross my arms and narrow my eyes on them. "Right, clearly we need to set some ground rules so you don't go around killing each other." I huff as Archel grins at me and Jago stares me down, not the least bit sorry. "Yes, he made me cry—" Jago growls and Archel palms a knife. "But that doesn't mean you can kill him," I finish. "That is between him and I, besides there are more important things to deal with than whose dick is bigger than whose, so you need to sort your shit out and get over it. Understood?"

"Understood, Princess. We can revisit the dick measuring in private if you wish." He winks. I look at Jago who grimaces. "Fine."

"Good boys." I grin. "Now, let's go find that woman and see whose ass we are kicking first! Team Piper the Asskicker unite!"

They all groan as I turn and head out of the tent. Maybe having three men isn't as difficult as I thought....

Chapter 8
A Queen

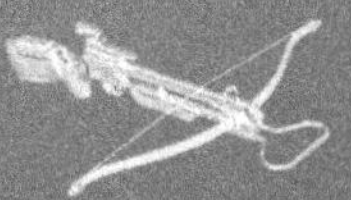

An hour or so later, we are gathered around a makeshift table, with Jago on one side and Archel on the other. I was excited just to be invited. I look around at all the scary mother- fuckers surrounding me, and wonder how Worth deals with them all until she stands up and clears her throat. Her eyes narrow on everyone, power emanating from her. It's what I imagine a queen looks like, so fierce, so determined.

Someone creeps up behind me and I jerk in my seat, grab- bing a knife until I spot it's just another person for the meeting, then, feeling embarrassed, I put my knife away and turn back to Worth as she starts to talk, focusing my attention on her as Jago's hand lands on my back and rubs, obviously noticing what happened. It would be nice, but Archel's hand lands on my thigh under the table and also starts to massage, and my head fills with thoughts of them both doing other things to me at the same time.

Bad, Piper, focus. War, bad men, things to do. Sex later.

"I'm going to make this fast and simple. We don't know if they are dead and we don't have time to stay and find out. If they are alive, they aren't opening that door, and you could all die waiting for it. If they aren't, then they aren't opening it for a reason. My people and I are leaving this afternoon, we still have a war to win, so before then, we need to come up with a plan for you." She looks around, stopping on the man she introduced as her father. He's familiar from down below, he was always nice. "I say you leave Paradise for good."

I watch as he leaps to his feet and stares at her in shock. "B-But this is our home! We don't know how to live out here!" he yells, as we all watch. Worth's men are starting to get itchy, so she lifts her hand to stop them from doing anything stupid.

"I feel like I need popcorn," I whisper to Archel, who grins down at me.

"Then you fucking adapt. Everyone else had to. It's time you stopped hiding in the bunker," she snaps and then looks at me. I want to shout, "Oh snap," but I restrain myself, which is harder than it sounds. "You offered your help, does that still stand?" she asks, so I sit up taller under her gaze, serious. I meant what I said, it's more than just about adventure, it's about saving lives now. A war would be bad for everyone, including my new family. If I don't join now, we will be dragged into it later, and I would rather it be now with someone like her.

Someone likely to win. A queen.

"Yes," I reply.

"Good. I need you to stay here for two days, that is all. Help them pack up and move out. There is an empty town near The Rim. It's called Spring, and it's probably the safest place, even if it's not as habitable as everywhere else," she instructs.

I bite my lip, but I have a better idea. She doesn't seem like the type to ignore someone and want all the power, so I give it a shot. "Can I offer another suggestion?" I query, raising my hand and she smiles at me.

"Sure," she agrees.

"We wait for two days, and if they don't open the door, we abandon Paradise like you suggested. Then we take them with us." I look at Archel then, hoping I'm doing the right thing. "To The

Forgotten. There is enough room and they will be better protected. They will need to earn their place, but the people are friendly and will help them."

"The Forgotten will accept them all?" she inquires.

I hesitate, unsure and not wanting to lie to her. "Not any who harmed those there. I speak for my people, and they will face punishment for that. The others, yes."

I lift my head and face her down, not backing off. They hurt my family, so they deserve whatever they get. "Then do that, your punishment and vengeance is yours to have, and Piper?" She leans forward, her eyes filled with a frightening intensity. I would really hate to be whoever has pissed her off. "Make them pay for what they did, make it fucking hurt."

I smile, I can't help it, as the others hail her and me. "Too fucking right, hotness." I raise my hand in a fist bump and she raises her eyebrows, making me sigh—hot, but clearly not used to people. "You're too hot to be dumb, you bump it with your fist," I explain, before grabbing her hand and bumping our fists together, then I pull mine back and make an explosion sound and gesture.

"It is sorted then," she declares, leaning back.

I spot Jago glaring at her, so I distract him. "I bet she has a bigger penis than even you. You should have a measuring contest," I whisper to him, and he turns to me with a snort.

"It's not sorted! My people should have a choice!" her dad shouts, and I lean back as I physically see her lose her shit on him. Her face goes cold and she spins and advances on him. Damn, popcorn is needed again. Why does the apocalypse have to ruin my dreams?

"Listen and listen hard. I will say this only once. My men, the people I love most in this world, are being tortured as we speak so I can babysit your fucking pompous ass. I don't give a fuck if you are scared out here, or that the last time you came outside was when you lost my brother and me. You will do as you are fucking told for once or so help me God, we will leave you here to die. You are being given a better choice than most—protection and a new home.

Everyone here had to earn that, had to fight for that, and you want to complain it's not fair? Life isn't fucking fair, sweetheart, but you keep on going, keep fighting, because it's the only life you get. So you are going to go back there and tell your people what is happening, then you will pack up. You will listen to Piper, you will do as she tells you, or you die, but I am not wasting another moment of my life on a man who left his own daughter to die at the hands of a madman. Not when the men who saved me and brought me back to life are suffering. Do we understand each other?" she finishes, her voice deadly. Everyone else is frozen, watching them as he shrinks back before her wrath. "I understand," he says thickly, and I wouldn't be surprised if he shit his pants. She is one scary woman.

She storms away then, turning her back on him and raising her voice. "Pack up! We are rolling out soon!" she yells, then strides away, her hands balled into fists and her body wired tightly. She disappears into her tent and I get to my feet, knowing now isn't probably the best time, but there will be no other. I gesture for Jago to stay there and go after her, finding her packing her bag in her tent.

"Worth, can I have a minute?" I ask, and she turns with a sigh.

"Sure."

I lick my lips and force my head higher. I won't back down, not now. "I want to help with the war, I think I can."

She raises her eyebrows, crossing her arms. "Piper—"

"No, I was always saying I wanted an adventure and, well, this is it. I can fight, I can lead my people. If you fail, you said it yourself, the Wastelands are theirs and they will probably kill us all. If I can stop that, I will. When I take the Paradise people back to my tribe, I will speak to them and gather our fighters." I'm not asking permission, not this time. She might be a queen, but I'm the leader, and she has my respect...and yes, fear, but this is important.

The thing is, that thing worth fighting for isn't always a person, it can be a place...and this place? This Wasteland is worth fighting for. No matter what.

She takes in my stance and smirks. "Good, then help us, fuck knows we will need every man we can get."

I relax then, I was ready to fight her if necessary...or run away, 'cause I doubt I could take this bitch in a fight. The tent pushes open and we both turn to see Evan, Archel, and Jago standing here, obviously looking for me. She groans. "This isn't a fucking counselling chamber, take your lover's spat elsewhere."

"Worth, I'm going with them," Archel says, shocking me.

"I know," she offers. He grins then. "I wouldn't expect anything less. Look after her and meet us at the front line," she adds.

"I'm going too, if she will have me?" Evan requests, looking at me worriedly.

I swallow but nod and a giant smile curls his lips.

"Shit, who's going to patch me up now, Doc?" she teases.

He laughs and narrows his eyes on her. It's cute they are friends, I'm happy for him. I'm glad he has others, and not at all jealous...okay, like ninety percent happy and ten percent jealous. "Stop getting fucking hurt. Don't let anyone else patch you up or do it yourself. I've seen your needlework on your skin already and it fucking sucks. No getting shot, stabbed, burned, tortured, or captured. I will see you after the Cities." He nods.

"Thanks, Doc," she replies. "I'm glad you found her," she whispers, almost too low for me to hear, and I watch his face soften as he smiles at her.

Okay eighty-forty, but I will totally work on it.

"You'll find yours again, Worth. They wouldn't dare die on you. You aren't saying goodbye again, not this time, and I won't sing you a fucking song like Vas," he jokes, making her laugh...

Okay like fifty-fifty.

"No goodbyes, not anymore," she agrees, and then hugs him. They embrace and I debate if I really like her at all, then I feel childish. They are friends, clearly, and share memories. I can't begrudge either of them that. Plus, there are other nice people out there, he can have other friends than me. I hear her whis- pering to him, but I let them have their peace and privacy. She pulls back then and looks at us.

"I'll see you at the front," she states.

"What? I don't get a hug?" I pout, and everyone groans, making me smile. "I'm just saying, thought we were going to all hug it out? No? Guess not." Jago huffs and grabs me, throwing me over his shoulder and making me laugh. As he walks out, I carry on talking.

He drops me to my feet outside when I shut up, and we look around before diving in to help pack everyone up. Before I know it, the bikes are in a line and everyone is ready to leave. I linger near the edge, watching them, and Worth sees me and heads my way, looking all sorts of sexy and badass in her leather biker getup.

"Hey." She nods, standing next to me and observing everyone.

"I gotta say, you don't seem weirded out by the three men thing," I comment, unsure what else to say. I was never good at goodbyes.

She snorts. "Three? That's nothing, come back when you have five."

I turn with a grin. "Five? Fuck, that's a lot of cock. Like, I guess I have three holes, you know, but do you take turns? Is there a schedule? Do they play pick a hole?"

She laughs and I feel high as hell making that happen. "If we make it through this, I'll tell you," she promises.

"I mean like, three, I get it, I have three holes, you know," I repeat, but she turns serious.

"Evan never stopped looking for you, and even when he thought he was going to die, all he thought about was you—that he never said sorry, that he never told you how he felt. Just thought you should know."

I stare at her profile, lost for words for a moment. "I loved him for such a long time, but I don't know if I'm that same person anymore," I admit.

"So? Be the new you and see if the love is still there. He's different too, I'm betting. Maybe this time, you can both love each other and get it right. Sometimes the person is right, but the timing is off."

"Fuck, you're smart. Brains and beauty, no wonder you have five cocks," I tease.

"Stay safe, Piper." She nods, starting to walk away, but freezes and grabs the goggles off her head and comes back, offering them to me. "You're going to need these out there."

"But they're yours," I reply, not grabbing them, so she throws them and I catch the goggles automatically.

"Then I'll get them back next time we see each other. Keep them safe for me." She winks and leaves, heading over to her bike.

I look down at them and smile, holding them to my chest. It means a lot, it's a peace offering from one woman to another. She doesn't know it yet, but we are totally friends—hell, girlfriends. After the war we can meet up, drink some beers, kick some ass, and talk about all the penises.

She doesn't look back, not once. I get that. I watch her leave, a new purpose filling me, one greater than I ever imagined. I won't let her down, I won't disappoint her people or mine.

Shit just got real.

It gets dark quickly, and there still isn't any contact from the bunker. I agreed to stay only two days, I will keep that prom- ise. With Worth and her people gone, the Paradise citizens seem more relaxed. I keep away from them, since I don't belong with them anymore, even if I promised to protect them. It feels wrong. Instead, I take Worth's tent —not like she is going to need it— and we lie our bikes out front like she did, making a ring of protection, while some guys called Lupin and Jason work on getting us a line to the bunker.

I'm also informed there is a shower out back. I plan to have one later, but for now I stand on the next building's roof, keeping lookout. I needed a minute, just some space to decompress after today. A lot has happened, blasts from the pasts, new friends, and a new job...it was a lot. I was really overwhelmed, so I slipped away from Jago's protection and headed up here, leaving him glaring at Evan.

I feel a shift of air behind me, and despite myself, I smile. "I know you're there, Shadow."

He laughs from the darkness next to me, leaning on the roof lip, looking out into the Wastes like I'm doing. "You always do, Princess."

I sigh. "You come to fight with me or ask me questions?"

He doesn't say anything, so I turn to him, begging him with my eyes.

"Archel, not now, please, I can't deal with anymore emotions or crying today, please," I implore, as he wraps his arms around me.

"It can wait, I would wait forever for you, for now this is enough," he whispers.

"I guess you kept your promise, though I don't think it counts if I have to help you," I taunt playfully, and he laughs, pulling me closer.

"I told you I would always come back to you, Princess, no matter what it takes. As you command," he whispers, and I pull my face away as he cups it, searching my eyes. "Are you okay? Do I need to kill anyone?"

"Maybe later." I sigh. "I'm okay, just a lot to take in."

"I bet, your boyfriend meeting your other two," he teases, and I narrow my eyes.

"Evan isn't my boyfriend." I huff and his grin grows. "Oh, so I am?" he whispers, leaning closer.

"Erm, I'm sorry, that answer is not available, please try again later," I offer, and he laughs, kissing me softly.

"Okay, how about then I just tell you. I am. I don't care who else you date as long as they aren't pricks, because then I will have to kill them. As long as I get you, I'm okay with that. You were with Jago when we met, I knew that, plus I've seen Dray and Worth with her men. It might even be nice having a family. Someone to protect you when I'm gone." He shrugs.

"You're weird, you know that?" I tell him and he grins. "Takes a weirdo to know a weirdo, Princess."

"Ugh, you got me there...now, be honest...you missed the fun bags, right? Is that what this war is really about?" I whisper in shock, and he stumbles back dramatically...

"Oh fuck, it is, you caught me!" he shouts in mock horror, then grins and scoops me back up. "Want me to go to war over your body, Princess? I will, and your heart."

"Cheese ball." I huff.

"Dance with me?" he whispers, looking into my eyes, the moon shining on our secret spot.

"There's no music...or people to play our game with." I snigger then turn serious. "Okay."

He grabs my waist and starts to spin me across the roof, making me laugh. He grins at the sound, stopping in the middle and just swaying us from side to side. "I missed that." He strokes my cheek and I lean into his palm. "I thought I was going to war without ever seeing your face again, Princess."

"Like you were worried," I scoff. "You would win it with your eyes shut."

But he remains serious, his eyes tracing my face like he really thought he would never see me again. "This life and the next, Princess, I want you in them all. I'm tired of fighting it. When we left, there was something between us...and I'm hoping that's still there for you, even with Jago and Evan back...I'm praying I still have a place in your life...and heart."

I swallow hard, looking into his eyes. "You do, my heart is big enough for you three. I'm coming to realise love isn't as simple nor as easy as I thought. It's possible to love more than one person equally. You all have something of me. Evan, I loved as a child, Jago as a woman...you as a warrior. You all had my past, different parts...now it's clashing together, and I hope you will all have my future. I don't know if it will work. I don't know if we will even survive long enough to find out. But I'm hoping we do, I've never backed down from an adventure, why would I back down from ours?"

He leans his head down and seals his lips to mine, telling me everything I need to know. He is with me, through it all, no matter what it takes. A noise has us pulling apart. Breathing heavily, I look over to see Evan in the doorway to the roof, staring at us in shock and pain, but he quickly clears it away.

"Jago is looking for you, as is some man named Lupin," he rushes out, before turning and running away. I sigh, life is difficult.

"Well, this should be fun. I bet he wants to kill me." Archel grins and I snort.

"Weirdo," I mutter, as we twine our hands and make our way off the roof.

Time waits for no man...or woman.

A nervous, weedy man is waiting with Evan and Jago down- stairs. He looks at me once before glancing away. "Worth told me to come to you when I had something..."

I wait, but when he doesn't finish, I nudge him. "Did you find something?"

"Oh, erm, I think so. I managed to get into the video feed, but it seems to have been shut off, so I can only access a select amount of footage from before it was shut down," he informs me nervously.

"Okay, show me." I nod and he rushes away as we follow after him to the bunker door.

He pulls out a screen linked in with wires, and displays it to me, pressing some buttons. The screen splits into four and my gaze darts between each one, watching as guards troop down the corridor, a destination in mind. If they were looking for explosives, wouldn't they stop? One heads to the control room and I see them typing away, obviously shutting everything down, but then my eyes catch on something else.

Captain.

My heart slams into my chest, fear mixed with anger. Storming down after them, he follows his troops as they head deeper and deeper into the maze of Paradise, and into sections I've never even seen before the cameras cut off. "That's where it ends, it was strange, they sent us up here for safety, but..."

"But it looks like they are searching for something, not checking for attackers or bombs." I look at him then.

"What could they be searching for?" he asks nervously.

"I don't know, but I know someone who might. Good work. Keep trying to get this door open. I'm thinking this is more about keeping us out than anyone in." I nod and turn to the others.

"We need to speak to Worth's dad."

Chapter 9
My Shadow

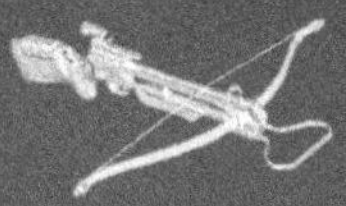

"I need to talk to you," I call when I spot him trying to build a fire. He looks up at me and nods before standing. I turn and head back to Worth's tent—or mine, I guess—not wanting anyone to overhear what I am going to ask.

Pushing past the flaps, I turn when I'm inside and cross my arms, narrowing my eyes on him when he steps through. Archel, Jago, and Evan stand behind him, not letting him escape as his eyes dart to me with a frown. "Please do not take this for disrespect, but they need a leader out there, and they won't follow a...erm."

"Woman," I interject.

"They know me, so I took over, it looks bad when you come and give me commands," he points out as he straightens.

Grinning, I step closer, making him uncomfortable. "I don't give a fuck. I'm not here to make friends or play nice, I'm here to save your ass, so stick your sexist bullshit where the sun don't shine, Papa Worth. Now, I asked you here because you used to lead, and I need to know some information."

"What information?" he questions, frowning at me, wrinkles crinkling around his lips.

"They are searching for something down there, something they needed everyone gone for, a secret, I am guessing, and I want to know what."

"And you think I know because?" he challenges.

"Because you are a politician, and you are all corrupt bastards who know secrets, so what are they looking for?" I repeat, as Jago snorts, crossing his own arms until we look like a big me and a mini me, how cute. Couples who fight together stay together.

He ruffles at that. "I am not corrupt. You forget who is top here with you—"

"Shut up." I roll my eyes. "I don't need your speech, just your information, so for God's sake don't monologue and just tell me what I need to know."

"I don't monologue," he argues with a huff, but deflates when I continue glaring at him. "I don't know, I don't!" he protests when I snort. "I was only signed into office five years ago. There are still a lot of things under military control that we aren't allowed to know, so it could be anything."

"Then there is only one way to find out," I muse. "Get down there and see."

Evan nods. "But how, Pip?"

"That geek will get us in, then we go in as a team and search, capture, and do some recognisance, like that game we used to play." I grin at him and he laughs.

"We aren't kids anymore, Pip," he cautions.

"Damn right we aren't. No way could my sexy ass fit in those vents, doesn't mean the same rules don't apply though. Go tell Lupin he has until dawn to open those doors." I look at Papa Worth then. "You're dismissed, go and suck your cock somewhere I don't have to see it."

Damn, this power is addicting, how does Worth do it?

"Brawler," Jago sighs, "it's lick your wounds."

"Same thing." I wave my hand, dismissing him, and turn away, throwing myself on the sleeping mattress. "Damn, so this is how a queen sleeps. Not too bad for little old pied piper of cocks," I whisper to myself, stroking the soft bedding.

"Princess." Archel laughs and then throws himself on top of me, wrapping himself around me like a blanket as we both giggle. "We should build a fort," he whispers, and I nod, looking into his eyes, ignoring the others.

"Do you think Meat Head and Doctor Dolittle will help?" he inquires, pretending to whisper again.

"Maybe, I could flash the fun bags and distract them, or hypnotise them," I offer, and he nods seriously.

"It could work," he muses.

"Or just say you hurt your ass again," Jago interrupts, and comes and stands over us, glaring at Archel. "If you start feeling her up, I will chop your hand off."

"You could try," Archel retorts, and snuggles closer, "but Princess will protect me."

"Ugh, men." I groan and slip out of his hands, offering mine to Jago who helps me stand up. I brush off my ass and look at them to see them tracking the movement with hungry eyes. "I didn't actually hurt my ass, Jesus."

Rolling my eyes, I walk past them and back into the camp, and I hear them scrambling after me. "Now, what did I hear about a shower? 'Cause there is sand in places it shouldn't be."

"This way," Evan offers, popping up behind me and looking beyond thrilled to be able to help. I follow him, Jago and Archel trailing after me, and he stops at what looks like a pumping station, puts in a code, and swings it open. "To the right, Pip." He smiles at me, but it doesn't reach his eyes as he looks behind me to see the other two.

"Thanks. Shadow, I need you to fill me in on what's been happening. Jago, go and check on how the Paradise peeps are hanging. Evan see if Lupin needs anything," I instruct, and he bristles and I sigh, giving him puppy dog eyes. "Please?"

He nods, flickering a look over my shoulder and then back to me.

"Anything for you, Pip," he murmurs as he leans closer, grasping my head and dropping a chaste kiss on my forehead like he used to when we were little before he walks away, whistling to himself. Jago watches him go with narrowed eyes.

"Someone needs to kick his ass to sort out the pecking order," he grumbles, and Archel nods.

"You first, then me." He laughs, and ignoring them, I head inside, stripping off as I go. I walk through another door and spot the shower in the corner.

Slipping inside, I flick on the water, jumping when it first comes out cold and then relaxing as it turns warm. Pulling the sheet over the cubicle, I tip my face back and let the dirt and sand wash away as I hear the outer door shut and then nothing. That fucking sneaky assassin, I know he's there.

"So, what happened when you left?" I query, as I scrub my body and hair, my voice muffled through the water.

"I met up with Dray and he asked me to hunt Worth down. She had been gone too long here at Paradise. I found her and we headed back for their Summit. It went wrong, Princess, and some of our people were killed. She ended up being captured by Ivar and her men were taken by the Cities. We tracked her up to the castle, but she had already killed the mad king and was being crowned queen, then we headed here," he recalls and I whistle.

"So, a lot."

"I missed you every day," he whispers, and I lock my lips, looking through the sheet, trying to see him.

"I missed you too."

"Doesn't seem like you did that much," he scoffs bitterly, and I sigh.

"Don't start, Shadow. I care for you all in different ways, you already knew about Jago, you said that yourself, and I did miss you, don't ever think I didn't. I slept in your shirt every night, not wanting to wash it to get rid of your scent, and every morning and night I stood waiting at the entrance to camp, hoping you were coming back. You can't hate me for deciding I was tired of being left behind."

He rips back the curtain and stares at me, his eyes dark. "You're right, I'm sorry, Princess. I won't leave you again." His lips quirk up. "I guess we can keep the big guy as a pet, is he house trained?" he teases, and I laugh, making his eyes drop down to my lips and then to my exposed skin like he only just realised I was naked.

"Archel?" I murmur, watching as his eyes go dark, locked on my body. My heart starts to race at the utterly devoted and hungry look in his gaze. We always danced around this, acutely aware I wasn't ready for anything physical. He was there to save me, to keep me alive, and put me back together again. He saw me at my darkest, my most vulnerable, and he stuck around, he made me laugh again, taught me to protect myself...and then he left, and only then did I realise how much he meant to me. That I craved his brand of darkness and crazy and I regretted never being with him, never finding out if he was as controlled in bed...or as strong. Fuck, I clench my thighs together. When he left, I was still a broken woman, and although the cracks are sealing together, I'm not perfect but neither is he. My shadow. My protector. The man who admitted he had been hurt like me, he knows that feeling. I want him, it's that simple.

It could fuck up everything, but I'm done fighting my own feelings, done trying to be everyone else's version of perfect. If they don't like it...fuck them. If Jago loves me, he will stick around, and if he doesn't...well, it will break my heart, but I can't force someone to love me and stay...just like I can't force myself to stop loving more than one man.

The world could just be very well ending, and I want to face that final goodbye knowing the feeling of this assassin's body against mine.

Decision made, I grin at him, but he stands there, his hand clenching the sheet like a lifeline, his eyes locked on the rise and fall of my chest.

He won't make the first move, I know it. Somewhere down the line Archel was hurt and violated like I was, and now he wants to protect me, even from himself, even if it's not what I want, so instead I make the initial move.

I step back and grin. "Joining me?"

He gulps, but lifts his hands and grabs his shirt, and in one move he yanks it over his head before kicking off his boots and jeans until he stands naked before me. This isn't like with Jago, I've never seen Archel naked. He's beautiful, all muscle, golden skin peppered with blond hair, and...scars, which only add to his raw masculine beauty. He's a survivor, a warrior, an assassin. I want to trace every cut, every lash, every last ragged memory.

Each one is a testament to his strength, to how strong he is, and each one fills me with desire, but he takes my silence badly and starts to turn away, so I hold out my hand. "What, I'm not allowed to look? You gawk at me," I scoff, and he turns back to me with a smirk.

"Oh, you can look, Princess, I would rather you touch though," he teases, hiding his vulnerability behind his flirty words as he steps into the cubicle with me, pushing me farther under the spray. He's taller than me, and sometimes I forget how big Jago is, but Archel is only a tiny bit taller, and our lips are close to touching right now, our bodies only a hairsbreadth apart as we just stare at each other, both of us panting, our gazes hungry but hesitant.

When we cross this line, there is no going back, Archel will be mine...but wasn't he already?

"Are you sure?" he asks, obviously seeing the desire in my eyes. He's asking if I'm okay, if not, I know he would back away, no matter how much he wants me.

"Don't get all shy on me now, Shadow, I heard assassins are good with their hands...that true?" I query breathlessly.

That control snaps and he rushes at me, slamming me back into the shower wall, no longer soft and teasing. The assassin is in his element, stroking my body with his weapon scarred hands, memorising my curves as he stares into my eyes, letting me see the wild power there, the strength and ghosts, everything that makes up the darkness inside him...the very thing that allows him to kill now allows him to hold me effortlessly.

"We are good with other things. Want to see, Princess?" he whispers against my lips teasingly, as his hands caress my curves in a gentle touch.

"Thought you would never ask," I murmur, sealing our lips together. This is no goodbye kiss this time, there won't ever be one again. With this kiss, I seal our promise, our promise of forever. The assassin and the forgotten. Two lost wanderers who found each other in the bloodshed in the sand out there, we were meant to be.

I feel his heart slam in time with mine as he groans into my mouth, his tongue tangling with mine before he pulls back and nips at my lips playfully, like the man himself.

"Archel," I gasp, as he draws away and runs his lips across my neck, lapping at the water there before leaving stinging bites that have me moaning as I clutch his head to me, tipping mine back to the wall as I close my eyes in bliss.

"You taste so good, Princess," he growls against my skin, as he traces his lips across my collarbone and then meets my gaze as his hands part my thighs and stroke the sensitive skin there.

"Yes," I groan, pushing closer, trying to get his hands where I need them.

He chuckles against my skin and finally cups my pussy, pressing against it as he nips at my skin. "Fuck, you are so wet," he breathes, as I rub myself against his palm, my eyes closing in bliss at the pressure, but it's not enough.

"Shadow, please," I beg, opening my eyes to meet his, and like those were the words he needs, he traces his fingers down my pussy and slips one inside me, teasing me before adding another and another until he is stretching me with them.

His hands are used for killing, they are his weapon, and right now they are aimed at me. He traces kisses back up to my lips and swallows my moan as he starts to slowly pull his fingers out and push them back in, fucking me shallowly, speeding up so slowly that I don't even notice it until he is slamming them inside me with such force, I hit the wall harder.

He swallows my moans, his other hand tweaking my nipple before tracing across my stomach and flicking my clit. He sucks on my tongue as his fingers throw me over the edge and I have to rip my mouth away to breathe as I come back down from the high.

He pulls his fingers free from my clutching pussy and steps back to show me as he wraps his glistening fingers, still wet with my release, around his cock, and strokes his hard length. My mouth goes dry, my thighs quivering as I watch him. His fingers were good, but I want his cock.

"Assassin," I hiss, narrowing my eyes on his. "Enough games, fuck me already."

"As you wish, Princess." He grins and moves so quickly that I don't even have time to gasp as he smashes me back against the wall and slams inside me.

Groaning, my head falls forward to his shoulder, my teeth digging into his flesh as he works through my tightness, only to pull out and push back in. Fuck, he's long, so long and feels so right buried within me, stretching me.

"So perfect, Princess," he whispers lovingly against my shoulder, biting down just like I am. "You fit me perfectly."

"Archel," I moan, wrapping my legs around him to hold him closer as he fucks me, slowly at first, tenderly. But our need is too great for slow and affectionate. I urge him on by kicking my heels and he obliges, fucking me harder, slamming my back into the wet shower wall with the force of his thrusts. His cock hitting that place inside me with each push and pull until I'm screaming into his skin, a wet wonton mess. I don't even know what I'm saying, begging, pleading, teasing...all of it for more of him.

And my shadow? Of course he does as I ask.

He fucks me harder, faster, it's brutal and fucking perfect. So smooth like the man himself, every thrust deliberate to bring me the most pleasure, his hands gripping my skin, playing my body like he does his knives.

Before I know it, I'm coming again, screaming my release into his skin as my pussy clamps down around his cock, and he still doesn't lose his rhythm. Fucking me through it, driving me higher and higher again.

"Please, please," I chant, my body his to do with as he pleases at this point.

"Princess," he gasps, the only sign of weakness he shows, until I notice the tremor in his hands, the twisting of his lips as he tries to hold back, to keep fucking me.

"I want to feel you come," I beg, and I do, more than anything.

He groans and slips out of me, leaving me cold and shaky as he drops my legs to the shower floor. With jerky movements, he grabs the shower curtain and does some weird hand flicks and then yanks me over, tying me up in it. My eyes fly wide as he hoists me into the air, the pole creaking but holding my weight, my legs barely touching the ground, the wet material suspending me for him.

Then he grabs my legs and holds me up, slipping back inside my pussy like he belongs there at all times.

He grins, his fingers gripping my thighs as he pummels into me, the new angle bumping my clit each time, leaving me moaning his name louder and louder. "God, too fucking good." He groans, his eyes pinching as he watches me. "I want to—" He gasps, his hips stuttering for a moment before they lose all rhythm and he just fucks me, all that power unleashed on me. "To see you come around me, Princess, you are too fucking beautiful when you do. Better than any fight or weapon," he pleads, his voice harsh and breathy.

I grip him tighter, my pussy aching in the best way, my clit throbbing, my nipples sore, and yet I want more. I want this man branded in me at all times, filling me up. The next time he pulls out, he does this little twist with his hips that has me seeing stars. He does it again and again until I'm screaming his name, wrapping my legs around him to keep him inside me. He groans my name and stills, his cock jerking in me as he fills me with his cum.

My eyes are dotting colours and I have to blink it away, to see his pleasure slack face before me. "Well, shit, Shadow," I gasp.

He nods, leaning his head against my racing heart. "You feel like home."

After we are both washed, dried, and dressed, he turns me around and plaits my hair for me before kissing me softly. "Now you look like the leader you are," he whispers, and my heart squeezes when there is a knock at the door.

"Brawler, it's time to eat," Jago grumbles.

Archel smiles. "Your other men are getting antsy to have you back. Wouldn't want to have to kill them, come on." He winks and twines my hand with his as he opens the door and pulls me outside to see Jago and Evan waiting there impatiently. I won't let them make me feel bad for spending time with Archel, though, so still holding his hand, I head to Jago and drop a kiss on his lips.

"Thanks, Beast. Come on, let's eat," I tell him, and wink at Evan as I skirt around them, pulling a chuckling Archel with me.

We grab some food that Paradise peeps are cooking and head to the table Worth was using, not wanting to sit with them. All my men and I sit together. It's filled with awkward tension, which Archel keeps breaking by making jokes. Once we have eaten, I check up on Lupin, but he isn't through yet, so I decide to go to bed.

Only when I'm in the tent do I realise the problem, they are all going to want to sleep with me. Faking confidence I don't feel, I turn to see them all waiting anxiously. "There's enough room for everyone, you can dick it out for the position next to me, but I'm going to sleep," I inform them, and kick off my boots and jeans before wiggling into bed.

I pull the covers up and see them all watching me before they look at each other and dive towards me, making me yelp and shield my face protectively. They all land on me in a heap, and try to fight each other to get beside me, causing me to giggle, I didn't expect Evan to join in, but he proudly rolls next to me and grins up at a disgruntled Jago, and while he is distracted, Archel steals the other's spot next to me and slides under the blanket, putting his arms under his head and grinning up at the big guy who narrows his eyes.

He glares at them both before his fire eyes light up and a small smile curls his lips. Oh God, no, what is he going to do?

"Fine, I'll get the best spot." He grunts and then proceeds to yank off the cover and slip under it, resting his head on my stomach as he forces himself between my thighs and settles there.

Well, shit, wasn't expecting that.

"Well played." Archel nods and scoots closer until we are touching, unlike Evan, who has left a gap between us.

He smiles at me. "Night, Pip." He turns over and presses his back to me before promptly going to sleep.

"Night, guys," I murmur, and close my eyes, warm as balls, but I daren't disrupt them so I go to sleep like a chicken in an oven.

I wake up disoriented sometime later, if the quiet outside the tent is anything to go by, but what they don't warn you about with being with so many men is...the snoring. Dear God, one stops and another starts, like they are an acapella group, the Dick Snorers. Groaning, I cover my eyes and try to go back to sleep, but they are too loud, even competing in their sleep to be the loudest, so I finally give up and crawl backwards from under Jago and slip out of the pile of men.

Grabbing my jeans and boots, I get dressed outside of the tent. Yawning, I look around to see only the patrols on the roof, since everyone else is asleep. I walk the perimeter and kick some sand onto the fire to put it out. I wave at Lupin, who is still at the door, and he waves back distractedly, so I leave him to it and instead walk to the pump station to use the water again while we are still here.

Inputting the code, I slip inside, wash my face, and gargle my mouth out. What I wouldn't do for some toothpaste right now. When I lift my head, I jump, spotting Evan behind me in the mirror. I spin and grab my chest, my heart racing. "Jesus, Evvie."

"Sorry, Pip." He winces and then scrubs at the back of his head. "I keep fucking this up," I hear him mutter, before he blows out a breath. "Can we talk?"

Licking my lips, I nod and lean back against the sinks. I said everything I needed to, I'm not sure what else he needs to say. "I want you to know, I'm really trying to be okay with you and... Jago and, erm, Archel. I am, I want to be part of your life, Pip, and if that means accepting them, then I'll do it." He nods, his lips flat, as if waiting for a reaction.

"In what way?" I ask, tired of dancing around my attraction to him. Once upon a time, I loved this boy so much it consumed me. I guess I'm asking if he ever really felt the same.

"Huh?" he retorts, his eyes crinkling adorably.

"In what way do you want to be part of my life? Brother?" He cringes at that. "Friend?" He shakes his head and I sigh.

"Evan, just fucking speak, man, I'm tired and overly warm and getting annoyed with the vague words and glances. What do you want?" I snap, throwing my hands in the air.

"You, always you," he replies, losing all hints of shyness as he straightens, a confidence entering his eyes that I have to admit is attractive as his lips curl up flirtily. "Always was you, Pip." He crosses the space between us, grabs my face, and presses his lips to mine.

I gasp in shock and he slips his tongue inside, entangling it with mine as he backs me into the sink with his hips, holding me there as he kisses me so desperately, so utterly consuming, that I don't know which way is up. He breaks away, both of us panting, and stares at me from inches away, his eyes completely open and hopeful. "I've loved you since I was a child, Piper, and into manhood. I followed you everywhere, protected you, loved you even when you didn't know it, but you deserved better than a bastard like me...but I won't ever give you up again. Keeping you at arm's length and seeing you with others was the hardest thing I've ever had to do. Maybe that's why I was so bitter and hateful. God, I was a prick, Pip, the biggest one on the planet, but love makes people crazy."

"Evvie," I whisper, eyes round. "Are you saying..."

"That I love you?" he says for me, smirking. "Isn't it obvious, Piper? I always have, always will. Jesus, your name was the first fucking tattoo I got. You drive me crazy, but in the best way. My life was so empty and boring without you."

"Erm, I'm sorry, my brain is shutting off...what tattoo?" I question, swallowing at his close proximity. I've wanted this for so long, and now that it's happening, I feel like I'm drowning in him. His scent, that smirk that is so Evvie, those twinkling eyes I love so much.

He steps back and I whimper, but he winks and rips his shirt over his head, and my eyes become lost in the hard planes of his chest and scrawling tattoo that I used to trace as he was asleep next to me, imagining him pulling me closer and whispering all these things he is saying now. With one chipped, black painted fingernail, he taps right over his heart, showing me one I never noticed before. Stepping closer, I hover my hand over it and look up into his eyes.

He nods and I trace the intricate ink which spells out "Pip," right over his heart. He shivers under my touch as I lick my lips, just staring at the ink. "I got it when I was fourteen. I knew then and there you were my forever, Pip, knew you would always be my one, my family. Now, I'm asking you, will you be mine? We've made mistakes, we've fucked up and been stupid...but if you'll give us a chance, I think you'll find that we would be amazing together. Will you, Pip?" he asks, his voice quiet and scared as he's lying all of his cards bare before me.

It's everything I've ever wanted to hear. This man had my heart before I even realised I could give it, and now he's showing me I've had his for just as long. We were both too blind and young to realise it. Sometimes, people need to break away to come back together, better and stronger than before.

"Yes, Evvie, God yes," I tell him, and meet his eyes with a watery smile to see his filled with tears as well.

He whoops and scoops me up, swinging me around the room like we used to before stopping and holding me against him. Usually he would let go and step back, putting distance between us. But that was before, now he holds me closer and I wrap my legs around his waist until there is no space between us at all.

Gripping his cheeks, I cover his lips with mine, teasing them with little pecks before he groans my name and I kiss him prop- erly. Letting our tongues tangle as his hands grab my ass and hoist me higher, gripping me as he walks us backwards and stum- bling over since he won't look away. My back hits the wall and I grunt into his mouth, gripping his hair and pulling him tighter as his hand pushes my top up, only hesitating for a moment before he strokes across my stomach and up my ribs, making me giggle into his mouth when he hits a ticklish spot.

Ripping my mouth away, I stare down at his closed eyes, his lips bruised from our kiss, his chest rising and falling heavily as he grips my breast with rough fingers. I tip my head back and he nudges it to the side as he kisses down my neck to my shoulder.

He jerks down my bra cup and twists my nipple, hard, tweaking and yanking it until I'm moaning and pushing into his hands. I didn't expect this from him, I expected him to be soft and hesitant, almost loving, but the way his hands are dominating my body...the rough way he treats me...

Sit on a dick and spin, it's amazing.

My pussy pulses like there is a direct line from my nipple to my clit, and I kiss along his cheek until my mouth meets his again, starving for his kisses after all these years.

He moans my name into my mouth, the sexiest sound ever as I grip his shoulders, digging my nails in to his skin to keep myself close.

Maybe this can really work, maybe I can have all three men I love.

A bang comes at the door, pulling us apart. "They are fighting! They are going to kill each other!" comes a scared yell.

I stare at Evan in shock. "Who do you...shit!" I yell, and he lets me go as we both scramble to the door and yank it open.

Only two people among us would be fighting, scaring people enough to reach out to me...Jago and Archel.

I'm going to kill them myself.

Chapter 10
Pecking Order

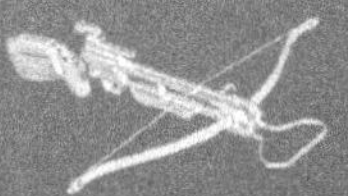

Fury twists inside me as I storm through the camp, drawn to the circle of people screaming and yelling. I barge through their masses until they part, and I see Jago and Archel.

Archel is dancing around while Jago tracks his movements, and then they meet in a flurry of punches and flashing of knives. I narrow my eyes, spotting a bruise appearing on my shadow already, and there is a cut along Jago's neck. They aren't playing, they are trying to kill each other.

I swear to baby Jesus, I'm going to chop both of their cocks off and make the others eat it, that way they can eat as much shit as they talk. Stomping between them, I stand there as they both stop. Jago has his fist raised, ready to hit Archel, who has a knife pointing at Jago's junk.

"Stop," I yell, my eyes narrowed as I look at both of them. "You throw another hit and I will leave you here to rot. Tent. Now," I bellow, before looking at the circled people. "Break it the fuck up! Shouldn't you be packing?" I shout, meeting their gazes until they break away, grumbling to themselves.

Glaring at both of them, I let them see how mad I am.

"Now!" I scream, before turning and heading to the tent, hearing their footsteps behind me.

Pushing through the flaps, I turn to scowl at them, beyond furious as they slink inside, their heads held high and grinning at me like they were just having fun.

Boys will be boys my arsehole, they don't get to try and kill each other. Only I get to kill them when they are being stupid fuckwits like now. Hands on hips, I take them both in.

"Well, nothing to say for yourselves? You giant, fucking turd-burgalars!"

Archel raises an eyebrow. "Turdburgalar?"

"It's better than assbandit," Jago says seriously, and he nods in understanding.

"You motherfucking men, just because you have dicks doesn't mean you need to act like one! I leave for five fucking minutes and I come back to you two beating the shit out of each other. You might as well have got your cocks out and seen whose was bigger!"

"Huh, where were you anyway, Princess?" Archel asks, changing the subject.

"None of your business," I sputter, and he grins, sharing it with Jago.

"I think someone made up with Doc, if her hair is anything to go by," Archel teases, making me huff in indignation.

"That is not the fucking topic at the moment, you two assholes—"

"And by her lips, I wonder if he is as skilled with women as he is with patients?" Jago adds.

My mouth drops open at how chummy these two are. "What the flying fucking cock tassels is this?" I yell.

Archel steps closer, curling around me until he whispers in my ear from behind. "We just needed to see who was the strongest, a pecking order if you will, we are good now."

"Are you freakin' kidding me?" I shriek, but it turns into a gasp when he kisses my neck right in front of Jago, who's watching us with curiosity before he steps closer and presses to my front until I'm framed between them.

"He's right, we are good now, we know where we both stand. There's enough of you to go around. Fuck knows you are a handful," he grumbles, and Archel snakes a hand between us and cups my breast, making my eyes widen.

"More than a handful," he teases, whispering against my skin.

"Does someone want to tell me what the hell is happening right now? I feel like I'm in a bad porno," I mutter, while Jago grins down at me, his eyes hungry as he tracks Archel's movements as he squeezes my breast.

"Do you want to be, Brawler?" he whispers seductively, licking at his lips.

"Dear God, you two have too many after fight hormones. Go stroke one out to a thought about a princess," I snap, and Archel laughs.

"You mean you, Princess?"

Shit, I forgot about his pet name for me.

"You two need to..." I trail off, searching for anything to say, but I'm at a loss.

"Thank fuck, she's run out of words," Jago remarks, before tilting his head down and kissing me.

Groaning into his mouth, I feel the desire Evan stirred up returning full force, especially when another set of lips kisses down my neck to my shoulder and nudges my shirt aside. Finished protesting, I let my thoughts go and concentrate on Archel's hand on my breast, stroking me through the material as Jago dominates my mouth.

He sucks on my tongue before pulling back and nipping at my lips, making me gasp, especially when Archel draws the skin on my neck into his mouth and bites down, making me jerk between them.

Tits on a prick, this is hot.

Archel's hand skates lower, letting go of my breasts to push up my shirt, then they both move far enough back to rip it over my head and toss it away until I'm in nothing but a bra, the cool air hitting me and making me shiver.

My eyes flick open to see Jago staring down at my exposed chest with a hungry gaze. I don't know why, but I expected him to be the super jealous type, hell, maybe that fight did sort things out for him... or he's just super horny.

Archel leans closer, whispering in my ear, careful to keep reminding me who is there, and the thought makes me melt back into him. Even now, in the midst of things, he is looking after me, aware of my new triggers and thinking of ways to help me.

"Look how wild you make him," Archel whispers for just me, licking the shell of my ear as his hands come back up and pull down my bra, pushing up my bare breasts for Jago's hungry gaze.

His eyes flicker back to mine, on fire like always, smouldering for me. He licks his lips as he watches me. "So fucking beautiful, Brawler."

"Yeah, Princess, so beautiful," Archel echoes in my ear, sucking my lobe into his mouth as Jago leans down and, without warning, sucks one of my nipples into his mouth.

Groaning, I anchor my hands in his hair, pulling him closer as I arch into his touch, the feel of his mouth on my nipple going straight to my pussy which is throbbing, begging for their touch.

Or anyone's really, she's not choosy at this point, the little hussy just wants to take a pounding and get off. And yes, I referred to my vagina as a separate entity, get over it.

Archel's hand comes up to cup my free breast, tweaking my nipple before rolling it between his fingers, both of them pulling a whiney moan from my mouth that has Archel jerking closer behind me, his hard cock pressing against my ass. Unable to help myself, I start rubbing against it and I'm rewarded with a grunt in my ear that has me shivering.

His hand releases my nipple and traces across my chest, almost touching Jago's head.

"Don't fucking push it," I hear Jago hiss to him, but Archel just chuckles and moves his hand farther down, tracing it across my belly to the button of my jeans.

Jago lifts his head, kissing along my chest and back to my mouth to swallow my moans as Archel flicks open my pants and snakes his hand down my panties to cup my wet pussy.

I lose track of whose hands and mouths are where, just giving in to the pleasure they are providing, forgetting all about their stupid fight outside, especially if this is how they make up for it.

Stroking along my wet heat, Archel sinks a finger inside me, making me groan into Jago's mouth as I pull him closer, my hands spanning across his chest to touch as much skin as I can get as I rock into Archel's touch.

"So wet, Princess," he coos into my ear, nibbling at my lobe again. "Did our fight get you all hot and bothered?"

That asshole, if he wasn't offering me the orgasm I needed, I would turn around and kick his pretty boy ass.

Adding another finger, he stretches me until I'm gasping into Jago's mouth, rocking my hips, fucking myself on his fingers as Jago's hands tweak my nipples. Both of them working together to bring me pleasure is too much, I can't take it.

I explode, my pussy clamping down on Archel's fingers as I scream into Jago's mouth. Archel chuckles in my ear. "So fucking hot, Princess."

A noise has me ripping my mouth away from Jago's and turning as I pant to look at the tent's entrance as I hear running feet.

Don't come in here. Don't come in here.

Of course they come in here.

The tent opens, making all of us look over to see a grinning Lupin there who takes in our position, turns bright red, squeaks, and dashes away.

"Fucking turds on a bird, can't a girl get laid around here?" I groan, dropping my head back onto Archel's shoulder.

"Guess not, Princess. Come on, let's see what he's done. I'm betting he can't look you in the eye again though." He laughs.

Just then, the tent opens again to show a bewildered Evan who spots us, his eyes widening in shock. His eyes flare with jeal- ousy, his lips thinning before he turns and storms away. For fuck's sake.

All I wanted was an orgasm, why do men have to be so needy and emotional?

"Uhh, looks like you are going to need to make up with your doctor again, Brawler," Jago observes as he steps back, and as we watch he frowns, reaches down, and rearranges the bulge in his pants.

"Fine," I grumble. "Being a leader sucks."

Evan won't talk to me or look at me, but he is waiting with Lupin over near the edge of camp...so that's good...I guess. Men, I swear they are more emotional than any woman I know. They act all hard and tough, but they are like those old candies, all soft and gooey on the inside...if the goo is annoying emotional baggage that you have to wade through.

I don't know how Worth does it with all those men. I'm struggling with just three. I knew I had three holes, but fuck, I didn't think about not having three hands to juggle them.

Stupid, Piper.

Deciding to be the mature one and not letting him shame me for my decisions and something I enjoyed, I head their way. He knew what he was getting into. I'm betting it must not have been easy to see me like that with them, and I am sorry for it, but I can't stop every- thing with Archel and Jago just so he can adjust.

Calmer by the time I reach him, I lay my hand on his arm and he looks down at me with cool eyes. "I'm sorry, Evvie, you shouldn't have to walk into that, even if you knew. We will have to set some ground rules. I understand you will get jealous and I'm sorry if that hurt you." I offer. There, that was mature.

His eyes melt and he smiles at me, but there's hurt still lingering in his eyes though. "You're right, I'm sorry too, I shouldn't have stormed away. I respect what you said and knew about them, it was just different seeing it." He scrubs at his face. "Especially after we were just, erm..."

I nod, wincing. "I'm sorry, Evvie, can we move past this?" I ask, searching his gaze, or will this be where we crumble after only just finding each other?

He licks his lips, darting a look to Archel and Jago who are standing with Lupin. "We can move past it. I may need to punch one of them at some point though," he grumbles to me, making me laugh.

"Sure thing, Evvie, I'll hold them down for you." Then I get serious as I look at Lupin. Like Archel said, he can't even meet my eyes, his face blushing so hard.

"What's happened?" I inquire, cutting straight to the point, trying to spare the boy some embarrassment.

"I, erm, we, you, er," he stutters, and Archel laughs, making me cut him a glare.

"Lupin, it's okay. Now why don't you tell me what was so important?" I request softly.

He huffs but finally looks up at me, a small smile on his face. "I opened the door."

Chapter 11
Ball of death

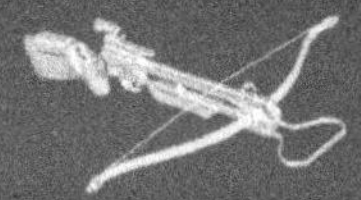

"You got the bunker door open?" I repeat, my mouth dropping open in shock. That thing is built to withstand wars and bombs...and this man managed to get it open?

"Yep, only managed to get it open a bit before the fail safes kicked in, but it's enough for someone to get through." He nods excitedly.

"Shit, we better get in there and make sure none of them come out." I look at Jago and Archel then. "Go."

"As you wish, Princess," Archel comments, and then bows before clapping Jago on the shoulder. "Come on, big guy, you can tell me more about how you think you kicked my ass."

"I did," Jago growls, and then looks at me with a soft smile. "Don't take too long, Brawler."

They rush off to watch the door and I turn to Evan. "Go tell Worth's dad to make sure they keep packing. We are leaving as soon as we get out."

"Out?" he repeats before he groans. "We are going down there, aren't we, Pip?"

"Hell yes we are. Come on, Evvie, where is your sense of curiosity?" I grin.

"It killed the cat, remember?" He smirks.

"Semantics, plus the only pussy is the one in my pants," I tease, and hear Lupin squeak before he races away. We both turn with a laugh and watch him. "Go ahead, I'll go get dressed properly and grab some weapons. Oh, I also want someone on the door while we are down there so no one can sneak out or in."

"Sure thing, Pip, you know this leader thing looks good on you," he observes, and I turn to say something just as he leans in to kiss my cheek like old times, making our lips crash together. We both freeze before he groans, grips the back of my head, and drags me closer, kissing me hard before pulling away. "God, I was an idiot for not doing that years ago. Go on, get dressed." He slaps my ass before turning, shoving his hands in his pockets, and walking away, whistling to himself.

Blinking in shock, I shake it off and rush back to the tent to put my bra on. No one can take me seriously if my nipples are pointing at them like a gun. I add my crossbow and katana as well, and when I look sufficiently badass, I head to the bunker door to see Jago and Archel arm wrestling.

Rolling my eyes, I prop my hands on my hips and cough at them. They break apart with a smile and turn to see me. Archel wolf whistles, running his eyes down my body. "Badass, Princess."

Jago nods in agreement as I peer behind them at the bunker door which, like Lupin said, is only opened wide enough for one person at a time to slip through. The inside is pitch-black, and I'll be honest, I would not be putting my back to it like these two so casually are. Maybe women are the smarter sex.

"You two finished or are you going to pork sword wrestle next?" I call.

I turn to see Evan jog up next to me. "Pork?" he questions with a frown, all serious. "Don't think we have any. We have some other meat, though, if you're hungry," he offers sweetly, making us all laugh as he glances between us in confusion.

Archel finally takes pity on him. "She's talking about the meat in your pants, Doc."

The frown melts into a smile as he winks at me. "She can eat that too if she wants."

"Evvie, you couldn't handle me eating your meat." I smirk as he gapes at me and turn to the others. "Gear up, we are heading in."

I feel like we are at the start of an action movie...or maybe a horror one. I'm in the middle, with Jago and Archel on one side of me, strapped to the teeth in weapons, the assassin in all black, including a hood. To my right is Evan with two knives strapped to his chest, wearing a black vest. We are all lined up as we stare into the abyss of the darkened bunker I once called home.

Evan grabs my hand and squeezes. "We got this, Pip."

"Let's go, Princess," Archel says. "See what you really learned."

"We follow you, Brawler," Jago adds.

I draw in a deep breath of the Wastes before stepping into that waiting darkness, my finger on the trigger of my crossbow. When nothing jumps out at me, I start to feel silly for being so jumpy. Flicking on the light Lupin found for me, I attach it to my bow and lift it, holding it before me as I start to cover the space of the garage where the patrol jeeps are left forgotten.

It's dark, cold, and so silent I can hear us breathing as we move deeper into the underground labyrinth. It was once filled with life, and now all that's left are the ghosts and the skeletal remains of a society. Pressing to the door that leads into the bunker, I wait for Jago to move to the other side before counting down with my fingers, then we both burst into movement on one.

I slide around the corner, pointing right as he points left, Archel moving in after us to watch our backs with Evan in the middle. We didn't discuss this, we just fell into a pattern, comfortable with fighting and working together.

A tap comes on my shoulder, so I start to move forward, my nose crinkling at the smell of rot. I have to move around the fallen bodies of soldiers and what looks like Berserkers that I'm guessing Worth took down.

I slide my feet along the floor so our booted steps don't ring out, and I hear Evan grunting as he tries to copy my movements, but I don't turn my attention away from the deserted hallway, knowing they could be anywhere and all it takes is a moment to catch us off guard.

When we reach the next corner, Archel and Jago move forward, so I turn to face the way we came, watching our backs as they clear the bend.

"Clear," comes a low whisper, so I move backwards until I reach the corner and face them as they move forward, Evan keeping pace beside me.

Lights are flickering above us, the siren ones. They are red and cast a creepy glow along the place. We find more bodies and have to move around them, and I hear Evan cough as he inhales. When I turn back, he's crouched down checking their pulse. Shining my light across him, I frown as he shakes his head and gets to his feet, following after me.

There are bloody marks all over and empty shells from guns. I almost slip on one as we head into the cafeteria, to find yet more bodies. Jago moves closer and lowers his head. "I say we go to command and try to get the cameras on to find where they are so we aren't blind."

"Good idea," I whisper, and circle my fingers to Archel and Evan who are searching. Archel nods and comes back, almost blending into the dark. Sometimes I forget he is the most feared assassin in the Wastes, but seeing him in action now, I can understand why.

It's in the way he moves—lethal, predatory, and hunting.

Evan, on the other hand, frowns at my gesture. "What the fuck does that mean? You want me to spin?" he hisses, and I can't help the snort that escapes me as Archel lets out a chuckle and Jago grunts.

"It means round up, we are moving on. Better keep up or we will leave you behind," Jago snaps back, before heading out of the door, leaving us staring after him in shock.

I don't miss the not so subtle dig because, well, I'm not a moron, but I really don't know what to say, so I just follow after him, wondering how Evan managed to piss off my beast.

We hit the next corner and wait there. Evan slams into Jago, glaring at him as I look around nervously. "What the fuck is your problem?" Evan hisses at Jago, who looks down at him with contempt.

"You are," he rumbles back. Their voices getting louder.

I cut Archel a look to see him leaning back against the wall, watching it go down with a smirk on his face. Goddamn it. "Keep your voices down," I snarl quietly, but they pay me no mind.

"What the fuck have I done to you?" Evan almost yells.

"Not to me, her," Jago growls, pushing off the wall and towering over Evan. "I was the one who found her sobbing her heart out because you were too much of a cunt with her. I'm the one that saw you break her heart, that's my fucking problem."

"She forgave me!" Evan yells, and I decide what the hell, I aim my bow at them.

"You two better shut the fuck up before they realise we are here!" I scream, just as an explosion rocks under our feet.

"I'd say we are too late for that!" Archel laughs, does nothing rattle him?

We all turn and peek around the corner to see a group of soldiers bearing down on us, guns aimed just as the lights flicker on above our heads. Fuck!

"Duck!" I yell, as I see one of them grab something and toss it at us.

It hits the wall and bounces towards us. All three men dive at me and cover me, pressing me against the opposite wall. We all freeze, but when nothing happens, I push free from their arms to see a round object on the floor.

"Wait here!" Jago hisses, before sprinting down the corridor and around the corner, no doubt to shut off the lights using the main switch located just beyond the door.

Arching my eyebrow, I look around to see them equally confused, so I pick it up. "What is it?" I ask dubiously, tossing it between my hands, but it slips and my finger gets caught in a metal tag and pulls it out. It clicks and we all stare at each other as I squeal and toss it right back around the corner. No thank you, ball of death.

Grinning, I look at Evan and Archel. "Well, no clue what that was—" Another explosion rocks the earth and we all stare around the corner to see bodies go flying. One lands at our feet, our ears ringing and eyes pained from the force of it.

"Oh God, is he dead?" I scream, glancing back at Archel and Evan in panic. I look at the hallway to see all the soldiers on the floor, blood and body parts everywhere. "He's dead, isn't he?"

I look back to them. "Did you...just accidently blow someone up?" Archel wheezes, leaning into Evan from laughing so hard. Evan pushes him away, even though he laughs too, so hard tears run down his face while I just stare at them in shock. I can hear more boots heading our way, but Archel and Evan just keep laughing. Right as one comes around the corner, Archel, without looking, tosses three knives. I hear them scream as they fall, the blades undoubtedly hitting their targets. "She-She blew someone up with a grenade." He gasps and looks at Evan, and they start laughing all over again.

"I didn't know it was a grenade! I panicked! You shouldn't throw ball-shaped objects at a girl if you don't want it smacked back!" I yell hysterically, which only makes them howl louder with laughter.

"Ball-shaped objects," Evan echoes. "It was a fucking bomb." I throw my hands in the air. "I was having flashbacks of sports class, okay? Where they threw balls at us and I panicked! I didn't expect this ball to go boom!" I mimic an explosion in my hands and they share another look before laughing again.

Men.

I turn to peer around the corner to see bits of material and bodies still almost floating. "Oh look, it's raining soldier," I point out helpfully, as I look back at them.

Archel bends over, gripping his stomach. "Oh God, please stop, Princess."

I hear racing feet and Jago skids around the turn. He blinks when he sees them laughing and strolls towards us, a frown in place as he glances between us. "I leave you for two minutes and you are blowing people up?" He huffs. "What happened to being silent, sneaking by, Ninja Piper?" he teases.

"Goddamn it! If balls fly at your face, you hit them back, stop judging me!" I scream.

"Huh, so you going to do that to my balls? 'Cause a warning would be good." He laughs, setting the other two hyenas off again. Well, la-di-fucking-da, I'm glad I could help them bond at my expense.

"Men," I mutter. "You blow up one person by mistake." "Eight people," Evan corrects helpfully, interrupting my rant

with a smirk.

Ignoring him, I carry on, "And then they act like they have seen the klutz of the century!" Looking down at the body of a soldier, I grab another grenade just to prove a point, tossing it between my hands dramatically as I glare at them. "See? Look! Not blowing up!"

Not watching my hands, I throw it slightly too hard and have to try and juggle to catch it, but it's too late. It falls to the floor and rolls slightly to the bend, the pin falling out. Laughter dries up as we all share a look and start running in the other direction.

Just as we leap into the cafeteria, it explodes, sending us flying farther into the room. Groaning, I turn over to stare at the ceiling as the others cough near me. "Okay, okay. Note to self, don't play with grenades, they aren't like balls and they don't like to be rolled in your hands like testicles, they tend to go boom...which now that I think about it is kinda like your testicles," I muse, making them laugh again.

"I think it's fair enough to say they know we are here," Archel jokes after they finish laughing. "I say we go to plan B."

"Which is?" I query, rolling to see him. He grins at me from his spot on the floor.

"Hunt them down, don't play nice." He winks.

"Hell yes, I'm down for that, let's go, Piper's Power Rangers!" I yell and jump to my feet.

"Piper's Power Rangers?" Evan repeats and then shakes his head as he climbs to his feet. "Nope, if we are anything, it is Piper's sidekicks."

"Speak for yourself, Doc, I'm no sidekick." Archel grins. "I'm not Prince Charming either, I'm the villain in the princess's story, and she loves it."

"Alright, Romeo, let's get moving," I order, as I follow after Jago when we start moving again. We want to surprise them before they get to us. We are all racing towards each other in an underground lair, after all.

It's taken us hours to clear two levels with no sight of any other soldiers. Everything is dead and abandoned. Frowning, I start to let down my guard. "Maybe that was all of them?"

"Then where is the captain?" Jago snarls, and I shiver, turning away so he can't see my reaction as we leave the gym and hesitate in the hallway.

"Let's check the cameras like you suggested instead of hunting randomly, we could be looking for days," I advise and he nods. "Lead the way. Archel, take the back, Evan, you are with me."

"Why am I always in the middle?" he grumbles, and I wink at him.

"So I can protect you like a damsel in distress."

He narrows his eyes on me and I grin at him until it melts away and he smiles. "After you then, Pip."

We start moving towards the command center as Archel speaks up. "Why do you call her Pip?"

Evan laughs. "Like pipsqueak. She was this tiny little girl when we first met."

"Awww, was she a little princess?" he asks.

"She was a terror, always getting into trouble and blaming me," he scoffs, but winks over at me.

"What about Beast Man, you knew him growing up too?" Archel questions.

"No," we both reply.

"Eh, dude probably wasn't ever a child, just spawned into a full-grown, angry-looking man," Archel teases, making me giggle. "I bet he was a cute child," I reply back, and Jago looks over

at me to see me checking out his ass.

"Not as cute as you when you get all flustered, Brawler," he teases.

I snap my mouth shut then as we concentrate on moving through the labyrinth. Jago is confident as he walks through the dark, obviously knowing where he is going. We hit a door down another random corridor and he nods.

I move to the side, watching our backs as Archel and him clear it. They come out a minute later and nod, so we all slip inside and shut the door before Jago presses something and the lights come on.

Archel stuffs a discarded jacket at the bottom of the sliding door to block the light leaking out into the hallway, giving away our position. Smart move. Looking around, I let out a whistle at what I see. Now this is a command center.

Screens cover the whole back wall. They are darkened now, but I bet they used to cover all of Paradise and the grounds outside. Four desks are curved before it with matching chairs. On the desk is what I could only describe as a control board with buttons and keyboards and big red buttons. The only other thing in the room is a cage in the back corner where they obviously used to store their guns. It's empty now and the gate is left open as if they rushed away in a hurry.

"Okay," I call, rubbing my hands together as I let my bow drop to my back with the strap. "Anyone know how to get them working?"

We all look at each other and then at the computers and camera, which might as well be from a different universe. "We could try just pressing buttons," I joke, and Jago snorts as he kicks one of the chairs out of the way and stares down at the boards, seeming to think, so I lean back against the wall and leave him to it.

"I think if we restart the system, I should be able to get the cameras back on, but not the lights if I hit the right sector. I'm not sure if it controls the door as well...but I think I can do it," he grumbles, typing away on one of the computers.

Who knew? Muscles and brains, what a hot combination. I say so and Evan looks at me in disgust. "Do you think I'm a girl? We might be besties, Pip, but I don't need to know how he gets your motor running."

I wink at him and he grins as we both turn back to see Jago muttering to himself and smacking away Archel, who keeps trying to press buttons. "There," he grunts, and we all look up in time to see the screens turn back on, fading to a black and white view of Paradise.

Some cycle through other rooms while others stay stationary. Moving forward, I lean in next to Jago and search the screens for signs of life. "There." I point to the very bottom right screen where I spot two soldiers outside a door, guarding it.

"What's that lead to?" I ask with a frown. It doesn't seem familiar, so I clock the number painted on the wall. "That's down below, where most of the rooms are abandoned." I look at Evan for confirmation then and he nods.

"We went down there a lot as kids to explore, there's nothing down there, well, not in the rooms we checked," he adds.

"Something is there, something worth killing and dying over," Archel states grimly.

"But what?" I muse.

Jago leans back, grabs his sword and gun, and looks at us. "Let's go find out."

Chapter 12

Revenge is a Bitch, so am I

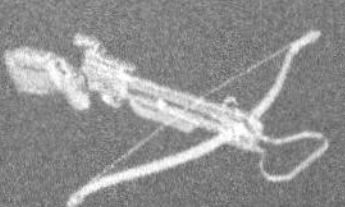

We move quickly and quietly down Paradise's hallways. I remember the way from when we were kids, so I take point, as Archel calls it. I spent a lot of time down here. It was somewhere to explore, somewhere free of adults where Evan and I could pretend for one minute that everything was okay.

There are rooms that were long since abandoned or locked. I'm guessing this used to be one of the locked ones. But what does it hide and why are the soldiers and the captain so bothered about getting to it now? So bothered they are willing to leave their people to die just to get their hands on it.

We reach the level, and in the stairway I press my fingers to my lips. I figured from the number on the door that it's right down at the bottom, but that doesn't mean they can't hear us. They all nod as I crack open the door and slip out into the corri- dor. This one is harder, they have the lights on down here.

It's slow going, sliding across the floor quietly as we sneak towards them. We are just turning our second corner when I hear a noise. I hold my hand up to halt them and tilt my head to listen before turning with a panicked look and pointing at another door.

Jago and Archel rush to the left, but Evan and I don't have time because they are on us. Looking around in panic, Evan yanks open the door closest and shoves me in, following after me.

The door shuts, the room submerged in darkness. We are so close we are touching, breathing each other's air, our panting overly loud in the quiet. Feeling along the wall behind me, I realise we are in a cupboard, probably a cleaning one. It's small and compact, pushing us together.

I hear them again, the guards, coming closer, their boots drawing near. Evan pulls me tighter against him as I stare at the closed door, wondering if they are going to find us and what will happen if they do.

They are right outside the door now, and my heart slams against my chest at the thought of being found even as I slip my hand down and grip my sword closer, ready to fight our way out of here if we need to, but Evan's hand comes up and grasps mine. Turning my head, my lips brush his chin and he sucks in a breath.

Time seems to stand still as I see him tilt his head down to mine, maybe to talk, maybe not...we will never know, because his lips brush against mine and we both gasp quietly.

Why does the dark always make things more exciting? A brush of a hand, a touch of lips? All my other senses are on high alert, very aware of him. Even though we are in danger, all I can think of is him.

"I love you, Pip," he whispers almost silently against my lips.

Tears fill my eyes, it's all I ever wanted to hear, and I'm done being angry or upset with him. We agreed on a new start, but that doesn't mean I still don't have all the feelings and love for him that I had before.

"I love you too, Evvie," I reply, and then his lips are on mine.

Moving hungrily, teasingly as he nibbles on my lips before I open for him, he tangles his tongue with mine.

I try to stay quiet, conscious they are right outside, but when his hand grips my hair and yanks me closer, a groan escapes. He swallows it down as he presses nearer, letting me feel the hardness in his pants. I want to make a joke about being happy to see me, but he is still kissing me.

He's hard and domineering, until I'm gripping his shirt to hold him close, weak in the legs from this dominant side of him. Fuck, I knew it would be hot as hell with him.

The door is wrenched open and we both turn, me with my sword and him with a knife, to see a grinning Archel and Jago there. "Doc and Princess, sitting in a tree," Archel whispers, and I roll my eyes as I put my sword away and take his hand so he can pull me out.

"Come on, love birds, they moved on, there's no one on the door. It's now or never," Jago tells us, and I let the fog of Evan's kiss fade as I grip my crossbow and aim it at the floor.

"Let's go find out what they are doing," I agree, and I trail after him, Archel and Evan behind us as we head to the once protected door.

Like Jago said, it's no longer protected, so all we have to do is hit the release button and it slides open. We are all ready, our weapons pointed, but we come up disappointed when nothing happens. Jago goes in first and I follow, noticing we are on what looks like a catwalk above a massive room. Peering over the steel rail, I spot the captain and a few soldiers below. I'm betting he doesn't have many left, but what catches my eye is what they are protecting...

"Are those bombs?" I hiss, and we all crouch, peering through the railing as the captain shouts orders to his men.

"They look like it," Evan confirms.

"I would say that one in the back corner near the silo is a nuclear warhead, I'm not sure if the others are." Archel frowns.

"What the fuck are they doing?" Jago mutters, and I look at him.

"Did you know we had bombs down here?"

He shakes his head as I look down again. "Me neither, feels like that's something they should mention at orientation." I snort. "Please don't venture outside or into the patrol areas and, oh, we are hiding bombs below our feet," I mock.

"What now?" Evan inquires.

"Now, we go down there and ask them what they are for," I reply. "They can't get out, and we can't leave them down here with that. There are only six soldiers and the captain, I think we can take them."

"Only six, what will the rest of you do?" Archel teases.

Jago nods. "She's right, okay, Piper, you're up here with the bow. Evan, watch her back and the door, the others will come back when they hear firing. Assassin, you're with me, we are going to sneak down there and kill them all but the captain. Piper, wait for my signal to start picking them off from up here." He turns then, probably sensing I'm about to argue. "We need you to watch our backs, Brawler."

"Got it." I nod and he leans forward, kissing me hard.

"Aim true," he whispers, before he starts to crouch walk away, keeping close to the floor.

Archel steals his spot in front of me and winks at me. "Don't worry, I won't let him die, watch my ass, won't you?"

"You got it, I do like that ass after all." I grin and he leans forward.

"Don't do anything I wouldn't do, Princess," he whispers, before kissing me softly.

"That's not a lot," I hiss back, as he follows after Jago, both of them disappearing.

"Well shit," I mutter, as I pull my crossbow around and perch it on a low rod of the rail, ready to shoot. "Evan, use my sword if you need to."

I'm trusting him to protect my back. I feel him press close to it, no doubt staring down at the door. Blowing out a calming breath, I resist the urge to search for my guys, keeping my aim on one of the soldiers closest to the captain.

A whistle comes and I let the arrow fly, reloading and moving on, knowing it's already embedded in his neck as I pick my next target and fire. Two down.

Jago emerges behind one and engages a man with his sword. As I'm about to fire at a third, Archel drops from the ceiling right on my target and cuts his throat. I don't fire again, not wanting to hit my guys, but I'm still protecting their backs.

The captain is standing behind the remainders with a gun in his hand. Jago kills two men quickly, and together they kill the other. They are turning to the captain when I see him lift his gun and aim at Jago.

I don't fucking think so.

I let loose another bolt, and it hits him right in the hand. He screams as he falls, the gun skating across the floor. I turn just as I hear the door opening behind me, but Evan is on it. He throws his knife at the first, and with a yell, he tackles the second and rains punch after punch down on him.

I leave Jago and Archel to restrain the captain, trusting them as I step up beside Evan to see the man's face is just mush at this point and covered in blood. "He's dead, Evvie, come on."

I tap his shoulder and he looks up, fists freezing mid-air. His eyes are wild, his lips curled in a snarl, and blood is splattered on his face. It might make me fucked up, but it turns me the hell on.

He nods and climbs to his feet, spitting down at the soldier. "Try to hurt my girl, I dare you," he snaps, before pulling his knife from the other corpse and turning to face me. "Come on then, Pip, let's see what that captain is doing."

"Then I get to have my fun with him." I grin, no doubt evilly, and he snorts.

"You do have a mean streak, babe."

"Too fucking right," I reply, as we head down the catwalk to a metal staircase. He helps me down the last step, his hands on my hips lifting me effortlessly before setting me down on the concrete floor.

Turning, I spot the captain now tied up to one of the bombs, and I can't help the laugh that escapes. Archel is leaning next to him, sharpening his blades without looking. The captain throws him nervous glances as Jago paces before him, his muscles bulging.

I know they both hate him, want to hurt him for what he did to me...but that's not their revenge to get.

Plus, it's bigger than me now, and we need to find out what he is doing with these bombs…then revenge.

As I step up in front of him, his eyes swing to me and he smirks at me viciously. "You," he spits.

"Me." I nod.

"Thought you were dead." He leans back in the restraints like we are at the dinner table.

"Sorry to disappoint, turns out I'm not that easy to kill.

Kinda like a cat," I say conversationally.

"Or a rodent," he concludes, and Jago snaps. He marches towards him and smashes his fist into his face. I watch in amusement as his head snaps back, his nose breaking with an audible crack.

"We need him alive, Beast," I tease, and Jago shakes his hand as he comes to stand next to me again.

We all watch as the captain groans, lifts his head, and looks at us, blood trickling from his busted nose, his lips pursed in pain, and his eyes pinched. "You work for me, boy, or did you forget?" he snaps at Jago, his voice thick.

"I work for her," Jago replies, jerking his head at me. "Figures, another dick following a cunt," he sneers, and I

wince for him as Jago smashes his fist into his face again.

Rolling my eyes, I step forward again. "As fun as it is watching him beat the shit out of you like the little bitch you are, we need to know what you are doing down here."

"Why would I tell you that?" He laughs.

"Well, him for one." I nod my head at Jago, who cracks his knuckles. "Him for two." I point at Archel, who grins and flashes him a blade. "Him for three." I jerk my head at Evan, who waves, making me grin.

The captain looks at him. "Those two I get, but him?"

"I can patch you up time and time again, keep you alive as they torture you. Problem?" Evan asks, and even I blink at the hate in his voice…okay then.

"So, what are you doing down here?" I question. "Protecting." He shrugs.

"I don't understand, what are you going to do with bombs?" I frown and he smirks.

"Of course you don't understand, that would require a brain."

Archel moves quickly, smacking him so hard his head jolts around and blood and teeth clatter to the floor.

"We went out there to protect our people, always the grunts, but someone made us a better offer." He grins, spitting more blood on the floor. "The Cities, they approached us on patrol, told us they knew Paradise was hiding a weapon, one that meant whoever controlled it would be in charge. They offered us a place in their new world when they took over, grunts no more. We would have everything we ever wanted." He grins. "They hide these down here, forgotten, didn't even try and use them. They could have controlled the Wastes with these weapons, but instead we hid down here and hoped no one ever found us. They were weak and stupid, I'm not. The Cities are going to use these to persuade those idiots who live out there to follow them, that this is their land now, to work for them, otherwise they bomb the North."

"They can't," I snap. "They need the North, they are running out of food and supplies. Kill us and kill their shot at the future of their people."

"They can always go south." He smirks. "They have already started exploring down there. Either way, they want control of the Wastes. With or without the people, dead or alive."

"Then we have to stop them," I exclaim. "We have to make sure they never get their hands on these bombs."

"Too late, they know we found them. They have sent patrols out into the Wastes to see if they can get through to us. If not, we are to put them in trucks and drive them to their borders where they will wait with our reward."

"You forget one thing, there are already leaders in the North. This is our land, our home, and we won't bow to any southern bastards! The bombs are ours now, we control their secret weapon... without them, their threats are useless. They will fall to the Queen of the North, and I will be by her side. You picked the wrong team, Captain, and you are going to die for it."

"You are all fucking savages, just playthings for my boys until we were put into action. They have had this planned for years, and no cunt, queen or not, is going to change that. The Waste- lands will fall and so will she."

Chapter 13
Princess Problems

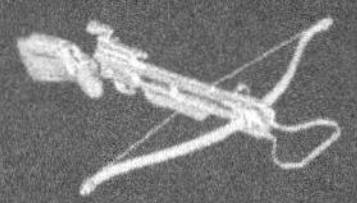

His words fall into the silence of the room until everyone explodes, yelling and moving, but I just smile and step towards him. "Well, really, I have to thank you for monologuing and telling us their plans and yours, makes this a lot easier, you know?" I look at my men. "And they say us savages are the idiots."

He stares at me with wide eyes as Archel starts to laugh. "Oh, Princess, one day I'm going to marry your crazy ass."

Okaaay, moving on.

"So what do we do with him now?" Evan inquires, and I see him inching closer to the captain as I turn to Jago.

"We kill him," I answer, and he nods.

"Make it hurt," he growls, eyes flashing just as we hear the sound of skin hitting skin.

We both turn to see Evan punching the captain again. He shakes out his hand and looks over at us as we stare. "He deserved it." He shrugs.

"Aww, now I feel left out, everyone has hit him but me." I pout.

"Hit him, Princess, it's a good stress reliever," Archel advises, leaning back against a crate.

"Remember how I showed you, don't break your hand on his face or I'll have to kill him," Jago warns as Evan nods.

"I'll get the med kit just in case," Evan mutters and walks away.

"You can't hit me, I'm your commanding—" I smash my fist right into his eye and yell from the pain as I grip my throbbing hand.

"Worth it," I chirp, before looking at the others.

I nod my head to the side and they follow me over to the corner of the room where the captain can't hear me. "We have a problem."

"What's wrong, Princess? I can kill him if you want me to. I can start by ripping off his balls and then I'll burn them so he doesn't bleed out, then flay his legs and arms—"

"Yeah, no, not that," I say, staring at him. "Though we may need to talk about your anger issues."

Then, I sigh. "We can't leave the bombs here unprotected and we don't have the manpower to take them with us, not to mention it would draw too much attention. What do we do?"

Jago grins. "Leave it to me." He looks at me, and Archel winks and saunters away as Jago moves closer, his eyes a low simmer. "Brawler, are you going to be okay with..." He gestures at the captain.

I glance back at the man who ruined my life, who changed it so dramatically, but knowing where I am now, I can see maybe everything happens for a reason. Maybe you have to walk through hell to live in heaven. I thought that when I saw him I would be...broken, scared, and weak, but all I feel is sorry for him. He is filled with greed and hate, and he will die alone and in pain. I'm not scared because my men are with me, and I know this man will never hurt me again.

But that doesn't mean he can live, he hurt me...badly, and if I don't, they will...Also, what if I let him go and he warns the Cities or hurts someone else? No, he needs to die, and it needs to be by my hands.

I need to put that part of me to rest, and I think ending his life will help me get over it, knowing the men who hurt me are all gone... it sounds wrong and normal people probably don't think about killing to help the healing process, but in this way, I don't think I care.

"He needs to die." I nod, resolute. "I have to do this, Beast, I have to look into his eyes when he realises all the pain and vile acts he has wrought have finally caught up with him."

"If you can't do it, one of us will for you," he whispers, stepping closer and wrapping his arms around me, pulling me into his warm embrace. "We've got you, Brawler. When you can't be strong, we will."

I breathe in his scent for a moment, absorbing his warmth and comfort before pulling away and leaning on my tiptoes, then I kiss him softly. "I know, I got this, you go sort our bomb problem, big guy."

He nods and kisses me again before heading out of the room as Evan comes back in with a med kit. Jago whispers something to him and he looks at me and nods before stepping back down here and setting his kit to the side.

"Right then, let's get this show on the road," I yell cheerfully. Strolling back over to the captain, I see him coming around.

I'm pretty proud I managed to knock him out, I'm going to ignore the fact that Jago probably set it up with his big ole punches.

Pulling my crossbow around, I load a bolt and aim it at his face. He needs to die, but I can't bring myself to torture him or make it last, it's not who I am. I will never be the monster he is.

His eyes clear, his lips kicking up at the corner as he stares down my bow to me. "Go ahead, cunt, it won't change what happened to you. You'll always be the useless little girl who couldn't even save herself."

I don't know why I'm hesitating, he needs to die. Maybe it's because I don't usually get time to think about it or second-guess my actions. It's spur of the moment and over quickly and usually to protect my friends and family...but now, I'm staring into his eyes and having to consciously pull the trigger.

"Princess," Archel murmurs.

No, the princess saves herself in this one. I pull the trigger.

Archel deals with the body, I don't ask how, I'm beginning to learn you shouldn't know everything...especially if it comes to an assassin and his obsession with killing and mutilating.

Evan checks over my hand and kisses it better before we go to find Jago. I collect the bolts I used and add them to the bow before we follow the bodies back to the bunker door where we find Jago waiting with a grin on his face.

"Your carriages await, my lady," he teases, and opens his arms to show the massive trucks they usually kept at the back of the bunker and under lock and key. They are the size of old-school oil tankers with massive beds in the back. "We put the bombs in here with some of the Paradise people, the rest can go on bikes and cars."

"Not bad, Beast Man, not bad at all." I grin, it's a good plan. We can't leave it here, the Cities know where the bombs are, so we can take it back with us and hide it where no one will ever look...with The Forgotten.

"Alright, let's go see if everyone is packed up. I want out of here before those patrols arrive," I call and they agree. "Jago, Archel, Evan, you start a system to move the bombs, I'll send down the biggest men I can find, okay?"

"Sure thing, Brawler." Jago nods and pulls his shirt off and passes it to me. My mouth goes dry as I check out his flexing muscles.

"Two can play at this game," Archel mutters, and throws his shirt at my face. I turn to see him winking at me, his golden skin on display.

Christ, it's an all-you-can-eat man buffet.

"Oh hell no, I'm not being left behind!" Evan yells, and I turn yet again to see him ripping off his shirt, grinning at me.

My brain is officially blown.

"Nipples," I blurt, looking between them. "So many nipples, why do men have nipples? It's not like they breastfeed, you know?"

"I honestly never know what you are going to say," Archel comments with a laugh. "Now, Princess, who has the best chest?" he calls, and I start to back away.

"Nope, no, not judging that. It's like how you can like three flavoured ice cream, you know?" I offer as they all turn to me. Holy vagina, this isn't fair.

"Yes, but you have a favourite," Evan points out.

"What's that?" I gasp, pointing behind them, and as they all turn, weapons drawn, I laugh and run away. "Later, suckers!"

I head back out into the sun, shielding my eyes as my gaze adjusts to the difference. I find Lupin waiting outside with two Paradise people. "Lupin, head in, there isn't anyone but our people left. Get that door open fully, will you?" I request, and he blinks but rushes inside. "Keep your eye on the door, if anyone but us approaches, you holler, okay?" I tell the guards, before rounding the building to find Worth's dad.

Everything is a go where we were camping. Everyone is packing up and rushing around nervously. I find him in the center, giving orders and helping pack. "A word," I order, as I walk past him and lean against the building in the shade, watching them run about.

He helps finish the sorting of some supplies before dusting his hands and coming over, looking nervously at me. "What did you find down there?"

"Did you know?" I ask, crossing my arms. "About the bombs?"

"Bombs?" he echoes incredulously, his eyes widening, and the shock isn't fake, it's real.

Well, shit.

Sighing, I scrub at my face before filling him in on what we found and the plan. "I didn't know, it makes sense now though. They were trying to take over Paradise, probably so they could control what was going in and out. Fucking traitors," he snaps. "Okay, I'll make sure they are all ready to go by tonight and send my biggest men over."

I nod and he starts to turn away before stopping. "Thank you, Piper. I know I wasn't gracious before, and I apologise for my rudeness. Not everyone is good with change, and I guess I am one of them. I shouldn't have taken that out on you, you were only helping. I've made them aware that you are in charge and to listen to you," he offers peacefully, before walking away and shouting some names.

When there are twenty or so good-sized men around me, I lead them back to the bunker and to my men who are in the garage waiting, with ropes and what looks like a pully system in place. "I brought you some men," I call.

"Leave her alone for one minute and she has twenty new booty calls," Archel jokes.

"Shush, Shadow, now get to work, my merry band of men! I want to move out at dark!" I yell and clap my hands. The Paradise men rush to help as my guys start giving out orders, even Evan.

I leave them to it because it seems they know what they are doing, but instead of going back outside to help pack, I slip past them and into the bunker, heading to what I used to call home.

I don't know if there is anything there I want to keep, but it feels like I need to say goodbye. I have no doubt this will be my last time here, especially if I don't survive the oncoming war.

I wander the familiar hallways until I come to my room, and then I press my hand to the scanner which allows me inside. Lupin must be doing his work, because the lights and air condi- tioning are back online now, illuminating the messy room I left behind.

Nothing has been moved, my bed is still unmade, my clothes are littered everywhere, and souvenirs and mementos of my life line the shelves, including pictures and teddies.

"Huh, wonder why they didn't clear this place out," I mutter, as I pick up one of my shirts and toss it towards the chest of drawers as I step farther in. I pick up a picture of Evvie and me when we were thirteen or so, both of us pulling silly faces and grinning like crazy.

"Because I wouldn't let them," comes his reply from behind me. I turn as I hear the door shut behind him.

Leaving me alone with Evvie in my room, old times anyone? Only this time we both know where we stand and we are a lot older and wiser, even though it wasn't that long ago.

"I thought you were helping?" I query, tilting my head, the photograph still in my hand.

"They told me they had it. I was on my way to pack up the medical equipment and drugs when I saw you slip in here, why? Don't want me here, Pip?" he asks, stepping closer, almost pressing me to the wall.

"Shut up, Evvie, just wondered why you had taken a page out of Archel's book and stalked me is all," I tease and he grins, tipping his head down until we are almost touching.

"Want to finish what we started in the closet?" he whispers seductively, his eyes flickering to my lips hungrily.

"Well, it would be rude not to...seeing as though you are shirtless and there's a bed." I grin but he shakes his head.

"No," he snaps, and then smashes his lips to mine, tracing them with his tongue until I gasp and then open them. He slips it inside and tangles it with mine as his hands go to my ass and hoist me up, slamming me back against the wall as he pulls his mouth away.

"No, I've had this recurring fantasy of slamming you up against the wall and fucking the sass out of you every time we had a stupid fight or you looked at me with those eyes..." He trails off then. "Yes, those eyes."

"Well, we can't let your fantasy down, can we?" I tease breathlessly. My hands have a mind of their own and trace down his neck to his shoulders to his pecs, feeling him up as I talk.

"Shut up, Pip," he groans.

"Make me," I challenge, and I see the glint in his eyes, the one he used to get when we fought or I made a bet with him. He slams me harder into the wall as his hand yanks up my top until it's around my neck and my bra is on display, he pulls down the cups and as I watch, he leans in and kisses across my chest to my nipple.

He sucks it into his mouth and bites softly before pulling back and giving the other the same treatment. Holding me up with one arm, he slides his free hand around and unbuttons my jeans before he buries his hand in my panties.

He cups my pussy through them, finding me wet. Evan groans against my nipple, the vibration travelling through me and making me shiver in need. Fuck, I like this side of Evan. There's no hesitation or holding back, showing me exactly how much he wants me, no games, no arguments.

For once we are on the same page.

Trailing my hand down his solid chest, I flick open his jeans and he rips his mouth from mine, dropping me to the floor before stepping back and shoving them off, kicking them away until he's bare before me. His cock is long and hard, thinner than Jago's but so fucking long. Jesus, my mouth actually waters until my eyes widen when I realise he has a piercing down there too.

"You pierced your cock? Did that hurt?" I ask curiously, and he laughs.

"Why, you going to kiss it better?" he counters huskily.

Instead of answering, I yank down my jeans and toss them and my boots aside, my top joins them next, then I'm naked as well. He licks his lips, his eyes running across my body, trailing a fire in their wake, like with each look he is actually touching me. The stark hunger on his face and the worship undoes me.

Not the least bit shy, I strut over to him, run my hand down his chest, and grasp his cock, rubbing at the tip where it's pierced before leaning in.

"Didn't you promise to fuck me against the wall?" I whisper. Like I wanted, he moves, faster than I've ever seen him move.

He grips my hand on his cock and shoves it away, then he spins me and pushes me against the wall before kicking open my legs and yanking my hips back.

Leaning in, he licks my ear as he rubs his hard cock along my pussy, wetting it with my cream, nudging at my clit and entrance until I'm moaning and pushing back into him. "You're not in charge of me, Pip. I might follow you around on everything else, but here? Between us? You are mine," he growls. "Mine to touch." He traces down my side. "To lick," he whispers and licks my ear. "To kiss." He drops one on the slamming pulse in my neck. My heart is racing so loudly, I can barely hear him over it.

"To fuck." He lines up at my entrance and slams inside me. Groaning, I splay my hands on the wall and push back, taking all of his long cock until he's balls deep and panting in my ear. Gripping my hips, he pulls out and pushes back in, slow at first, working through my tight pussy before speeding up. With each thrust, I'm thrown into the wall. It's hard, wild, and oh so fucking delicious.

Pushing back to meet him, I turn my head and he kisses me, swallowing my moans. Only when we break apart to breathe does he speak again. "Want to know why I got the piercing?" he questions.

My brain is foggy with pleasure, so it takes me an embarrassingly long time to nod.

"For this," he murmurs, before tilting my hips farther back, and with each thrust it drags along the nerves inside me, making me yell. "Saw it in a textbook, wanted to try it out on you."

His fingers tighten on my hips, digging in, the pain maddening as he fucks me against the wall. But it's not enough for him. Just as I'm about to come from his cock alone, he pulls out of me, ignoring my whine, and twirls me until my back hits the wall again.

Hoisting me up, he slams back inside me, making me moan. Wrapping my legs around his waist, I dig my nails into his shoulders. I've been dreaming of this forever. My first ever orgasm was with my fingers in my pussy while imagining him, and now it's happening... and it's better than I could have ever imagined.

It's perfect, like two halves fitting together, we move as one. Our bodies were made for one another, our names on each other's lips.

Pulling him closer, using the wall, I rock my hips to meet his punishing thrusts as I yank his head to mine and kiss him, telling him how wild he drives me, how bloody turned on I am. He groans into my mouth, a sexy rumbling sound, before his hand slips between our sweaty bodies and rubs my clit.

"I want to feel you come around me, see you scream for me. Know you're mine." He gasps as he drives into me again and again until I'm a mess, words spewing from my mouth unchecked as my nails cut down his back, unable to help myself.

It's too much, too much pleasure, I can't handle it. His hands, his mouth, his cock...fuck.

I come apart in his arms, screaming his name, my nails clawing into his back again, my legs tightening around him to keep him inside me. He groans and bites down on my shoulder to muffle his yell as he comes, filling me with it until we both collapse back against the wall, panting and sweating, but satisfied as hell.

"If-If that's how we are ending every fight, we should do it more often," I joke breathlessly and he laughs, making me gasp.

"I agree," he murmurs, kissing where he bit my shoulder before pulling back and looking at me.

Reaching up, I push his sweaty black hair out of his face and smile at him tenderly. His eyes soften as he looks at me lovingly. "Pip —" He starts then grins. "You're my world, you know that?"

"I love you too, Evvie," I murmur.

"I, erm..." He blushes, actually blushes, which I didn't think he would be capable of with his cock still buried in me and his cum dripping down my thighs. "I've never done that before," he admits, and my eyes widen.

"Wait, hold the fucking bombs, I was your first?" I ask in shock. He nods, his cheeks blazing again. "But-But you seemed to really know what you were doing!"

He grins. "I have very vivid fantasies and I've read a lot of books, I always wanted my first time to be with you."

I blink, feeling guilty as hell, and he must see it, so he kisses me. "Pip, I don't care I'm not your first, as long as I'm your last...or I guess one of your lasts."

"You are," I promise. "I'm sorry you can't be my only."

"Nah, don't be, love, it's actually a relief." He grins.

"A relief ?" I parrot with raised eyebrows and he laughs.

"Not like that, just that, this world is filled with things that want to kill you and I've never been the big fighter type, so I'm glad you have men who can protect you when I can't and help look after your heart and happiness. I guess they aren't too bad if you get over the wanting to kill each other thing," he admits and I smile.

"Thank you, Evvie, thank you for never giving up on me."

Chapter 14
Road to home

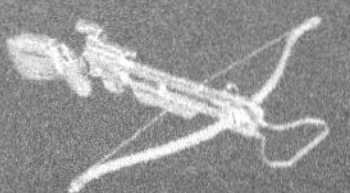

"Come on then, Evvie, I'll help you pack your office," I offer, and he kisses me before setting me down gently.

Heading past him, I spank his plump ass, making him yelp while I grin. I flick on the water, praying it's still working, and almost happy dance when it comes on. I take a quick shower. The water is cold at first, but soon warms up. I'm going to miss this.

Evvie slips in with me and we wash each other, which ends with me feeling him up before I force us to get dried off and dressed. Grabbing one of my bags from the drawers, I toss in a few clothes and some of my mementos before looking around and joining Evan at the door.

"I guess this is goodbye," I mutter.

"Think of everything that is to come," he murmurs, rubbing my back.

Nodding, I blow out a breath. "I'm not good at goodbyes, so... yeah, see ya, thanks for the memories and the walls to fuck against." I salute the room before pressing the close button, hearing Evan snort.

Tangling our hands together, we head down to his office. He opens the door and everything is like I imagined in my memories. I

"

hop up on the bed and swing my legs, watching as he meticulously grabs everything he needs and adds it carefully to a large bag. He looks over at me and smirks. "Thought you were helping, Pip?"

"I am, I'm your cheerleader." I wink and raise my arms. "Go, Evvie, grab those drugs and then come over here for a hug!"

I fake scream and throw some imaginary pom-poms at him as he turns around, muttering about crazy girls. I watch him pack up all the supplies we will need, he takes pretty much everything, mentioning something about casualties of war, and when he's all packed up, I grab one of his bags and mine and head back upstairs to find the others.

In the garage, they have one of the bombs loaded into the trucks, and the space is empty, so I'm guessing they have gone to get another. I add my bag to a random truck and Evan sets his in there as well. "You can ride in here," I tell him.

"Where are you riding?" he asks, leaning back against the truck.

"Your girl rides bikes." I wink and look over as a noise comes from the doorway. I watch them heave one of the bombs through, all of them sweating and grunting, holding on with pink, straining arms.

Evan and I rush over to help, and the next four hours are spent in a sweaty mess hoisting bombs around.

It's dark, the sun has just set, and we are all packed and ready to go. The trucks are with their drivers in the bunker, filled with Paradise people and their possessions. Waiting on the back of the bike, I grip on to Jago while Archel is next to us on his. He is going to ride at the back of the procession and watch our backs as we lead them to The Forgotten.

Here's hoping Trev understands.

I nod at Archel and his whistle cuts through the air—the signal. The trucks and cars start up, the bike purring beneath me. Lights flood the area from behind us as I pull down my goggles from Worth.

They know the drill, they stay close and we move fast, we aren't stopping until we reach home, not with the cargo we are carrying.

I tap Jago on the shoulder and wrap my arms tighter around him as he revs the bike and pulls away. I glance over my shoulder to see the trucks pulling out slowly and following us. We make sure to have the bombs placed in the middle, our last defence in case we are attacked, but with a convoy this size, I'm reckoning we won't be.

Turning forward to face the Wastes, I hunker down as we slowly set off across the sand, gradually speeding up to a pace the trucks can keep up with. The hours pass sluggishly, my legs and arms aching from holding on, but we have a long drive ahead of us so I let my mind wander as I hold on to my man.

My eyes close at one point as I relax into him, not quite asleep but not awake, just lost in the in between as the miles pass. I try to think of my parents, but I can't even remember them anymore. Their faces are blurry, hazy almost, from the years. For so long I tried not to think of them, it hurt too badly, but now, when I want to, I can't, but the feeling...the love they had for me is still there.

And the pain? The pain is fleeting, but it reminds me that although they are gone, no one ever truly leaves us, not if you love them.

"Evan, this is Piper, her parents are...well, they are gone like yours. She will be staying in these quarters with you until she is older. Will you look after her for us?" comes the motherly sweet voice of the plump older lady holding my hand. I look at the angry-looking boy just a few years older than me and want to cringe. He nods at the woman, acting like an adult, not a child, but when his eyes turn to me, they soften, a smile curling up at his lips, and he steps towards me from the many empty beds.

"Hi Piper, I'm Evan," he introduces himself, his voice gentle and low. "Hi," I whisper, looking at him then to the woman.

"I'll leave you to it. I'll be right next door if you kids need anything," she tells me, and crouches down to see me better, pushing the hair off my face. "I'm sorry, Piper, I really am."

Then she leaves me alone with this boy, a stranger in a strange empty place. I turn to see him, wrapping my thin arms around my young torso and stare at the ground. "Hey, Piper, which bed do you want? They are all ours, we are like the king and queen of the castle, see?"

I look up to see him grinning, his arms spread wide when I hesitate. He lets them drop and steps closer.

"It's okay, Piper, I'll look after you now, always, okay?"

Worry shoots through me for a moment at what I've agreed to do, not fear for me...but for them. I promised to love them, to protect them, yet I'm leading them into a war...I know we need to fight back, protect our people and land, but if I lost one of them. I don't know what I would do, how I would cope.

But even though I'm scared for them, I won't back down. People are looking to me now, counting on me, trusting me, and maybe, just maybe, I can make a difference in this world.

Maybe I can achieve my parents' dreams and find my own in the meantime.

❧

The sunlight hits the sand and shines brightly through the world. Banishing the dark and illuminating our trucks and convoy. We keep driving, but we are on high alert. We saw no one through the night, but during the day we are a big, noticeable load. I keep my crossbow in my hand as we drive, scanning the horizon. My back starts to ache and we have to stop for two hours for a pee break, where we switch off driving. Jago grabs on to my hips and takes over spotting as I focus on finding the best way through the Wastes and back to The Forgotten.

The hours drag on, sweat drips down my face, and my clothes are sticking to me, and sand hits my goggles and bounces off until, eventually, the sun starts to set, and yet we are still driving.

Tonight I can finally see the signs we are almost there. We passed the church a few hours back and the world is almost ending, the sounds disappearing, the life of the dead land gone... until I see the tunnel up ahead.

I hear Jago whistle and gesture as we slow down. Shit, I didn't think about the fact that the trucks are tall. I wonder if they will fit under. I stop just in front of the consuming darkness and hop off to look at Jago, who climbs off too, and stares at the tunnel with a nod.

"It will fit, will be tight, but we will fit. We will take it slow. Why don't you ride ahead and set off a warning so we aren't attacked as we come through?" he suggests.

"You sure you will be okay?" I ask nervously.

He grins and strides closer, kissing me as he lifts me and places me back on the bike. "Go, they only listen to you, we will be right behind."

Pulling my goggles down, I turn and rev the bike, riding into the darkness and leaving my men to sort out the rest of the people. I have my own challenge ahead, assuring the people of The Forgotten that we can exist in peace, that the people they ran from started a new life and need their help.

I make my way through the tunnel and out the other side, where the trees grow and I can smell home. It hits me, the scent of fire and cooking meat, and as I draw closer, I hear the laughter and chatter of my people and I realise...this is home.

Right here.

Out there might be my adventure, but home is where you always find your way back to...and it's not always a place...it's the people. And these people, these people who saved me and took me in when I was broken beyond repair, fixed me back up, and welcomed me with understanding arms that allowed me to grow without fear or hate... these people are my home.

When I round the trees, two patrols step up to meet me, so I pull up my goggles and kick out the stand before slipping from the bike with a groan. Jesus, my thighs hurt, like I've been clenching a man between them for hours...least that would be more pleasurable.

A familiar face steps forward and I grin. "Simon," I greet him.

He smiles at me and scoops me up into a bear hug. "Thank God, we were getting worried." He drops me back to my feet and steps away, looking behind me. "Where's ya big fellow?"

"Coming, we need Trev...Simon, we have some visitors coming and not a lot of time to explain, can you grab him?" I request sweetly.

He nods. "Wait here," he tells me and rushes away, even though I saw the questions in his eyes.

Waiting with the other patrol, I cross my arms and search the camp. Everything looks like it did when I left, which is good. "No attacks?" I ask the young man whose name I'm not sure of.

"No, sir, I mean ma'am, I mean, er..." He stutters nervously. "Piper is fine, what's your name?" I inquire with a smile. "Dez, Simon has just started training me in patrols." He

grins, looking excited.

I know the feeling. I hope that doesn't fade for him.

Trev comes running through the camp on Simon's heels and examines me with concern. "Okay, I don't have a lot of time to explain, but I need you to trust me, I had no choice—"

"Sir! Sir! Trucks! Lots of trucks coming through the tunnel!" comes a yell from a patrol rushing down the road.

Trev frowns and glances from me to him.

"Yeah...about that." I laugh. "They are with me, they are coming to live here."

Chapter 15
Homecoming

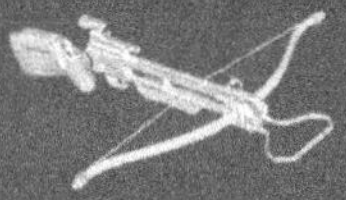

"Piper, what do you mean?" he asks.

I give him a quick rundown of events. "I'm sorry I didn't have time to ask. If you want to turn them away, I under- stand and I will find somewhere else. There is a town some-where called Spring we could try...but I couldn't leave them there. They were sitting ducks and not all of them hurt us, they are inno-cent. I couldn't live with walking away."

He blows out a breath. "Okay, and these bombs?"

"They are deactivated, from what we can tell. It wasn't safe to leave them there. I figured we could hide them here while we assimi-late the new people, put them to work, make them part of it, and if they don't fit they can leave. Three warnings, I figured?" I offer hopefully.

"Well, we can't turn them away to die," he muses, tapping his chin. "Okay, bring them in. We'll hold a meeting in the morning. Tonight, I need to know everything that happened, after we hide those bombs." He turns to Simon then. "How about behind the tent, between the old shack and trees?"

Simon thinks about it for a moment. "It could work. We will leave them in the trucks and cover them, no one will be the wiser."

"Good, grab some men," Trev orders, and then looks back at me. "Well, let's welcome the new members, shall we?"

I nod. "Thank you, Trev, I truly am sorry about the lack of warning."

"It is okay, Piper." He grins, placing his hand on my shoulder as we hear the rumble of trucks heading our way. "You did what any leader would, you made a decision in a hard place. We will make it work one way or the other, but I will need your help to calm our tribe."

"Of course," I agree instantly, and watch the trucks roll around the corner. Jago is hanging from one of the doors, and when they stop with a hiss before us, he leaps off and heads my way.

I can hear our tribe drawing closer, their fear and panic melting when they see us waiting. They whisper behind us, shouting questions as people start to leave the trucks. Jago joins me at my other side as Archel zooms around the trucks and skids to a stop beside us, winking at me. "No followers, we are safe, I doubled back just to check."

Trev snorts. "Should have figured you would be involved, Shadow."

"You know it, old man." He laughs as he climbs off his bike and Evan breaks away from the nervous crowd of Paradise people to head over to us. He is grumbling the whole way, but it melts into a smile when he sees me.

"Next time, someone else is playing peacemaker with those people. I wanted to cunt punch at least half of them," he complains, then looks at Trev.

"Trev, this is Evan, he's my family," I say in introduction, and Evan grins at me before extending his hand. They shake and Trev looks at me.

"I'm glad you found him, now let's see what we are going to do with all these people," he mutters, but with a small smile.

Just then, a scream breaks out and we turn, all pulling weapons, until we realise it's a man breaking from the tribe behind us, shock on his face and tears in his eyes. "Willa?" he yells again, and a small woman rushes towards him from the nervous Paradise people.

He breaks into a sprint and scoops her into his arms, both of them crying into each other's shoulders. Just then, more and more people start to come forward from both sides, greeting people they know. It's emotional and I feel myself leaning closer to Jago. He wraps his arm around me as we watch families, lovers, and friends reunite.

"Well, at least we don't have to worry about them fighting." Trev laughs and then claps to get everyone's attention. "These are our new members. I need you to offer them homes, beds, food, clothes, and sanctuary. They are one of us now, make them feel welcome. We will assign jobs tomorrow. For all you newbies, this is our home, respect us and we will respect you. You have three warnings before you will be exiled. Everyone works here and pulls their weight. Understood?" he calls loudly, and agreement and murmurs go up. Then I step forward.

"If anyone has any issues with the newcomers, come to Trev or me, we will deal with it. To everyone from Paradise, this isn't the bunker anymore. Up here, it's hard, but this place...this place is truly paradise if you let it be. It's time to embrace the world and stop hiding," I shout, and a cheer goes up from my tribe and even some members of Paradise. I spot Worth's dad hanging around looking out of place. "Okay, the men who moved the bombs before, help us now, then you can all rest! Let's go!" I order, and they all break away to do as they need to.

"Papa Worth," I call, and he looks at me before coming over. "Trev, this is the leader of Paradise. I think we can find a place for him, won't we?"

"I would think so. If you represent your people, it would be good to have your council and help to get them settled," Trev declares, clapping him on the shoulder, and starts to lead him away.

"Get settled, Piper, and then come find me," Trev calls over his shoulder.

"Sure thing!" I agree, before turning to my men. "Well then...this is going to be a tight squeeze in my house."

"No kidding," Archel mutters.

"I'm dibbing big spoon!" Jago adds, making me laugh as I grab our bags.

"I'll take these to the house, you guys going to help move the bombs?" I tell them.

"Men strong," Archel mocks. "Move bombs." "Dude, you are so weird," Evan mutters.

"Come on, Doc, let's go show Princess how manly we are!" he jokes, and they all head over to help move the trucks and bombs as I grab their bags like a pack horse and trek through the camp to my hut on the hill.

I see the newbies looking around, someone is giving them a tour, while others are offering food. Despite their differences, they are welcoming the very people they left...it gives me hope.

Panting with the effort of being a packhorse—I swear their bags are even heavier than mine—I dump them inside the door of my hut. Everything is where I left it at least, not that I expected it to have been moved. At this rate, I'm going to need an extension.

Curious why the bags are so heavy, I peek in one which I'm guessing is Archel's...the guy hasn't even packed clothes or under-wear...it's just filled with weapons! I guess I'm not surprised, but Christ, I don't even know what half of this stuff is!

"I think we are going to need to put another bed in here," Archel jokes from behind me. I spin, glaring at him for sneaking up on me.

"Dude, I will put a bell on you!" I tease and he laughs.

"To think, I thought you always saw your shadow," he purrs, stepping closer, prowling towards me like he always does.

"I only see you when you want me to, assassin," I retort, and he grins, letting me know I'm right.

"So, Princess, going to share your castle with your men?" He corners me against the bed, his hands darting out and gripping my hips to pull me closer. "Won't they get jealous when they see you sleeping in my shirt?"

"Who says I will be sleeping in clothes?" I counter, and he groans just as another voice comes from the door.

"New house rule, all dudes must wear clothes. I don't want to see swinging cocks in the morning," Evan mutters, stepping in and looking around.

"We all wear clothes," Jago agrees, but then looks at me with fire in his eyes. "Apart from you, Brawler, feel free to walk around naked."

"These two are a bad influence on you!" I accuse, and he grunts in agreement.

"He's right, we are going to need another bed," the big guy adds, and with all of them in here, I have to admit it's a tight squeeze—not that I mind being squeezed between them.

"I'll get us one," Archel says casually, before dropping a kiss on my nose and rushing into the night.

"Don't steal it! Or kill anyone!" I yell after him, and I hear his chuckle float to me. He is going to steal one.

"Okay, which side of the bed am I on?" Evan inquires, looking around.

"I'm closest to the door," Jago snaps. "And Piper."

"Fine, I'll take the other side of her and the wall," Evan mutters, rolling his eyes at Jago. "What kind of crazy person wants to be closest to a door where they could get attacked or killed anyway," he grumbles to himself, as he drops down on the bed.

There are bags under his eyes, which are bloodshot, he's tired, we all are. "Sorry, you guys get some sleep, I need to go and talk to Trev," I tell them through a yawn.

"No, we will go with you, Brawler," Jago states with a hard voice, giving Evan a glare, who grumbles again but gets up.

"Like we would leave you. Lead the way, Pip!" he declares.

I guide them down from the hill and through the camp to the tent where I find Worth's dad and Trev talking. When I walk in, Trev turns to me with a smile. "Okay then, Piper, I have learned some of what has happened, but why don't you fill me in on the rest and I can help you work through it?"

I sit down, and Trev passes us some tea while I explain everything that happened involving the war and the promise I made to Worth. When I'm done, he is stroking his chin. "I see, okay." He nods and looks at me. "What's your opinion on this war?"

I sit up taller, knowing he is coming to me for advice and will really listen. "That it's coming one way or the other, and we can either choose to be part of it or be left broken in its wake. They won't stop with Worth, they will take all of the North, and when we don't fall in line, they will kill us, the bombs show you that. I think it's time to fight, that for once we can't hide. This time there is no running. We have to take a stand, all of us, or we all fall."

My words land hard in the silence, and I fight the urge to fidget as he examines me. "That is a very mature perspective." He nods with a small smile. "As you can understand, I am hesi- tant about leading our people into a battle if we don't have to."

"Of course, they are my people too, but this battle? It's coming no matter what. Wouldn't you rather it be on our terms?" I point out and he laughs.

"Very true, ah, assassin, what are your thoughts on this war?" Trev calls, and I turn to see Archel sitting in a chair next to Worth's dad, who turns to see him there in shock, the sneaky man.

"I agree with Piper, and not because I enjoy a good fight." He becomes serious then. "I've seen the devastation it can cause, but whether we want it or not, it's coming, and all we can do is decide where we stand. I know I want to be on that front line, helping to protect the people I love. Live or die, we do it together."

Licking my lips, I stare at the blank expression on his face before he turns and winks at me.

"And think of all that fighting and blood, won't it be glorious, Princess?"

"Then I will need to step up our training," Trev comments with a sigh. "They have been practicing and we have some good talent, but not nearly enough warriors."

"We will do what we can. For now, we all need to rest, we haven't slept in days and we will think clearer on a less tired mind. We have time to decide how to approach this war, but one way or another, we will be on that front line," I state with conviction.

"Very well, get some sleep, I will see you in the morning," he replies, but his smile is strained, his face lined, the news taking a toll on him.

"Goodnight," I call, before heading back to my hut, my men on my heels.

When we get inside, I can feel them hesitating nervously, even with the extra bed which Archel has pushed up to the other. There is only a small walkway between the door and the beds now. But I'm too tired to care, so instead, I take off my boots, jeans, and shirt, knowing I'm going to be surrounded by boys and skin and bound to get hot. Crawling into bed, I am wearing only my bra and panties. When I'm under the quilt, I turn to see them all standing at the entryway, staring at me with hungry but tired expressions.

"Come on, it's time to sleep. You can all try to kill each other in the morning, but for tonight, let's just get along." I sigh, my eyes closing with the softness and warmth surrounding me.

I hear them whisper something to each other before the bed dips, then I grunt as someone crawls over me. My eyes open to see Evan pressing his back to the wall and cuddling under the duvet beside me, his legs tangling with mine. I slip into his arms, resting my head on his chest as another body presses to mine from behind. I glance over to see Archel with Jago on the outside. "Night," I murmur around a yawn, and as soon as I close my eyes, I fall deeply asleep.

"Piper!" comes a scream that jerks me awake. Archel is on his knees in an instant, his sword out, and Jago is crouched in front of me protectively, but it didn't come from outside, it came from inside. A whimper comes then, and I turn to see Evan reaching for me in his sleep, his face split with panic.

He calls out my name again, the heartbreak and fear in it making me almost cry for him. What happened to Evvie to make him have nightmares? Was it just losing me, or was it something else?

Like he did so many times before, I scoot closer and wrap my arms around him, kissing his head softly. "I'm here, Evvie, I'm here," I repeat, until he settles down with a sigh and a grumble, cuddling into my embrace and falling back to sleep.

Jago and Archel climb back into bed without a word, the assassin draping his arm and leg around me and Evvie, holding him too. "Our fears have a way of manifesting in our sleep, that dream he is having? I've had it too," he whispers in my ear.

We are family now, and Archel is showing me that. Despite the jealousy and anger, he is holding Evvie, helping him through the nightmares. My heart slams into my ribs, so filled with happi- ness that tears erupt. I bury my face in Evvie's hair and settle between them again.

"I'll keep watch over him, get some sleep," Jago grumbles.

"Thank you, big guy, love you," I whisper, as I start to fall back to sleep again.

"Love you, Brawler," comes the hushed reply. "Love you, Princess," comes another.

Chapter 16
Old Friend

"Brawler, come on, wake up, you need to eat," comes the order.

Groaning, I flip over and bury my face in something warm and shaking with laughter. Cracking open my eye, I see a bare chest and follow it up to find a grinning Evan.

"Come on, Pip, you get mardy when you don't eat," he begs softly.

"Traitors," I mutter, and flip over to see Jago already dressed and waiting at the edge of the bed. "Where's my shadow?" I ask, scrubbing at my face.

"Who knows, probably scaring children." Jago snorts. "We left you both to sleep as long as we could while we checked on everyone, but breakfast is ready."

"Alright, alright," I mutter. I slide from the bed and stumble into Jago who catches me.

"Sit down before you fall." He grins down at me, eyes on fire.

"Coffee, need coffee," I groan.

"Sorry, Brawler, none here," he tells me, before grabbing my shirt and pulling it over my head, and then starting on my jeans. I get to my feet as he buttons them and pushes me back down, grabbing my ankle to place it on his leg. Pulling on my sock and boot, he sets my foot to the floor before doing the same to the other. He is just lacing up my boot when Archel pokes his head around the door and wiggles his eyebrows at me.

"Thought I would find a threesome, gotta say I'm disappointed," he teases, making me laugh. "But ah, well, I brought you a present, Princess."

He comes into the room and produces a steel mug from behind his back. I see the warmth wafting from it and a delicious, familiar scent hits my nose... "Is that coffee?" I almost scream and tackle him. "God, tell me it's coffee."

"It's coffee," he agrees, and thrusts the mug at me before I hit him. I cradle it in my hands, staring down at the brown liquid in the mug, tears filling my eyes. "Fuck, don't cry," he implores. "I remembered how obsessed you were, so Jago and I stole all the coffee from Paradise while you were screwing Doc's brains out."

I ignore that and take a sip, groaning in bliss as my eyes close. Dear God, it's like the best form of liquid in my mouth. I must say that out loud because someone groans.

"Shush, leave me alone," I snap, and pull it closer. "How I have missed you, old friend," I tell it as they watch.

"Want us to leave you alone with it?" Evan laughs behind me. "You laugh, but I would. I would make love to coffee, and I would have its bean babies," I murmur, as I chug the goodness and wipe my mouth before passing the mug to Archel. "More please."

"As you wish, Princess." He bows and rushes away.

"Come on, you need to eat as well, coffee isn't a food group," Jago warns.

"It totally is, big guy." I pat his chest, and feeling more alive, I saunter out of the hut, leaving Evan swearing behind me as he rushes to get dressed to follow us.

I weave through the tables near the fire and pick the closest one, dropping down as Jago and Evan sit on the other side. Maria heads over and passes me a plate.

"God, it smells so good, thank you," I tell her, and she smiles at me.

"No problem, you are getting too skinny again, sweetie, eat up. Your shadow is brewing you more coffee, and don't worry, he has told everyone that they can't touch it, or him or Jago will beat them with their own intestines." She laughs.

"How romantic!" I grin and dig into the food before me.

Archel places the mug in front of me then and slides in beside me. "I know I am, you are so lucky, Princess," he coos.

"Hey, I kill people for her," Jago growls, narrowing his eyes on him.

"I patch her up after she beats them up," Evan interjects. "Wow, you really have it all covered," Maria teases and walks away.

"We do," I agree, my mouth filled, making them roll their eyes.

When I've finished eating, I sit back as others start to join us. Some are tribe members just asking questions or updating me on their training, while some of the Paradise dwellers thank me or let me know their worries and complaints, and before I know it, hours have passed. This being a leader business isn't easy.

"Killing people is easy," Archel laments in his seat, slumping against the table.

"Why don't you go? Jago and you could help restart the train- ing, see where they are," I suggest, and he perks up and looks at the big guy in question, who stares at me with a pained frown.

"Brawler, I'll end up killing him." He groans wearily.

Laughing, I lean over and drop a kiss on both their lips. "Be good boys and you will both get a reward."

"As you wish, Princess." Archel grins, jumping to his feet. Jago blows out an exasperated breath, but stands, and throws me one, last pained look. "Be good, come and get me if there's trouble, Brawler."

I nod and sit back in my seat with Evan just as Simon comes over and drops into Jago's vacated spot. "Enjoying being back?" He grins, and I throw my fork at him just as an explosion rocks the area.

I shoot to my feet, gripping the table as Jago and Archel race back over to me from the treeline, but my eyes go to the rumbling mountain where it came from. I can see a small plume of smoke there now. Once the rumbling and earth shifting is finished, everyone around us turns their eyes from the mountain back to what they were doing.

Me? I narrow mine on Simon as Archel and Jago reach me, and start to fuss to check that I'm okay. "Those are no protective land mines. This occurs way too often, and everyone around here is used to it, suggesting it happens a lot, so tell me, Simon...what are you hiding in those mountains?" I demand, slamming my hands down on the table. I am tired of being lied to and deceived.

He shakes his head, gazing around at everyone else. "Piper, I don't know—"

"Don't you dare fucking lie to me. I have people depending on me now, do not treat me like a child. What are you hiding in those mountains?" I yell.

He nods, looking defeated before leaning closer. "Not what... who."

After he dropped those words, he hustled me into the main tent where Trev is still speaking to Worth's dad. He takes one look at us and his smile fades. "If you'll excuse us?" he offers to Papa Worth, who stands with a nod at us and leaves.

Only then does Simon speak. "We need to tell her about them." He jerks his head to the right, where the mountains are, and Trev winces but waves his hands at the empty seat.

"Sit, won't you?" he asks, and I narrow my eyes, annoyance flaring over me at something all these people know that I don't.

"I'll stand. Now tell me who the hell is hiding in the mountains and why do they keep setting of explosives?" I snap, and then turn to look at Archel. "Do you know anything about it? I swear to God, assassin, shadow or not, I will cut off your cock and give it to Jago to torture."

He simply grins. "I know nothing for once, Princess." Then it fades. "I'm in the dark as much as you." And doesn't that just annoy him, I can see it in his eyes.

So whoever they are hiding, protecting, they managed to keep it even from Archel. Trev sighs again as Simon sits. "It was not to lie to you, I can promise you that, Piper. It is both to protect us and them. They have been a tribe secret since we first came here. This was their land, their home. They let us move in, they helped us set up and build these structures you see around us, but they preferred the mountain, so they went back home and we promised to keep their existence a secret. To protect them like they did us. All they wanted was to be left in peace, Piper, surely you can understand that?" he pleads.

"Who are they?"

"People, just people like you and me." Simon snorts and Trev grins. "Well...a bit eccentric and obsessed with building weapons like the bombs you heard. It's their way of life, they are warriors, healers, and fighters...they are The Lost."

Chapter 17
Don't Die

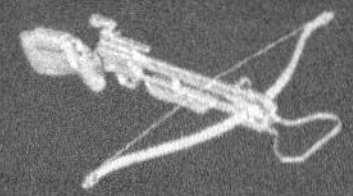

"The Lost?" I echo.

"Not all those who are lost are wanting to be found, Piper, they are happy with their world. Their people, they have built a whole civilisation in those mountains, with traditions passed down from their grandfathers to their fathers and so on. They...are different than most."

Sighing, I finally sit down. "Different how?"

Simon and Trev share a look, and Simon leans forward, clapping his hands between his parted thighs. "They don't want to hunt out there or pillage, but they are...warriors. Obsessed with honour and fighting. It's like they have been preparing for some- thing, even though I don't know what and I never dare ask. They are scary men, Piper, and barely speak to us. We live in harmony because of those who came before us, that is the only reason why they allow us to live. Out in the Wastelands, you have your clans...your Berserkers and Seekers who have myths around them, but the scariest people of all are the ones you know nothing about. That's what they are. They are like us, human, and yet they are not at the same time. They are rigor- ously trained from children in harsh environments, like the stories of old...but they have certain craftsmanship for bombs and mines. Almost like they worship it."

Trev shakes his head. "Not worship it, they once feared the very weapons that could wipe out worlds within a blink of an eye, but what they fear...they conquer, and they made those weapons their own. To protect, not kill."

It's a lot to take in, a secret clan that even the people here fear and do not speak of. "Have you ever met any of them? Their leader maybe?"

"Once, when I was younger, he was scary, very scary. It was a peace meeting, and they went back their way while I stayed here. They are good men, just terrifying...do not mistake that for kindness. No one comes back from those mountains alive." He sighs. "Not even our people if they are stupid enough to venture inside."

"You got that wrong, I am," I retort, and then wince. Okay, not my smartest come back, but still.

"Piper," Trev starts, but I hold up my hand.

"We have a war to win, and you just told us of these mythical warriors...we need them. I'm not going to demand they help, I will ask nicely and try to avoid their bombs."

"It will not matter, they won't let you leave," he snaps. "You cannot."

"I can and I will. I will do whatever it takes to keep our people safe. If that means venturing into death mountains, I will do it, if it means begging these mountain men for their help...I will. I have survived a lot worse, but if we are not careful, we will lose this war and all of our people...and they will lose their home too. I will make them see that, we have no choice, Trev, you said yourself, our people aren't ready, aren't warriors. We need fighters and as many as we can get. It can't hurt to try," I reason, softening my voice at the end, seeing the worry in his gaze.

"Piper, these are not just men...they are death itself. The lost souls everyone fears, please do not do this," he pleads.

Getting up, I crouch before him and clasp his hands. "We both know I have to, otherwise why would you have told me about them? Logically, you know what I am saying is true," I say sweetly. "I will try to be careful, but we have to take this risk and it cannot be you. If I fail, you must lead our people, they will not all follow me yet. You didn't accept this mission, I did, I made an agreement with a queen and I plan to keep it. I have two choices—die tomorrow on a mountain trying, or on the front line fighting. Either way, I will know that I did everything I could." I squeeze his hands in reassurance. "I am going, will you help me?"

I wait with bated breath as he searches my eyes. He must see my determination, because he sighs and he seems older now... defeated. "You know I will. Piper, promise me one thing...please, please come home."

"I won't make promises I can't keep, but I promise to fight my hardest to," I agree.

"I will see what I have that could help you." He nods and stands, pulling me to my feet. "You are better going in the daylight. They will not think you are attacking them then... though that doesn't mean they won't kill you on sight."

He moves away, going over to a chest in the corner and opening it. "I think I have a map here that they left, it just shows the entrance to the mountains in case we ever needed it, not that it will do much good, but..." He grumbles to himself and digs around as we wait.

"Piper," Simon starts.

"I know." I nod. "Keep training our people. I'll be back before you know it."

"If anyone can, it's you," he states, and scoops me into a bear hug. "Be safe, good hunting," he whispers, and then places me on my feet and strides from the tent.

I watch him go before my eyes drift to my men who are all suspiciously quiet, but this will not be the end of it, I will hear their thoughts as soon as we leave.

"Here it is," Trev yells, and passes over an old, folded up piece of paper. "Take supplies...and Piper? Show them your backbone, they will respect that."

I nod, putting the paper in my jeans. "Anything else?" "Yeah, don't die." He grins and I laugh.

"Got it, well, I'll see you when we're back," I tell him and he nods solemnly.

"Then I won't say goodbye."

Smiling, I turn to my men and leave the tent, ignoring the fear clenching my gut. I would be a fool not to fear what Trev does, but that fear won't stop me.

Not now. Not ever.

Chapter 18
The Mountain Man

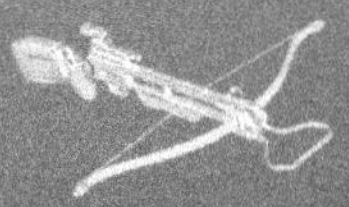

"**D**id you hear the part where he said nobody comes back alive?" Evan huffs, racing up behind me. Turning with a sigh, I face them all down, crossing my arms as they stand before me in a line.

"I did, I'm choosing to ignore it." I grin. "Of course you are."

"Evan, they are warriors, we need them. We need everybody we can get. Trev said so himself that they are the best, the scari- est. Surely it's worth trying to get them on our side? Worst case, we don't, best case, we do."

"I would think worse case would be dying," Archel points out helpfully.

"Nope, told you we are ignoring that," I counter with a smirk. "Look, you don't have to come, but I have to try. Worth is counting on us, I want to protect this place, my home, my friends...and you guys. The more fighters we have on our side, the better. Jago, how many soldiers do the Cities have?"

"Lots," he grumbles, "with guns."

"Exactly, we need every advantage, and surely a terrifying race of warriors obsessed with blowing shit up is exactly what we need? It's worth the risk. Everyone is counting on us, looking to us. Now's the time to have courage, courage doesn't always mean you make the right decision, but you do so honourably. I'm tired of being the underdog. They want to underestimate the North, then let them. We will show them exactly what we are made of."

"Fuck it," Jago grunts. "I'm in."

"You are getting good at the whole motivational speech thing, Princess." Archel winks. "Deadly mission where I get to test myself against warriors? You know I'm in!"

We all look at Evan then, who throws his arms in the air in defeat. "Fine, someone has to patch up your crazy asses."

"Yes! Come on, my merry men, let's grab our bags and some supplies and head into death mountains." I start to whistle as I walk away.

"That's probably what they are actually called," Evan grumbles, but follows after us as we head back to the hut.

We didn't unpack our bags, so I grab one, pull out some clothes, and add some water and fruit in there, making it as light as possible. I load up my weapons too, making sure to add my katana at my side and my crossbow over my back. I even slip a knife into my boot, and when I turn around, I spot Evan strapping on his knives. Archel is all ready to go, covered in weapons and black.

Jago ties back his hair and fastens on as many weapons as he can carry before looking at me. "Well, Brawler, least if we die, we die together."

"That's the spirit!" I cheer.

I examine the map Trev gave me, which shows a passage between the crevices of the mountain hidden at the base past my house. Not wanting to be questioned about where we are going, we decide to leave straightaway and take his advice to go during the daylight.

As the tribe's noises fade away, our legs aching from the climb over the sand-covered rocks to the base of the mountain, I push away my fear, it has no place right now.

When we stand at the bottom, I have to crane my neck back, and even then, I can't see the top of the mountains. They seem to reach into the very sky themselves. Before us lies a pitch-black fissure, cutting between the orange mountains, just wide enough to go in one by one. On Trev's map, it outlines where the mines are too, but they are marked with a symbol they must use for the people of The Lost.

It has two crosses and then a line down the middle, similar to lightning. I run my eyes over it again before putting the map away. I'm going in first, it's my idea, after all. Taking a deep breath, I soak up the last of the heat before throwing back my shoulders and stepping into the dark crevice.

When nothing happens, I test another step, making sure to keep my eyes on the ground for mines. The farther we venture in, the more the temperature drops, until it's almost cool. At least I'm not sweating, that's always a plus.

I find the first mine fifty meters in, marked by the symbol. I know it's triggered by pressure, so I step over it very carefully. "Mine," I call out, and turn to watch them all step over it—apart from Archel, who jumps because he likes to show off.

When they are all past it, I turn back to the front. At least my eyes are adjusted to the dark, but everything is still in shades of grey, even the tiny stones beneath our feet are grey. The walls of the crevice have water dripping down the grey and black rock. The plants that are growing in here are vines, crawling across the stone like a living entity, popping up from the ground to try and trip you.

It's slow going, and I can feel the time slipping away as we keep walking. We encounter five more mines before I see the sliver of daylight up ahead. No wonder people die in these mountains, they might even give up going ahead if they didn't know anything behind us existed.

There is a tight squeeze before us, the jagged rock closed in, I even have to turn to the side to squeeze through, so when I see Jago grunting and struggling, I worry he won't get past, but he manages to. Archel just climbs over it and lands on sure feet on the other side. Evan is right behind me waiting, in case he needed help.

"All good?" I question, but even as quietly as I talk, my voice echoes around before being swallowed by the rock, the mountain.

"Good, Princess," Archel replies. "Brawler," is all Jago says.

"Let's keep going, this place gives me the creeps," Evan grumbles, and I nod, turning to face the front again just as rocks seem to rain down from the top of the mountain, tiny orange pebbles crumbling upon us.

Covering my head, I wait for them to stop, and realising none hit me, I push up to see Evan covering my head. "Thanks, Evvie," I whisper, and peer upwards, but I can't see anything.

Is someone up there?

Blowing out a breath, I step forward again, but as if my thoughts are running away from me, making me imagine things, or am I? I can feel eyes on us. I shiver under it. Are they watching us right now?

I can't tell if it's my imagination or not, but I keep going, unwilling to turn back at the first hurdle.

"Eyes," Archel whispers, and I nod my understanding, he can feel it too. So they are watching. I guess I should have expected that. Anyone who land mines the way into their settlement is going to have sentries as well, after all, these people don't seem to be the most welcoming.

I head towards the light ahead, climbing over rocks and stones and two more mines until we reach the end of the fissure. We stand in the dark, peering out into the light. I feel them crowding behind me, looking as well, and when I peer back, I see Archel hanging from the side of the wall to survey beyond us. That man.

It opens up into what looks like a flat area of the mountain, with two more up ahead from what I can see. It's like The Forgotten, though, as plants are growing here, and trees, mixed with sand and death. There's a skull painted in what looks like blood on a sign before us. A clear warning to turn back.

"They are going to be watching out there, nowhere for us to hide," Archel points out.

"Then let's hope they are bad shots," I murmur, and step into the light, my heart slamming as I wait to be gunned down, but when it doesn't come, I blow out a breath and walk forward, moving around the sign.

No one jumps out at us, or even moves. It's empty, so we keep walking, but I can still feel the eyes on us, watching, waiting...for what?

Standing in the middle of what I now realise is a circle hidden behind the peaks of the mountains, I spin around, noticing everything is orange out here. So bright and different from the tunnel we just walked through.

"Brawler," Jago snaps, and I look back at him to see him staring upwards. I follow his gaze to see what has caught his attention. It looks like a rock...until it moves.

A person.

They stand up with a gun held in their hand, and more emerge from the rock face, blending there, but now they want us to see. Lots of them, with guns, spears, and bows, all pointed down at us.

Their faces are covered by masks, some spiked, others plain, one even has a gas mask on and it is a terrifying sight. I spin in a circle to see them everywhere, all watching us...but what are they waiting for? A boom sounds...a clap?

I turn to see a man materialise in front of us, his hands poised, he made the noise. A roar goes up among the gathered warriors watching us, all eyes on him as he steps closer.

I swallow the urge to move back...because this dude is a fucking giant.

I thought Jago was big, this guy is bigger, almost inhumanly so.

The lower half of his face, from his nose down, is covered by

a black leather mask, silver spikes pointing out of it. His eyes are strange as well, one blue and one brown, both locked on me. Big, slanting eyebrows arch over them. He has blond hair, the sides shaved, long at the back. It's tied into a ponytail and brushes the back of his neck. I can see the beard hiding beneath the mask as well. He looks feral, like a big mountain man. Black marks, intri- cate almost, cover the left side of his face, wrapping around his bright blue eye and trailing down his neck to his bare, barrel chest.

That's right, he's shirtless, and holy fuck. He doesn't have the lines that my men do, no, he's too big for that, like a powerhouse. He has a huge, wide chest, his pecs bigger than my head, with the black markings covering it, running down the lines of his hips to the low slung leather pants, which are painted on to his massive thighs and legs, ending in black boots that are covered in spikes as well. He's like the advert for post-apocalyptic fashion.

He looks scary as hell, but something about those eyes draws me in, so I step forward, his eyes lasering in on me, ignoring the men gathered at my back who are inching closer.

"Greetings," I offer. Fucking greetings? What the hell, Piper? "I am Piper, from The Forgotten, I come to speak to your leader. There is an emergency or we would not dare cross on to your land," I call loudly, my voice echoing around.

A murmur goes up among the men on the mountains, a gibberish of sorts, setting me on edge, but the big man doesn't speak, just steps closer and examines me before starting to circle me. "Would that be possible?" I inquire, always needing to fill the silence.

I start to turn to keep him in my line of sight, but he picks up the end of my braid and looks at it before dropping it. When he reaches my front again, he stops.

"We mean no harm." Laughter goes up among the others then, like they find the idea of us being a threat hilarious...okay then. "Please, it's an emergency."

He steps back, nodding at me, and turns and starts to walk away.

Er, am I supposed to follow him? When no attack comes, I stare at his retreating form, and he stops and turns to look at me, his eyes narrowing, and jerks his head. Okay, guess we are.

"And I thought Jago was the quiet one," I mutter, but follow after the silent giant.

"No shit." Archel laughs. "Dude is massive, reckon I could still take him though."

"Nah, I could." Jago grunts.

"Shame," I hiss, and when we are almost at the big guy, he turns and starts to walk away again.

"What do we do?" Evan questions nervously, looking around at the men perched on rocks still aiming at us.

"We follow him down the yellow brick road," I answer seriously, before twining my hand with Archel's and tugging him along as I start to skip after the big mountain man, singing. Archel chuckles and copies me, joining in even though he clearly doesn't know the song, so he mostly just makes up his own lyrics.

We walk for a while before we reach what looks like a cliff. I stop, unsure on where to go, but the big man doesn't hesitate, he just steps off the cliff. A scream leaves my throat as I rush to the crumbling edge to see him falling to a ledge below. He lands on bent knees and stares back up at me, and in his eyes I see a challenge to keep up with him.

Well, I've never been one to back down, so I take a few steps back.

"Pip, no—" Evan yells, as I leap from the edge.

I bite my lip to stop the squeal from coming out as I fall, my body turning weightless before I hit something hard with a grunt. I look around with wide eyes to see the big guy caught me in his arms. He places me on the ledge and I grin at him, but he turns away.

I glance up to see Jago and Archel already leaping after me, mid-air as if to catch me. Evan shakes his head, but throws himself off as well. Jago lands in a crouch, fist to the ground, Archel lands on light feet, and Evan...he falls over onto his ass with a pained yelp.

"That was so much fun!" I grin at them.

"You are fucking crazy, Pip," Evan exclaims and I nod.

"Best people are." I wink and turn to see our guide already moving on.

He grabs on to the mountain and leaps across a small opening to another ledge. "Dude, this is like an assault course." I giggle before I throw myself across the chasm and land right against his back.

He turns and peers down at me before lifting me and placing me to the side. "Whoops, sorry about that," I chirp.

"Goddamn it," I hear Evan mumble, before he lands next to me, this time on his feet. Jago and Archel make it across and we look at the big guy who turns and starts moving again.

The ledge abruptly ends, but he turns to the left and disap- pears, so I follow after him blindly. I have to blink against the dark before I realise the path is now leading us...into the mountain.

He speeds up then, almost jogging, and we have to run to keep up as we cut a path through the mountains, until suddenly, he stops. I almost run into his back again, but manage not to this time, stepping up to his side instead, almost panting, and my eyes widen in shock and awe.

"Holy shit," I mutter. "They don't live *on* the mountains... they live *in* them."

Chapter 19
Clay

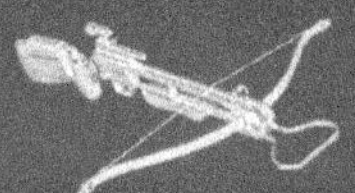

Spread out below us is isn't just a village or a settlement...it's a whole civilization. Lights hang from the mountain's ceiling, the bulbs flaring, and down beneath I see them carry on. Houses are built into the side of the mountain in different layers until they reach the floor. Big and small, some brick, some wood, and some I don't even know what they are made out of. The ones hanging in the air have walkways between them, wooden slats with ropes on either side. It's beautiful and not what I expected.

The man gives us a moment to gape before following the winding path, which leads downwards through the center of everything. I spot women, children, and more men than I could have ever imagined. They look hardened, like fighters, every single one, and oh so different than I envisioned. All with long hair, braids almost, and some wear the same markings as our tour guide, while others don't. But they all look happy.

This place is incredible, no wonder they protect it so fiercely, it's a slice of heaven cut into a mountain.

People stop and stare when they see us, obviously not used to visitors. Some of the buildings have handmade signs, crudely painted. I see the universal sign for doctor on one, a blacksmith on another, and what looks like a bar and then a shop. The town seems to be divided into sections, the base units on the floor are shops, while the surrounding buildings are houses. We move through it all to the other side, where a large, slightly elevated building stands, actually built into the brick, some of it stone, some wood, with an opened doorway.

He heads there, ignoring the men stationed out front, and the rock and sand beneath our feet changes to stone as we step inside. Tables run down both sides, filled with benches and chairs. But nobody is sitting there at the moment. The ceilings are high, and open into the top of the mountain to see every- thing. At the very end is a raised dais with...a fucking throne. A serious-looking throne made out of what looks like skulls and blades. It's cool as hell, but also terrifying, as is the man seated in it, watching our approach.

Our guide stops before him and slams his arm into his chest before bowing his head and moving to stand beside the man on the throne, watching me again. Okay then, I'm guessing this is their leader?

"Thank you," I tell him, and incline my head before turning to face the man in charge.

"What are you doing in my mountain?" he calls, his voice rumbling like the rocks. He's a big man, thick. He has long grey hair, curling around his lap in a braid, shaved on the sides too. His thin lips are currently pursed at us, and one eye is missing, but he doesn't try to hide that, the other is a cornflower blue. His face is mottled and pale, strange, but it makes sense since they live down here. He has more grey scars across his face and chest, and the paint across him is red, not black like our guide's. He is bare chested in just black trousers.

"We came to speak to you of war, of a fight facing everyone in the North," I start, and his eyes narrow as he leans forward.

"Your north, we are not part of you, we may live side by side in peace, but that only affords you so much, do not push it," he snaps, and I nod in understanding.

"Of course, we are lucky and grateful that you let us live to see your magnificent home," I offer sweetly, and he grins, sitting back.

"I like you," he mutters. "You speak of war...a fight?"

"Yes, it is facing us all, that is why we are here. To beg for your help," I implore, but a gong sounds, ripping through the room, and shocking me so much I gasp and turn my head.

"Take them to your house for the time being, I will discuss this with them later, for now it is the time for the tested to return," he orders, and rises like a sleeping mammal, all grace as he steps down. Without another word for us, he passes by and leaves us with our tour guide.

"That went well," I mutter.

The tested? What does that mean? Everything is so strange here. At least they didn't kill us yet, though, that's good...I think. Unless they are just playing with us, but something tells me I have intrigued him. That means he will keep us alive for now.

The tour guide turns to us and then starts walking again, straight past us. Okay then, back to playing follow the giant, silent mountain man. I wonder if he is unable to talk or chooses not to. For some reason, I have a strange need to hear his voice, to see if it matches the man himself.

We follow him from what I am going to dub the throne hall, and to the right of the building where a walkway is cut into the mountain side, a slim, narrow path that leads upwards. He heads that way, so we stomp after him. The higher we get, the worse my breathing becomes, like there isn't enough air. I'm guessing it's from the altitude.

We pass huts and small buildings and yet we go higher and higher, across walkways and bridges until we are in the very highest point of the mountain where a large building rests between walk-ways. No wonder he wanted us here, we would die trying to escape or get lost. He heads straight into the building, so we follow—is this his house?

I stop at the open doorway and watch as he strides inside, grabbing a long brown thing from a chair near the door.

He throws on what looks like a fur coat—still bare chested—which is a brown and white colour, and hangs to mid-thigh, moving like a cape as he walks. The action is strangely sensual, and I can't draw my eyes away from him, there's something so captivating about this silent man.

Continuing to ignore us, he moves deeper, so I step inside. The house is open planned. There is a kitchen and dining room to the left, and a living room of sorts to the right. In the back corner is an old steel bathtub with a bucket beside it, and taking up most of the back is a huge bed covered in more furs, closer to the floor than a real bed frame.

The whole place is lit by candles and mismatched lights, the floor a mix of carpets and wood. It's nice in a, erm...post-apoplectic way... nice for a cave, that's for sure.

"So this is your place?" I call, and he just carries on walking. "It's nice, like the...erm, fur everywhere, real Viking type getup you got going. Did you get a discount?" I snap my mouth shut when Archel laughs behind me and the big guy turns to look at me, eyes narrowed. He must understand English, because he brought us here to their leader, unless he is always ordered to do so and didn't understand a word I said.

"You speak English?" I ask, and when he just stares, I carry on like usual. "No speak English?"

He narrows his eyes further and I fidget nervously. "Just... like, where do we stand on the English?"

Instead of answering me, he reaches behind his head. I hear my men draw their weapons, but he pays them no attention as he unlocks his mask and pulls it away from his face, tossing it on his bed and revealing the bottom half of his features. I don't know why I expected him not to have a mouth or something, but he does...a very fine-looking mouth as far as mouths go. A solid nine out of ten.

I was right about the beard. It's the same dirty blond as his hair and covers halfway down his neck and cheeks. His lips are very plump, especially for a man, and a pink colour, tipping up at the sides. He has a strong, square jaw and high-arched cheekbones.

"Piper, it's rude to stare," Archel admonished me, but I can hear the playfulness in his tone.

The guy smiles slightly and I point. "Ha! Yes to the English then!"

That makes him frown and turn away again. Damn it, I thought I was getting somewhere. His braid moves as he does, and I realise it goes all the way down his back to his bum, not stopping at his neck like I thought.

Looking around, I decide to get comfortable if he isn't going to kill us, so I head to the wooden chair near the firepit to the right and slump into it, stretching out my legs. Archel follows me, sitting on the floor and pressing his head into my lap, so I comb through his hair.

Jago stands near the door with his arms crossed but leans back, which is as casual as he will get. Evan hesitates for a moment before joining us, not daring to sit on the other chair, so he sits on the floor next to me.

"How cool is this place?" I tell them. If he doesn't want to talk to us then we might as well talk amongst ourselves.

"Who knew this was hiding in the mountain?" Jago agrees.

"I like these people. Did you see that blacksmith?" Archel coos, his eyes closed as he leans back towards me. "Remind me to get you something from them before we leave."

"You going to buy me a new knife?" I tease and he grins.

"Anything sharp and shiny to keep my killer princess happy." He grins as I start to plait little sections of his hair.

"So, do we just wait here, you reckon?" Evan inquires, nudging closer to Archel to get to me.

"I guess so, could be worse, our heads could be on spikes or something." I laugh.

"We don't spike heads, we use their skulls for our decorations," comes a new voice. I turn to see the big guy watching us. Holy fuck, was that him? His voice was thick, rough, and unused but sexy as hell, dark, and low. It even sends a shiver through me—okay, so the voice matches the man. It's all he says and then he turns away again.

I look at the others with an open mouth and excited eyes to see Jago shaking his head at me. "Don't push it, Brawler."

"What a neat idea, we could decorate our house with skulls. Archel and Jago, provide the skulls. Evan and I will decorate," I offer.

"Hey, why am I stuck decorating?" Evan grumbles.

"I'll help, means I can feel her up," Jago remarks, making me laugh.

"I bet if we talk enough, he will get annoyed and have to speak to us," I muse.

"Or kill us," Archel points out.

I hear the mountain man grunt and head our way, slumping into the other chair and watching us, the firelight illuminating his odd eyes which I am partially obsessed with.

"What's your name?" I find myself asking.

"Clay," he rumbles, and I have to clench my thighs together.

Jesus, a voice has never affected me like this.

"Is that short for something?" I press, watching him too. "Like... Claymond?" I blurt, and then wince.

"Like Claymine," he fires back.

Okay then, so obsessed with bombs and things that go boom they named themselves after it...it is kind of a hot name though.

"Dude, once you start talking, you don't stop, do you?" I tease with a smile. He just stares at me, so I try something else, anything to keep him talking in that sexy as sin voice. "The mark- ings on your chest, are they tattoos or...?"

"It's made from dust of the mountain and water, it is a symbol for our warriors," he replies curtly.

"Oh, that's cool, and your leader has red?" I question, and he inclines his head.

"What's the tested? That's what he was going to see, right?" I ask, wanting to keep him talking and learn more about these people.

"It is when our children become warriors. They are tested in the ways of the old. Sent out into the mountains, they must survive a night out there alone, if they make it back, they are proclaimed."

"Proclaimed?" I repeat with a frown.

"Yes, proclaimed a true warrior." He stands then, looking at us. "You all stay here."

He turns to walk away, so I leap to my feet. "Wait, what?" "Sleep, tomorrow you will see our pascha," he rumbles,

before striding away.

Okay, conversation over, I guess.

He doesn't come back that night. Deciding it might be rude to take his bed, we steal his fur blankets instead and curl up near the flames in a big puppy pile. It's a good thing we have time before we have to meet Worth, but I am betting it isn't going to be easy to convince them to help us win this war.

They have the numbers though, and from the fighters we have seen...we need them. And maybe, just maybe, they need us to bring them back to this world and make them part of it. So they are not alone.

There is a reason they exist in peace with The Forgotten. They need them to protect their secret and homes—well, entrance to their homes. Maybe I can use that with the pascha? I think that's what Clay called him, it must be the word for leader.

I sleep well despite being a in a strange, threatening place, and when I wake I find Clay there, sitting in his chair, leaning forward and staring at me. When he notices I am awake, he gets to his feet.

"Pascha will see you now."

Chapter 20
Prove Myself

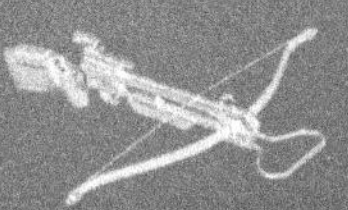

We are led back down the inside of the mountain to the throne hall where the leader, pascha, from yesterday, is waiting up on his throne again. His one eye tracks us like you see in animals until we stop before him.

"Tribes members," he greets, his eyes running across us and landing on Clay. They seem to communicate silently before he looks back at us. "War?"

Wow, no beating around the bush.

"War," I agree. "The Cities, have you heard of them?"

He scowls. "We do not worry about things beyond our mountains."

"They are a huge civilisation with more people than the whole north put together, they have soldiers, cars, weapons you can't imagine...and they are coming north. They plan to either bend us to their will or kill us all," I say bluntly, and his eye narrows, the other one too, though there isn't an eyeball there... creepy. "We are meeting them head-on, all the clans of the north are, but we need as many warriors as we can get. I have heard stories of your warriors' abilities and the way you wield explosive material like we would a sword, and came to ask your help."

"And why would we help?" He snorts.

"Because if you do not, The Forgotten will fall, and so will your protection against the world. They will no longer be your buffer and we all know you need them for that. The Cities will come here, and they will kill you all in your mountains. Fight with us, or die hiding," I snap, and step closer. "You speak of your courage, your warriors, who you have been training since children...to what? I think for this very day! What kind of warriors would you be if you hide in this...this lonely mountain? You may not want to be part of our world, Pascha, but you are, and our world is being threatened and you have the means to save it. Will you really sit idly by on your blade throne? What kind of leader would that make you?"

The room goes silent, I feel all eyes on me, but I don't break mine and the pascha's staring contest...well, erm...eye, I guess.

"Say you are right, say I agree with everything you are saying... why would I trust my men with you? I could not leave my haven, my people need us here to protect them...why would I send them with you? A stranger. You may be Forgotten, but I do not know you and my men...my men only trust men stronger than them, and you are just a little girl with a big mouth," he taunts.

He thinks he is insulting me, but he has no idea that I hear that on the daily. "Then let me prove myself," I yell, and turn to see rows and rows of people gathered behind us now. They must have come in during his speech. They watch us carefully with distrust in their eyes. "Your word! Give me a task, let me prove myself to you and your warriors, and when I complete it..." I turn to the pascha then with a wink. "And I will, you agree to help with the war, send your people with me. You have never met anyone like me, Pascha. You are right, I'm a little girl with a big mouth and an even bigger stubborn streak. I have been killed once before, and I don't plan on dying anytime soon again. Whatever you throw at me, I will defeat it...how do you think I earned the men with me, trust and love?" I step closer to him then and tilt my head down in respect. "Your word, you give me a challenge...a test like you do your men, and when I complete it, your warriors will follow me into the Wastes to fight this war."

He watches me, analysing me, and murmurs go up among the warriors in the room. "The stash," Clay rumbles, and the pascha flickers him a glance, a small smile coming to his face.

He booms out a laugh and grins at me, sitting forward on the throne. "Fine, little warrior, you want to prove yourself ? We have a deal if you can complete the testing."

I nod and he continues, "Complete the task that not even some of our best warriors could, and you will have anything you wish!" he booms, and a roar goes up, but he stands and they turn silent. "A couple of weeks ago, the eaters moved in just across our land, blocking off our supplies. We keep some out there in case of an attack, so our stash isn't all in one place. We have sent warrior after warrior after them, but so far none have come back. They are smart, vicious, and using the mountains. You want to prove yourself ? Go through eater land, get us that stash, and come back, then we can talk." He grins.

Well, fuck, I guess I got what I wanted, but fuck that doesn't sound good.

"Any rules?" I ask, tilting my head back, ignoring the hissing of my men. I won't let them second-guess me, we need them. That's all there is to it.

"You go alone, you have twenty-four hours, and you may take any weapon or supplies you wish, but if by tomorrow night you are not back when the moon rises...I will throw your men from this mountain and you will never return to your war. Or you can leave now, and I will escort you home, your choice."

"Piper," Evan hisses.

"Princess, even I'm agreeing with Doc on this one, it's a suicide mission," Archel grumbles.

"Brawler," Jago starts, and I turn to see him analysing my face. "I trust you, if anyone can do it, it's you."

My eyes widen. "You aren't going to stop me?"

"I wouldn't even dare try, not when you have your mind set to it. I'm terrified, but...if there's one thing I've learned from loving you, no one in this world can stop you when you set your mind to something. So you want to prove yourself, you will, but if you don't come back I'm going out there and I'm dragging your ass back myself and tying you to our bed," he snaps, stepping closer and ignoring the audience. "Understood, baby?"

"Understood, big guy, don't worry, I got those skills." I wink and he snorts.

Archel moves closer, searching my eyes. "Move quick, stay low, and get the fuck back here, Princess, or I will have to kill all these mountain people," he snaps, his eyes narrow.

"Shit, I'll get the med kit ready, don't you fuck up your body too badly," Evan yells, and I turn to see him with his arms crossed. "You got this, Pip," he adds, and I grin, turning to look at the pascha.

"When do I leave?"

Packing my bag on Clay's bed, I feel the others staring at me from across the room. I sigh and look up to see them all there. "Guys, I'm coming back, okay?"

"Why the fuck can't we come with you?" Jago snaps. "We could sneak," Archel offers.

"They would notice and she would forfeit," Clay rumbles near the fire.

"Forfeit?" Evan echoes. "Die," Clay clarifies.

"Brilliant." I grin and then let it flow from my face. "Clay, may I have a minute alone to say goodbye?"

He looks up at me from the fire and nods, rises, and leaves with no more words. They all surround me as quickly as he leaves, embracing and kissing me. I can taste their worry and fear on their lips, not that they will speak it out loud.

"I need you to trust me, I need you to be strong for me, okay?" I ask. "We don't have long, if I don't make it back—" They start yelling in outrage, but I carry on, "If I don't, you must escape and get back to The Forgotten and to Worth, promise me?" I demand, searching all of their eyes.

"Anything for you, Princess, you know that." Archel smirks and then swallows. "Plus, if you die, I might as well die in a war too, no point in living."

"I promise," Jago grunts.

"Evvie?" I murmur, looking at my reluctant lover.

"Pip, don't ask me to leave you out there. I lived without you once, I can't again," he begs, his eyes filled with tears.

"I need you to do this for me, Evvie, I need you to trust me this time," I implore, stepping closer and cupping his cheeks.

He closes his eyes and blows out a breath before opening them again. "I trust you, I promise, Pip," he exclaims, wiping at the falling tears. "I'm not good in a war, though, so I will stay behind as a distraction for these guys to get out. You die on this mountain, then so do I," he states strongly, without compromise.

"Fuck, we should have said that," Archel grumbles.

"Too late," Jago retorts. "Plus, Brawler is coming back, she learned from the best, after all."

"Fuck." Archel groans. "Here, take some more weapons." He starts pulling knives from his body and strapping them to me as Jago loads up my bow and checks out my sword. Evan adds some bandages and pain relievers to my bag, explaining what I can use them all for. I watch them, beyond lucky.

"I love you all," I say, and they all stop, blinking mid-action.

"We love you too, Princess, now you fight like a demon and come back to us," Archel orders, and I nod.

As I turn to grab my bag, I see them share a look and know they are planning something—fine, let them. I trust them, and they have already promised me to go if the worst happens.

I just hope it doesn't, because come sunset tomorrow, they are leaving me and joining the war.

"Come with me," Pascha calls, and I turn to my men and blow out a breath as I shove my arms through the pack.

"See you tomorrow, have a coffee waiting, won't you?" I joke, and I kiss each and every one of them before ripping myself away and following the pascha. If I stay longer, I won't want to leave, I will curl into their arms. So instead, I walk away and I don't look back, even though I can feel their eyes on me the whole time.

The pascha heads to the left of the throne room and there, built into the mountain, are steps leading up. I follow him up and out, fresh air hitting me in the face, and I realise we are on the top of the mountain. The night is just closing in, the sky fading from orange to black, the moon peeking through. He steps to the very edge of the cliff on the left and I follow him, staring down in shock.

"Is that the sea?" I inquire, peering down at the almost black-looking waves crashing against the bottom of the cliff we are on.

"Yes, the Dead Sea," he agrees, and I scoff.

"Why is everything dead? Can't it be like, I don't know, the pink sea?" I grumble, and he looks at me with a raised eyebrow.

"Because everything in it is dead," he points out.

"Ah, I see, kinda gives it away in the title," I quip, and he sighs.

"I hope your honour serves you well out there in the planes, Piper, as much as you think I am unfair, I am rooting for you," he assures me, and I look over at him. "You are right, we have been waiting for this, but if I order my men into battle behind an unproven woman, they would turn on you the very second you left. We are not like the men out there or even the ones you brought, they kill and enjoy it. This is the only way." He looks tired now, and I realise this man is barely holding his people together. I guess being the leader of a scary as hell warrior army would do that to a person.

He moves over and points into the distance where something is shining, a light maybe? "See that?"

I nod and he carries on, "That is where you need to go, it's an old electrical or cell tower, we can't tell. There is a concrete building beneath it where we stored our devices as a fallback position."

"How do I carry them back?" I finally ask.

"In there is a truck of sorts, load them into it and drive here. There is a path to follow, which you will see once you are in the building." He glances back at me and points before it. "About fifty meters in front of it is a ravine where the eaters have set up camp and are sleeping. It is closed in on either side with cliff faces, your only choice is to go through it."

"Brilliant." I groan. "How do I get there or do I have to figure it out?"

He grins, flashing sharpened teeth that have me blinking. "Follow the trail of course, your time starts now. Good luck, Piper of The Forgotten."

Then he turns and heads back into the mountain, leaving me alone on the top of it with nothing else to go on but a glint in the distance. Okay then, it's time to get to work...this will be easy...right?

Chapter 21
Run, Little Warrior

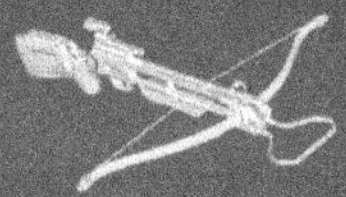

Perched on top of the mountain, I stare at the blinking in the distance before surveying the peak. I see a path I didn't notice before. A trail, one I wouldn't have caught unless I was looking. I'm guessing that's the way, otherwise why would he have brought me up here? It wasn't to show me the Dead Sea, that's for sure.

I stop myself from looking over the edge as I crouch walk down the trail. It's rocky and more like a swathe cut into the rock, which I hear crumbling down the side of the cliff, but I still don't look. Nope, I don't know if I'm afraid of heights, but tonight would not be the night to learn that I am.

It's slow going and I'm aware of the time passing, so I try and pick up the pace, almost jogging when the path widens and zigzags down the mountain. There are a few places I have to climb, my fingers getting cut gripping the sharp rock, leaving my blood behind, but I carry on.

It takes me a good couple of hours before I reach a plateau on the mountain. The trail doesn't continue down, so I start to walk across the ledge until I notice a gap and another ledge farther down. I can barely see in front of me, the dark setting in, so I would quite literally be flying blind.

Fuck it, lady up.

Stepping back, I get a good run and leap into the air. I'm airborne for a moment before smacking into the ledge, getting a grunt knocked out of me and rolling a couple of feet...and right over the other side.

A scream escapes my lips as I grab on to the ledge, my hands grappling for purchase on loose rock and losing my grip. Looking down into the black below, I get my ass into gear and yank myself back over the edge.

Landing on my back, I laugh as I try to catch my breath. Well, that was fun. Staring up at the starless night, I force myself to get to my knees and then to my feet. One of my ankles twinges, probably from landing on it wrong, but I ignore it. I don't have time to be hurt. Wiping my hands on my jeans, I grimace at the pain the movement caused, and I hold them up to the moonlight and see they are cut. Fuck.

I set down my pack and wrap some bandages around them to soak up the blood, otherwise I am going to keep slipping. Zipping my bag shut, I hoist it up and put my arms through it before looking over the edge of the ledge. There is one farther down and wider apart this time.

Shit stick. Okay.

Piper, you can do this. Time is ticking down and there is no way I'm getting my men killed. I step back to the opposite edge, my heels hanging over the side. Crouching slightly, I burst into a run and fling myself off the ledge. My arms windmill as my hair flies behind me, my stomach in my throat for a moment before I hit the other shelf on the very edge. My arms spin as I try to stay on it before I throw myself forward and land on my hands and knees.

"Fucking hell," I mutter. "Why do I agree to this crazy shit?

Oh, that's right, 'cause I'm crazy," I mumble to myself, as I get to my feet and look around, peering into the dark. At least there are no more ledges. I glance back to see I'm almost at the base of the mountain, where there is what looks like a dirt path leading off into the dark.

Yellow brick lane, here I come.

My eyes adjust and I use the light of the moon to see in front of me as I start to jog down the lane. I'm going to need as much time as possible to get around the eaters and load up the truck— at least with the truck, I can make up some time on the way back...if I get that far.

Every single noise has my head snapping around, searching for eaters jumping out of the dark to attack me. My body is strung tight, and I know I need to loosen up, but there is no one here to protect my back like usual. I haven't been out in the world alone since my attack, but I'm stronger now. Better, faster, a warrior.

Regulating my breathing, I concentrate on the slap of my feet against the dirt as I run, the moon following after me, the moun- tain fading into the darkness behind me.

After a few more hours of twisting and turning and running in the dark, I know I am lost, so I stop and press my hands to my knees as I catch my breath. Thank God I'm sleeping with three men so my stamina is good. I grab the water bottle from my back, though, and take a sip, saving the rest as I stand for a moment, not wanting to sit because I know my muscles will lock up.

After a few minutes, I hear a noise, an unmistakable crunching of stone. Grabbing my crossbow, I place my back to the wall behind me and search the darkness for the sound, keeping my breathing even as I aim. I see the shadow against the other wall move and loose an arrow. I hear a thud on impact, but load up another and fire as I walk towards it, shooting arrow after arrow before grabbing my sword.

"Come out, you eater piece of shit," I snarl. "Try and eat me if you dare."

I stare at the dark, waiting, my heart racing and my hands turning slick with my sweat. Maybe I got the bastard? But no, just as I am about to investigate, the shadow moves again, forming into a person-like shape before they step forward, the moonlight illuminating him.

"Clay?" I gasp, as I stare at the big mountain man.

His mask is in place again, but it's him and he's holding all of the arrows I shot in one hand...did he...catch them? What the hell?

"Are you following me?" I snap, not putting down the sword.

He holds the arrows out to me and I notice cuts along the palm of his hand. Stepping forward, I take them back and load them into my bow, watching the whole time, but he doesn't speak.

"Don't get mute on me now, why are you following me?" I demand and point my sword at him. "I have to do this alone, that was the rule...unless...are you here to watch me for them?"

"I'm here to make sure you get back alive," he rumbles suddenly.

"Why?" I ask, dropping the sword, my arm aching from holding it still for so long. "That wasn't the test..."

"You have your reasons, I have mine," he grumbles, and then turns and starts to walk down the path heading in the direction I was going. "Are you coming?" he calls.

Fuck, I rush to catch up, his large strides eating across the dirt. "I have to do this alone or die, your own words."

"They will never know," he says without looking at me.

I reach out and grab his arm, stilling him. "Why? Why help me? You don't know me."

He looks down at my hand, just stares at it, so I slowly retract it. I'm betting not a lot of people touch this man and live to tell about it. "Does there have to be a reason?"

"Yes," I nod, "there does. He said he sent his best out here and they died, so why risk it if you don't have to? I'm no one to you, just a stranger here to ask for your help."

"Exactly, you risked everything to come to us. That takes courage. You have honour, little warrior, maybe I want to see how far that will take you," he explains, looking down at me. "And your men tried to make a deal to help you, they didn't know I already planned to."

Yep, sounds like them.

"And if we die?" I challenge, eyebrow arched.

"Then at least I die fighting, it's an honourable death, better than standing on a mountain," he offers, his tone playful. Well, I never.

"Come on then, Mountain Man, we have a test to pass and a war to win!"

Ww walk in silence after that. I have to run to keep up with his long strides, I must look like a child next to him. The silence isn't uncomfortable though, we both understand why the other is here even if we don't know each other—it's for similar reasons...mine for family...his for honour. I can understand that.

The moon is high in the sky and I'm betting it must be very early in the morning, we have a few hours until sunrise, and I want to make it to the tower before then, easier to get around the eaters. Not that I know how we are going to do that.

I hear them before I see them—the snap and growl of their no longer human mouths, their howls, the high-pitched noises they make at each other, filling the once quiet night. Crouching down, I slow my breathing and try to stay silent, hoping they can't scent my blood.

"Have any suggestions?" I whisper, as he stands next to me, not even crouching, crazy bastard.

"The ravine is slimmer at the top to the left, I scouted it the other day. We can jump it, but then we will have to run like mad." He glances at me and grunts, like the sound of rocks hitting together. "The tower runs its own electricity and the fence is electric. That's why they haven't gotten in, they have learned their lesson from others being fried. If we can get behind it, we are safe for a while, they won't lose interest, but won't get through."

"So your plan is to run like fucking hell?" I grin. "I like it, okay then, Mountain Man, looks like we better get ready."

He nods and turns back to the front. "What a glorious way to die fighting though," he grumbles before striding forward.

"Wait," I hiss. "I wasn't ready," I mutter, but chase after him.

We curve around a bend and I spot the ravine up ahead, and

behind it, the tower, which is at least two hundred feet behind it. Oh yeah, we will just run that. Fucking hell, maybe he is a crazy bastard.

"Run, little warrior," he orders, just as the first howl goes up and they start to pour from the ravine like a bubbling sea of disjointed bodies.

"Fuck!" I yell, and burst into a sprint, Clay right beside me, keeping pace. He doesn't leave, he stays beside me as I swing my crossbow around and fire blindly as I sprint. I hit a few, but I don't want to use all my arrows, so I grab my sword as we approach the ravine.

One leaps at him from the right, and he simply grabs it mid-air and snaps its neck, tossing it back to its friends without losing his stride. One rushes me and I slash out my sword as I pick up speed, seeing the gap approaching. Why the fuck am I doing so much jumping tonight? But just as I'm about to leap, one grabs my ankle and tackles me to the ground.

I go down hard with a grunt to see Clay already on the other side. He looks back and whistles, and the rest of them turn to him. I watch with wide eyes as they rush him. Fuck. He fights them all, killing as many as he can as a distraction while I stab into the one at my feet who is trying to claw its way up my body. I finally get it in the eye and kick the carcass into the ravine. Step- ping back, I see Clay surrounded by dead bodies as more broil over, fuck. He's going to die in a pile of eaters because of me.

Not today, motherfuckers.

Throwing myself over the ravine, I land in a roll and come up with a katana in each hand, and wade into the pile, slashing and grab- bing, blood splashing me, but I still keep going until there is a gap.

"Run!" I scream, and we both break away just as he tosses some- thing that looks like a stick at the chasing eaters.

I race towards the tower up ahead, shining like a beacon in the night, my breath sawing out of my chest, my legs aching just as the ground beneath us rolls and an explosion sounds behind us, followed by another two.

"Keep going!" he yells, as he reaches my side. The gate is up ahead, twenty meters.

Ten. Five.

I can feel them behind me, snapping, their claws outstretched. Clay puts on a burst of speed and yanks the gate open, holding out his hand to me as I drop my head and give it all I have, my arms pumping.

I reach for him, my fingers touching his as I feel claws swipe across my back. Crying out, I let him yank me through. I fall to the ground on top of him, but he rolls and he's up in an instant, slamming the gate shut and hitting a giant red button on the left.

A siren cuts through the air just before the eaters smash into the fence...only to fry. I get to my feet, wincing at the pain in my back. I can feel blood dripping from the wound, but I ignore it as I sheathe my sword and watch the eaters stick to the fence, frying, as inhuman screeches leave their mouths. They fall to the ground eventually, the smell of burnt hair and skin making me gag.

The ones behind them get smart and don't come close, just pace back and forth, snapping at each other as they watch us. "Eat that, you motherfuckers!" I whoop and turn to Clay. "Well, Mountain Man, we made it."

He spins to look at me. "Come on, let's get inside and look at your wounds," he rumbles.

I agree. Now that the adrenaline is wearing off, exhaustion is setting in, followed by a blinding agony. He must see it on my face, because he covers the space between us in two steps and scoops me up, holding me to his huge chest as he heads towards the building set under the tower.

What a strange day.

Chapter 22
Two Lost Souls

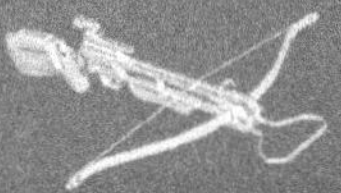

He carries me into the building, which is unlocked and dark, and places me on something solid. I turn on my side, wincing as it pulls at my back. The light flickers on overhead and I get a good look at the inside. It resembles a radio center, with controls over on one side and sofas and a TV in the corner. There are stairs up and down in the middle, and I'm lying on a table.

"On your stomach, we need to wash out the wounds," he orders, so I do as I am told, turning over with a whine and prop- ping my chin on my arm as I stare at him. He moves around the room, flicking switches before returning to me. He checks out my back without touching it and then disappears upstairs before coming back with a wet towel. "This will sting."

"There are some med kits in my bag," I tell him, and he nods and slaps the towel onto my wounds, making me yowl. It's echoed outside by the eaters, so I bite down on my arm to stifle the next cry as, with gentle strokes, he silently cleans out the lesions.

The cold disappears and I slump into the table, but he's back in a minute, and with no warning he sprays something that stings. Groaning, I squeeze my eyes shut and suck in breaths as he stops and then spreads something warm and liquid feeling across the cuts.

"Okay, I'm going to wrap it, sit up," he commands, so I do, my head swimming from the pain. He holds me until I'm steady and then looks at me. "Shirt off," he demands.

I hesitate for a moment, having a flashback of my attack, but this man has only helped me, so I pull it off and drop it into my lap. He averts his gaze kindly and grabs a bandage, wrapping it around my torso before ripping it and tying it off. It's tight, but my back actually feels better, less pained at least. He snatches my shirt and helps me back into it as I rest on my side and watch him.

He removes his mask and rubs at his mouth as he looks around. "We wait here for a few hours, can't drive until sunlight, rest for an hour. I will load the stash into the car," he mumbles and turns away, but I grab his hand on his way past, ignoring the harsh, rough quality of it.

"Thank you, Mountain Man," I say with a smile.

His mismatched eyes land on me and seem to soften for a moment before he steps back and disappears, heading down- stairs. I take his advice and close my eyes, giving my back time to heal—a little, at least. I should feel guilty he is doing the heavy lifting, but he offered, so I can't really complain. Plus, I wouldn't have made it this far without him, I know for sure I would have died out there.

The mountain man saved my life...why?

I rest my eyes for a moment, but with the howling and cries of the eaters outside, I find it hard to rest. So I throw myself off the table top, stumble to my bag, and take some pain pills before sitting back on the table for a moment and waiting for the meds to kick in.

I can hear banging below, where he's moving the stash I was sent to get, so even though my back is still hurting, I get to my feet and head downstairs, using the railing to support me since my legs are still a little weak.

Holy momma, I actually stumble down the last two stairs at the sight before me. It's not the weapons and explosives laid out throughout the room like an armoury...it's the man currently heaving them across the space, bare chested, to the truck—well, if you can call it that—in the corner.

Yes, I've seen his naked chest before, but right now he has no mask on, his hair is tied on top of his head to keep it out of his face, and his eyes are focused in concentration. His muscles bulge with the heavy lifting, and when he bends over, those trousers he is wearing leave nothing to the imagination.

Now, I've never been an ass girl myself, I can appreciate a good round handful, but this man...his ass is as tight and round as two peaches pushed together. My mouth literally goes dry as he stands back up and effortlessly lifts two huge boxes, one in each hand like they weigh nothing.

He heads over to the truck—again, if you can call it that. After all, it has no roof or doors, it's just a skeletal frame and a huge open back, which he is piling high. It does have wheels though, so I guess that's a blessing. When he turns around, he lifts his impressive arms to wipe at his face and spots me. Clay tilts his head in question. I guess we are back to the not talking thing again, so in answer I step down and start to help him carry things.

He plucks the box I am carrying out of my arms and tosses it into the truck before pointing at some smaller ones on a table with narrowed eyes, obviously not wanting me to overdo it or bend over to get the bigger ones on the floor.

I nod in understanding and start to move those as he goes back to calmly heaving missiles and explosives. I peer into one of my boxes and spot wires and what looks like triggers. When the truck is as full as it is going to get, I step back and wipe off my face, sweat dripping down it. I can feel it trickling into my wounds on my back, but I don't think it will hurt much...right? God, Evvie is going to have a shit fit when he sees my back…I wonder if I can get him to kiss it better? Or Archel, or Jago… hell, all three would be good.

I'm in a world of my own, imagining all the dirty ways my men could make it better, when Clay scoops me up again, making me yelp. He doesn't look down at me as he takes the stairs two at a time and places me carefully, more carefully than the explosives, onto the table and then points in my face with narrowed eyes.

Yeah, I get the drift, stay here, be good.

He starts to walk away backwards, his eyes still locked on me, and I can't help but smile as I swing my legs back and forth, watching him. I don't think the big mountain man knows how to deal with me. He comes back a few minutes later and rounds the table, peeking under the bandages with a grunt before stopping in front of me.

"Why don't you sit?" I suggest, and he looks at the chair and nods, dragging it over and sitting before me, his hands loose between his thighs, eyes focused on me.

"Why don't you talk much?" I inquire. We are going to be stuck here until sunrise, so I might as well do what I do best—talk.

"Does it bother you?" he counters, his voice making me jerk, it's that sudden.

"No, I talk enough for four people, I'm just curious why. Most people love the sound of their own voice and have a million thoughts and questions in their brain to get out," I explain helpfully.

"You do talk a lot." He grins, it's a quick flash, and then it's gone. "It's simple, when you don't talk, you are listening. You learn more, see more, things others might miss. It makes me a better warrior."

My eyes widen. Okay, wasn't expecting that. "Wow, no other reason?"

He laughs then, a short sharp sound. "You are smart, I don't like people. Most are stupid and when you don't talk, they soon grow bored with you and then I don't have to kill them."

Laughter tumbles out of me. "You don't talk—" I gasp for breath, ignoring the pain the laughter causes. "Because if you do, people talk back, which you find stupid, so you would have to kill them?"

"Pretty much." He nods, his lips twitching as he watches me.

I laugh harder, but then gasp in pain, stilling. He jerks, his hands reaching out to me. "Are you okay?"

"I'll be fine, I've survived worse," I reply weakly, and then sigh. Remind me not to laugh for a while.

"How so?" he asks, watching me closely. He's like Jago in that aspect when he watches you, observing you intently, noting every little nuance of your person. Every twitch, facial expression, storing it away. Oh, I have no doubt he has already analysed a million ways to kill me in a second, but instead he is talking to me...even though he doesn't normally talk to many people. I feel kinda special.

"That is not something even I want to talk about," I whisper, looking away. He can undoubtedly see the horror and pain in my eyes that simply thinking about it causes.

"Our warriors go through a test when they finish their train- ing. It can be at different ages depending on their experience and skill. For most, it is around their sixteenth cycle, mine was when I was ten." I look at him then, that's the most I've heard him say, but he surprises me more by carrying on.

"We live with our families until we are proclaimed. My mother had died in childbirth, but my father raised me. One day he went out, out into the Wastes on the orders of our pascha. Him and a group of our warriors were sent to see what the world has become. He didn't come back." He doesn't lower his eyes or look away, he lets me see the memories, the pain in those eyes. No hiding for him, because in his vulnerability, he finds strength. "I begged the pascha to go after him, and he told me if they found their way home, they would, if not, it was an honourable death. But he was my father, my only family. So I snuck away, out of the mountains, and into the world to search for him."

"Did you find him?" I query softly, entranced by his story. "Yes, but not alive. They had been attacked by eaters. There

were three still there, and I killed them with my father's sword and brought back their heads as proof. I presented them to our pascha, and he rewarded me by proclaiming me. I became a warrior, one of the youngest. I avenged my father, and in turn I found a strength in me I didn't know I had."

I blink at him, unsure what to say for once.

"What I am saying, little warrior, is tests come in all shapes and sizes and it's not getting knocked down that is the hardest, but getting back up. That is the true mark of a warrior, a fighter."

He stands before I can reply and strolls away, out the door. I hear the noise of the eaters increase for a moment before the door shuts, and then a few minutes later he comes back. "Two hours until sunrise," he murmurs, then sits back down.

My eyes are locked on him though. "You are right." I nod. He exposed his pain, so I sigh and sit up taller. "I was not born into The Forgotten, but a place underground far from it, similar to your mountain. It was all we knew, we didn't know the world out here, but I wanted to. So I trained, I fought to become a warrior, to become the best I could. The man with me? The big guy? He trained me, and we started out into the world. We protected our people, but not everyone wanted a woman as a warrior," I explain snidely. "The people I trusted, the leaders, they betrayed me. They sent me out there to die, only I didn't, but sometimes I wonder if it would have been kinder than what they did to me."

I look at him then with cold, angry eyes. "I got back up, I didn't want to, I wanted to die from my wounds some nights, but I couldn't. Not with them still out there, so I got back up. I fought every day, sometimes just to get out of bed, to get dressed. The tasks that everyone took for granted, I struggled with. But I kept fighting, and along the way, I found people to fight with me. I found a new home, a new people, and it gave me a purpose and reason to keep going. So I did," I tell him, then lick my lips. "Then, I met Worth. You should see her. A true queen, a warrior like no other, covered in the scars of people who tried to kill her, to keep her down, yet she wears them with honour. Men fall to their knees in front of her, and they would follow her to hell itself, but not just because of who she is but what she stands for. A better world, a unity, all fighting together to protect our home. That's why I'm here, for her, for me, for everyone like us who was hurt. I got my revenge and it did nothing, but this? This fight will. I've finally found what I was searching for, and I don't plan on letting it go." Staring into those mismatched eyes, I continue, "I understand you, Mountain Man, more than you can imagine. Despite the world that divides us, we aren't different. We are both just trying to protect those we care for, a home, and I guess that makes us allies."

"I guess it does, little warrior." He grins.

"Why do you call me that? It's not my fault I'm a normal, human size and you are a giant." I laugh, breaking the tension.

He winks at me then, actually fucking winks, holy vagina. "Because of the men who follow you and the way you stood up to the pascha, people only follow leaders. Warriors. You are a tiny, pocket-sized warrior." He shrugs.

Shaking my head, I grin at him again. "Knew you liked me, you find me enchanting and lovable."

"More like annoying and irritating," he scoffs. I nod seriously.

"I'll take it."

"This war, do you think you can win it?" he questions randomly, and I lift my head before turning onto my side and laying it on my arm. I had laid down to ease my back, and he found a blanket from some-where and covered me with it. For such a big warrior, he sure is a softie.

"Yes," I tell him. "I have to, otherwise what am I fighting for?"

He nods and turns quiet again, so I close my eyes and let him become lost in his own thoughts...for a moment. "Your pascha, would you follow him anywhere?"

"Not everywhere. Sometimes you have to have blind trust in your leaders. Follow them into the gates of hell itself, even if they are wrong, but I wouldn't for him. I haven't found a person I would do that for, not yet," he whispers.

I go silent again and close my eyes. I can feel him staring, but it feels kind of comforting, so I relax into the table and before I know it, I've nodded off. The clanging of the gate wakes me, and I jerk up with a whine at my stiff and aching back.

He is ready to go, just crouching next to the table, watching me.

"It's time," he instructs, and gets to his feet.

Chapter 23
Tradition

He helps strap on my weapons, his touch gentle but sure, and then we head downstairs to the truck. "Does this thing even run? It looks like you took two cars and they fucked and made this monstrosity."

"It runs," he offers, and gets into the driver's seat.

"Fuck it," I mutter, and climb into the passenger seat. At least they are leather. He flicks on the ignition and revs the engine a few times, and I look around. "Wait, how do we—fuck!"

He races forward, heading straight at a wall, but at the last moment...it moves. It goes up and we fly from the building. I have to grab on to the skeletal door as we go airborne, and we land on the dirt just before the gate. I look back to see the wall closing up again as we race to the exit, which opens as we approach. The eaters slip through, but when they spot us, they give chase as we kick up dirt, heading to the ravine.

One leaps from the cliff face and lands on the hood, making me yelp as I try to get my crossbow up, but it gets caught between the stick and the seat. "Fuck, flying dicks, fuck!"

Reaching through the empty door, it wraps its hands around my neck and yanks me forward. I react and punch out, splitting my knuckles on its teeth, but it flips backwards from the car.

"Take that, you cocksucker!" I yell as I sit back, just in time for the car to come to a skidding stop.

"What are you doing?" I yell, looking around, but he calmly turns off the truck and gets out. I slip into the driver's seat and stick my head out of the door to see him approaching the eater that grabbed me. My mouth drops open when he stabs it in the face and chops off his head. It dangles from his fist as he unhurriedly walks back, despite the thundering steps of the approaching eaters, and he holds it up to me.

"For you," he offers.

"Fuck, okay, get in!" I scream, noticing the incoming horde.

He leaps into the passenger seat and proudly displays the head on the dash like an ornament. *Fuck, my life is weird*, I think as I hammer my foot onto the pedal. The car fishtails, but I grip the wheel and straighten us out, making sure to build up speed as we approach the ravine.

"Hold on to your big ass balls!" I yell, just as we hit the lip and fly over the gap, landing hard on the other side.

Looking over my shoulder, I see the eaters still giving chase, but as I watch, we start to lose them, the truck too fast, and eventually I can't see them anymore. Blowing out a breath, I concentrate on driving, following the dirt path through the mountains.

I finally see why we had to wait for daylight. There, up ahead, is a tiny corner that I would have never noticed, but I do now. Swinging the truck right, I almost slam into the rockface I jumped down last night, and instead we head through a tiny passage, the sides of the truck scraping along the walls until we break free on the other end and into what looks like a slowly inclining hill leading to the mountain.

"Sure as fuck hope the truck makes it," I mutter as I change gears, and slam my foot back down on the pedal.

"It will," he states calmly, as the head rolls around the dash, leaving a trail of blood.

We drive steadily up the rockface, my heart hammering in my chest and my hands gripping the wheel. At any moment, I expect the vehicle to give out and go rolling back, but we keep going, and only when I see a darkness ahead, do I squint and steer towards it.

It turns out to be a hole into a cave, a big cave, and when I see the trucks waiting inside, I know we are almost there, so I stamp on the accelerator and we shoot forward, heading right for the gap.

We skid into what appears to be a transportation hangar, and I pull on the handbrake, breathing heavily as I look around. "We made it," I whisper, and then whoop, staring at Clay. "We made it!" I shout louder, and a clapping comes from the right-hand side.

"That you did," the pascha says as he steps forward. "Clay?"

Clay nods. "Was waiting at the bottom of the mountain to alert when she was back," he replies, and then winks down at me as he climbs from the car and offers me his hand. I accept, wincing at my back as I hop down. When my feet hit the sand-covered floor, I look at the pascha.

"I did it, I passed your test...now will you keep your end of the deal?" I inquire, feeling nerves starting to build in my stomach as he stares at me.

"Come with me," is all he says, and then he turns and starts to walk away, so of course I run after him.

He takes me to a chamber where a deep blue pool with smoke rising from it awaits. He looks to me then. "Bathe and then dress," he commands, before leaving me with Clay.

I turn to him with a frown. "Is this normal?"

He nods, returning to his silent ways. "When will I see my men?"

"Soon," is all he says, and then he crosses his arms, his legs braced apart, and watches me without any hint of humility or shyness as he waits. He doesn't plan to turn away, and asking him to would show weakness. He is, after all, a warrior. A mountain man, rough and untamed. He waits, his mismatched eyes observ- ing, anticipating...assessing.

"Do not keep the pascha waiting, little warrior, he is not a patient man," he rumbles.

Nodding, I keep my eyes on his, wanting to see a reaction as I slip off my top and bra, and then kick off my boots and trousers until I stand bare before him. His eyes do not drop, they are still locked on mine.

Turning my back on him, I step into the pool, the warm water making me sigh as I sink in deeper until I am submerged, washing away the blood, sweat, and battle.

When I break the surface again, I turn my head to see my mountain man sitting on a rock, sharpening his swords with a whetstone as he watches me, not the least bit ashamed for me to see him staring, but now, in those eyes, I see something...some- thing no doubt reflected back in mine.

Hunger.

Why does this man call to me? I have three, yet I find myself drawn to him...I do not know. A problem for another day, one where I don't have three worried lovers waiting and a pascha of a mountain to submit to.

I wash quickly, the pool rinsing away my pain and the exhaustion in my muscles. I can actually feel my back mending and the pain...the pain is disappearing. "How?" I ask, my eyes wide.

"Minerals and salts from deep in the earth, they gather in this natural pool. Good for healing and rejuvenating, nature's medi- cine," he reasons and I smile.

"Bloody hell, you have magic water," I tease, and he laughs, throwing back his head and letting it boom around the cavern.

"Magic water, as you wish, little warrior. Now come, I have your clothes." He puts away his weapons and stands, pulling a parcel wrapped in brown material and twine from behind him. There is no towel, so I step towards the edge and he extends a hand, helping me over the pool's lip and back onto the cold cave floor.

This time, I see his eyes drop to my body, it's not a quick, sneaky look either. He takes his time, running his gaze across every inch of skin until I know he could point out every scar or birthmark. I stand taller, his eyes giving me confidence, his hunger calling to mine. Licking at my lips, I reach for the parcel in his hands. He holds it for me as I undo it to reveal a small leather binding of sorts and some black trousers.

I pick up the brown leather, noticing it's a top, one which will show off my stomach, arms, and cleavage.

"It is tradition, and necessary," is all he says.

Well, okay then. I hold up my arms, knowing I can't get into it alone, and he places the rest on the rock before stepping forward and helping me pull the top over my head. His knuckles graze the sides of my breasts, and I inhale sharply as his eyes flicker to mine, watching me as he does it again on purpose as he tugs it down and settles it into place. It feels like a second skin, hugging my breasts and protecting my ribs, ending just before my navel. It's not restricting, and I thought I would feel naked, but if anything, I feel...feel like a warrior.

He grabs my trousers and kneels before me, holding them out. Resting my hand on his shoulder, I lift one leg and then the other as he slips the fabric over my feet and up my ankles, his pinky finger tracing along my bare leg as he draws them up and settles them low on my hips. They are tight fitting as well, but with enough give to move. Only then do I realize I am still touching him and his head is level with my pussy.

His eyes slide up to mine as he sits at my feet. "Are you ready, little warrior?"

"For what?" I ask, my voice slightly breathless. "Your future," is all he says.

How fucking ominous.

We leave the cave, and I follow him through the winding passages until we somehow end up back in the throne room where I see my men, The Lost, and the pascha all waiting for me. Lanterns and fires line the way, an entry made between the droves of people. Clay storms down the middle with me behind him. My men wait near the pascha, their eyes running over me in relief. All I can do is smile at them. I have a feeling that if I break whatever tradition this is and race to their side, it would be bad.

When we reach the front, Clay drops to his knees before the pascha and then gets back to his feet to stand at my side. A stomping starts, the crowd chanting until the pascha rises, then it goes silent. He waits for a moment before addressing the throng.

"Warriors, you are gathered here for a proclamation for one outside of our ranks and mountains, one who sought to prove herself and has done so a thousand-fold. A true warrior, Piper of The Forgotten, do you accept our title?" he calls.

"I do," I reply, not really sure what I'm accepting...like, do we have a contract? Is there a reunion? A dress code? Who knows, but it sounds fun and it's not really the time to ask, so for once I remain quiet.

"Clay, do the honours," Pascha orders, and then looks at me. "Kneel, warrior."

I do so, but tilt my head back and meet his eyes, making him smile as Clay kneels before me, a bowl of black ink in his grasp. He dips his fingers into it, swirling them around before lifting them. "A warrior's mark is to be worn with pride," the pascha booms.

Clay meets my eyes with a smile, and I reach up and grasp his beard, tugging on it to gain his attention. "Don't draw a dick," I joke quietly, before letting go.

I can see him fighting back a smile as he ducks his head and his cold fingers touch my bare stomach. I jump at the first touch, but steel myself as I feel him painting an intricate pattern. I don't look, not wanting to see it until it's done. It's strange, but I trust this man implicitly.

When he pulls his fingers away, he looks up at me with a frown before turning to his pascha. "Red," he calls, and I watch the curious smile that crosses the one-eyed leader's face. No one moves until that man nods, and then suddenly there is a bowl of red paste before Clay. He turns back to me and carries on painting before sitting back. He observes his artwork with a smile and then stands, offering me his hand. The pascha steps forward and gives me his as well. I accept them both and they hoist me to my feet.

"You are lost no longer," he calls, and it echoes around the cavern, a cry of my new people. I raise my head from the bowed position as he beckons me to stand, my marks standing out proudly on my stomach and chest. "For when we are lost, we are waiting to be found...Piper, you have been found. You are worthy, you are one of us. For you, we will fight!"

A cheer goes up, and I wink at my men as the pascha addresses me. "They are yours, but they must come willingly. Call your warriors," he instructs, and turns back and sits on his throne.

Okay, er...here goes nothing.

I turn to face the crowd, scanning the hundreds of faces all staring back at me. Each and every one a warrior.

"Who will stand and fight with me?" I call, legs braced, my warrior's mark on display.

A chant goes up, but men hesitate, though, until Clay drops to his knees before me, two blades held in a cross above his chest. "I, Clay of The Lost, stand with you, little warrior. I will fight, and I will stand and die at your side if the gods will it."

With his declaration comes a ripple, and voices call out as men and women step forward until I have more warriors than I know what to do with. Clay joins me at my side.

"You're their pascha now. They will follow you to this war and the gates of hell. Do not lead us wrong." He stares down at me as the weight of the responsibly hits me.

A pascha. A leader.

But to me, I still feel like Piper, I hope that is enough.

Chapter 24
Pascha

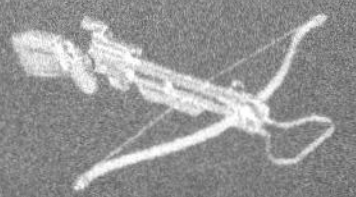

After my proclamation, I am allowed to rest, and we retreat to Clay's house. My body is exhausted, but as soon as we get into the privacy of the dwelling, I am embraced by my men. I know the warriors, my warriors now, are preparing to leave. Tomorrow, I lead them from their mountain and to war, but tonight, tonight I get to enjoy my men.

A burden of command.

They check me over, their words mixing together as they talk rapidly until Evan shouts at the other two to back off, taking charge as he examines my back. He declares that I don't need stitches, but cleans it and wraps it, and with a narrow-eyed look at me warns me to rest.

"Yes, Evvie." I grin and he sighs, leaning closer and kissing me.

"Fucking worst twenty-four hours of my life. Thought I was done being without you. Never again," he snaps.

"Never again," I agree, and kiss him back before Archel tosses him to the bed effortlessly and takes his place.

"Never doubted you, Princess." He smirks before dipping me for a kiss, making Evan shout about being careful even as I laugh. He spins me into Jago's awaiting arms, who wraps me up, making me sigh at the warmth and feeling of family. "Missed you, Brawler," he murmurs.

"Missed you too, big guy," I reply, and cuddle into his embrace.

"She needs to rest," Evan snaps, and I sigh, kissing him before heading over to the bed and jumping on it.

"Resting, see?" I snark, noticing Clay sitting by the fire, watching us. They follow my gaze and watch him before looking back at me.

"Oh God," Evan groans knowingly.

I regard my guys with a smile. "Can we keep him?" I ask. "He's not a fucking pet, Brawler, he's a crazy madman who

likes to blow people up and kill them!" Jago protests.

Archel snickers. "We keep *you* and you kill people."

"And don't forget we have an assassin and not to mention Piper's propensity for blowing things up," Evan interjects.

"One time!" I yell, and turn to him. "You blow people up one time and they never let you forget it!"

"Do I get a say in this?" Clay calls from the fire, and we all look at him.

"No," we say in unison, which makes me smile.

A yawn splits my lips and I fall back onto the surprisingly comfortable large bed. "We'll talk about you keeping a pet moun- tain man tomorrow," Archel teases. "Tonight, rest, Princess."

They climb on around me then and pull me into their arms and heat. With them I'm not a leader. Not a pascha or a commander. I am simply Piper.

My eyes find Clay's in the light of the fire, and I watch it dance in his mismatched gaze before I sleep.

I wake up warm, the snoring of my men surrounding me. I'm on my back, their arms and legs thrown across me in slumber. Blinking away the sleep, I look down at the drawing Clay did yesterday for the first time.

It consists of lines and marks, black outlined in red. One looks like a sword, the other is like the zigzagging of the mountain. It is beautiful, and when I touch it, I realise it is dried and not the least bit uncomfortable.

"It is the story of your test," comes his rumble, and I lift my head to see him standing at the edge of the bed, watching me. "Come, little warrior, you must eat. Today we leave our moun- tain and follow you into a strange world. You will need your strength." He turns then and disappears, allowing me time to wake my men and get up.

"Ugh, tell your new pet it's too early," Evan laments and snuggles closer, dragging me away from Jago, which starts a tug-of-war between them until I grunt, slip from their grasp, and kneel on the bed, looking at my three sleepy lovers.

"Come on, wake up," I demand, and Jago opens one eye, grins at me, and goes back to sleep. "That's an order from your pascha." I sniff, raising my chin in the air and crossing my arms.

Archel laughs at me—laughs! "She's cute when she tries to get all bossy on us."

"That's an order," Jago mocks, making my mouth drop open. "It's an order!" I huff, and Archel opens his eyes, flips onto his

back, and stretches like a giant cat.

"Yeah, we hear you, Princess. Bring that adorable ass over here and order us to do something more interesting," he teases.

"Damn it, I'm a leader now, you should listen to me," I whine, not at all leader-like.

Jago darts up, grabs me, and pulls me back into his arms, barring me there as he locks his legs around me. "Sleep," he commands, and then closes his eyes as I just lie there as his captive.

"I need more submissive men," I mutter.

"Nah, you like us rough and dominant." Archel laughs, making me blush slightly.

"My mountain man would listen." I pout.

"Then find him and be quiet. Don't you know we are trying to sleep?" Evan grumbles, but kisses my shoulder to lessen the blow.

"I'm hungry," I say, and that gets them moving. They are out of bed and dressed before I can even sit up.

"Come on then, Brawler, why didn't you say so?" Jago growls.

"Yeah, Princess," Archel adds.

"All you had to do was ask, Pip," Evan chimes in. Dear God, what have I done?

By the time I'm dressed, Clay is back with enough food to feed, well, an army...or my guys. I watch them devour it with an open mouth. Even while they eat like animals, they still make sure to pass me a bit of everything until I can't eat anymore, then they finish off what I left.

They even start talking to Clay as I watch, and I notice he fits in with us seamlessly. Joking with Archel about weapons and comparing swords with Jago, even discussing the medical proper- ties of the water and plants they have here with Evan. It's like he was made to be with us.

"So, Clay," I start, and he turns to look at me. "When will the warriors be ready?"

I'm conscious of the time it will take us to travel home, grab our warriors, and then get to the front line. We don't want to be late for the war. "In a few hours," he informs me. "Not to fear, little warrior, they are all excited and nearly ready. It has been a long time since they tested themselves in battle."

"Crazy mountain people," Evan mumbles, making Clay laugh.

"Good, can you show me to the bathroom? I just had to pee into the rock last night, I really don't want to repeat that." I ask him, rising from the table. They all jump up and my eyes widen. "I meant Clay, unless anyone else knows where it is? In which case you are all assholes watching as I almost peed on the poor people down below."

The others sit down, making me laugh, as the mountain man

leads me from his home and to a cave a few feet away. He points at a hole and then turns and protects the entrance of the cave. Well, that's one item off the bucket list.

I finish my business and wash my hands in some water coming down from the ceiling before shaking them dry and tapping his back. He grins and leads me back to his house where we spend the next few hours helping him pack and just learning how to be with each other. He will be spending a lot of time with us, after all, and he knows how to command the warriors, which I will need.

When he is ready, we head to the throne hall where the pascha is waiting. He embraces Clay before looking at me. "Good battle, Pascha Piper, may the gods smile at you." He nods and I shake his hand and turn to face the awaiting warriors.

They are all staring at me, waiting for my command.

Gazing at the amassed warriors, I look to Clay for courage and a guiding hand. He doesn't disappoint. Those mismatched eyes meet mine with a confidence I could never fake.

"You, Piper, are my pascha, the one I have been waiting for. I would follow you into the gates of hell. I trust you, your honour, and courage, little warrior. Lead us home."

Trooping through the mountain pass with over three hundred warriors behind me is an experience all right. I can feel their eyes on me as I lead them, followed by my men. It takes us just an hour to reach the crevice, but another hour to get all my warriors through it one by one. Once we are on the other side of the mountain, looking down at the green of my home below, something settles inside me.

I wait for them to gather behind me before beginning our trek down the mountain. We run into Simon and Trev who are waiting for us, obviously seeing us coming. They stand next to my house at the base, their faces covered in shock, but they quickly recover and smile at me. Simon embraces me like normal, while Trev just shakes his head.

"Should have known you could do it." He laughs, his eyes sparkling. "Come, tonight they can all rest and eat here, tomorrow you can set off with all your warriors and ours to the war. Tonight, Piper, we celebrate."

I have never seen the camp so full. There are mountain men spread everywhere. They watch everything with a strange intensity, sticking together on the outskirts, but at least they are here. The Forgotten people seem terrified of them, but me? Not so much. I trot over to a big group of them and smile with hand- made alcohol clutched in my hand.

"You know, you could smile. Make yourself more approach- able, show off a little, maybe get laid. We are going to war, after all," I tease. They continue to stare at me, so I sigh and crouch down, meeting them head-on. "Huddle up, warriors," I command, and they all instantly move closer. "Mingle, have fun, do whatever you want tonight. That's an order from your pascha. Tomorrow we leave and might never come back, don't waste another second. Is that under- stood, warriors?" I demand, my eyes narrowed, meeting each and every one of their gazes that I can.

"Yes, Pascha," they call, and I fist bump the one I can reach. "Good, go," I order and get to my feet, sipping my drink as I watch them brace themselves and join the festivities.

The moon is full above me, the trees swaying in the breeze, the fires of the perimeter strong. I watch everyone laughing, having fun, even my men, and a smile curves my lips. They deserve this night, they deserve this forever, but sometimes you have to fight for what you want.

It's a sordid reminder that I am the reason these men, these people, might die. Their blood will be on my hands, and with that I don't feel like celebrating anymore, so I down my cup and slip away into the trees to check the perimeter, to take over for someone who wants to participate. I blend into the dark, moving through the trees on silent feet and letting the quiet soothe me as I venture deeper than ever before. I don't stop at our normal patrol routes, I keep going, hiking up an incline until I find a massive boulder at the base of the mountain, high enough that it looks out over the land and trees. Climbing it, I sit cross-legged, staring out at the Wastes before glancing back at the fires of my home.

Blowing out a breath, I lie down, my hands beside me, and watch the moon and stars above. My parents used to tell me tales of cities so big and high you couldn't even see the stars anymore, something called pollution, but here, now? They shine bright, the night sky filled with them. Who knows, maybe the earth is recovering.

Healing.

Maybe all it took was a mighty fall, wiping out the humans who hurt it until only the strong survived.

I can understand that.

I let my thoughts float away, my head empty for once as I stare up at those stars. I feel close to my parents for a moment and my heart flip-flops. I wonder if they would be proud if they could see me now.

"Leaders seek solace with the gods and Earth before a battle. Is that what you are doing, little warrior?" comes a rough voice, and I grin as I sit up and turn around, trying to spot my moun- tain man. But I can't.

Not until he breaks away from the rocks down below a little, blending there so completely I skipped over him. How long has he been there? I don't ask, it doesn't matter.

"In a way, just having a moment before the madness of the next few days. Who knows what will happen or if I will even survive it, I just wanted to spend one more minute in this world." I shrug and he nods, leaping and landing onto the boulder next to me, the move so smooth I laugh. He sits down beside me, his feet dangling over the edge of the rock, and I go back to lying down, staring at the sky. His presence is comforting and quiet, just like I was craving. He is so close his arm brushes mine, but he doesn't move away and neither do I.

"You said you would follow me, why, because I am a pascha now?" I query curiously.

He turns to me, his mismatched eyes locking onto mine. "No."

"Then why?" I press, tilting my head to see him better, our fingers so close now I could reach out and twine them.

"Because you are a true warrior, I saw a spark in you. One that won't be put out, one I have been searching for since I was a child. You remind me of why I fight, Piper. What it means to be a warrior. I follow you because in your presence I feel something I never have before."

"What's that?" I whisper, searching his eyes, my heart racing, stomach clenching.

"Love."

My eyes fly wide and he grins. "I see the way you are with those men and your people. You love so deeply, so freely, expecting nothing in return. It's so beautiful, so simple, and it kindles a yearning in me," he growls, smashing his fist into his chest. "In here, to find that, to find somewhere to belong, and I think I have...here at your side, wherever that leads me."

What do I say to that?

I dart my tongue out to dampen my lips, and he tracks the movement with his eyes before reaching out and brushing his thumb across the path my tongue just took. My breath catches in my throat as I watch him. This fierce mountain man surprises me at every turn. He admits he's looking for love, someone to hold... after all, isn't everyone?

"You always have had a destiny, little warrior, everyone on this earth does. And I think mine is you."

"You should trade yours in," I joke. "You got a bad deal there."

He smiles slowly but doesn't answer me, just turns back to the stars and looks at them. So I do the same, but my heart skips a beat when he finally crosses the distance I wasn't brave enough to, and covers my hand with his rough, warm, bigger one.

"You will do great things, Piper, and I will be there to see it," he murmurs to the sky, like a declaration, and I shiver from the force. This man is something else. Just like the others, he appeals to me in a way I can't describe, but I feel guilty for wanting him, even if the guys didn't seem to mind.

They each feel like a piece of my puzzle, slotting back into place.

I turn my head, my gaze searching his face to find answers to questions I don't even know how to ask. He turns and catches me staring, his eyes dropping to my lips once again as I suck in a breath, almost shivering from that look alone.

In his eyes, I see a question. I could turn away now and he wouldn't try, but I don't want to. My own words to my warriors echo through me. This could be one of my last nights on earth. I don't want to die with regrets, and not letting Clay kiss me? That would be a regret. So I gather my courage and lean towards him as he closes the gap, tilting his head down. His eyes remain on me the whole time, checking that I'm sure...until our lips first touch, and then he groans and closes them, cutting me off from the power of his mismatched gaze.

His mouth parts as I trace my tongue along his plump lips and sweep it inside his mouth, his own tangling with mine. Clay's big hand grips the back of my head as he kisses me desperately, but so sure, so confident...owning me.

Like I was made to be his.

I moan into his kiss, leaning into his wide chest and soaking up his warmth as he dominates my mouth, licking and sucking and kissing me with such ferocity, I have to clamp my legs together. Need, one so strong, rushes through me, and it's the most natural thing in the world to get to my knees without breaking our kiss and swing my leg over his lap until I am strad- dling him.

He angles his head up as his hands come to rest on my hips, grasping the skin there as he drags me higher up his thighs until I am perched on his hard, thick cock. We both groan then, swal- lowing each other's sound of need. This isn't a first kiss, this is a last kiss. For him at least. I can tell in the way he touches me, he doesn't plan on letting me go.

I hear a noise, a clearing of a throat, and we break away. I scramble to my feet and look around, breathing heavily, my heart racing and pussy wet. Clay stands next to me, sword out and ready, but we both relax when my shadow breaks away from a tree, and strolls out into the open with a shit-eating grin. Guilt cuts through me for a moment, but he winks to let me know it's okay, he's okay with what he saw.

"So here you guys are, come on, mountain weirdos, they are playing a game, and if we have to then you have to," Archel calls. I smile at Clay, and he jumps down from the rock and reaches up, helping me down, his hands on my hips, lingering there for a moment longer than necessary when my feet touch the ground. His kiss still fresh in my mind.

"Let's rejoin our people," he murmurs and I nod.

We spend the rest of the night drinking, laughing, and playing games. I even get Archel to sing for us, and we stumble back to our hut, squeezing into my bed...apart from Clay, who insists he is fine on the floor.

Tomorrow comes all too soon.

Chapter 25
Fucking Delight

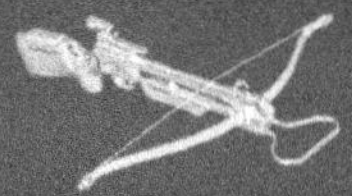

"**A**re all the warriors accounted for?" I call again.

"Yes, little warrior," Clay responds.

"Do we have all the medical equipment we need?" I blurt.

"Yes, Pip." Evan huffs, even though I've asked him eight times already.

I turn to Archel and Jago, and Jago's eyes narrow as I open my mouth, and before I know it his hand is covering my lips. "Hush, Brawler, we have everything. Everyone is here. We are ready, just breathe," he orders. So of course I lick his hand, making his lips quirk as he pulls it back.

"Breathe, yeah, I can do that." I nod, sucking in big lungfuls of air and ignoring the nerves rattling around my body and my mind, which is going a hundred miles an hour, shooting out random questions and thoughts faster than I can even speak. "There was this one time, there were like four of us playing hide and seek. Two boys and another girl, the girl wanted the boy who was trying to catch me, stupid Cathy, didn't she know Tommy only wanted me? Anyway, we were playing hide and seek, and I got so excited and nervous I forgot to breathe. So

225

there I was, hiding and not breathing until I eventually passed out, hidden behind this plant, you know? Someone ended up walking past and finding me and freaked out, thinking I had crawled behind this plant and just died." I nod and then suck in a breath. "Long story short, breathing is good, Cathy is stupid."

They are all just staring at me, mouths open and moving as if they don't know how to respond. My excessive breathing is the only sound between us until Archel starts laughing. "I seriously never know what you are going to do or say, Princess."

"Because I'm a fucking delight." I grin and turn to face everyone waiting for my orders. We have to take the trucks we brought here, it's the only way to transport all of our new warriors. They seemed concerned at first about riding in what one of them dubbed a 'metal beast,' but Clay told them to warrior up…or something more inspirational. We have four trucks, ten bikes, and three jeeps all waiting to go. Not including my men and I, there are over five hundred warriors in total. I hope it's enough.

Some of The Forgotten chose to come with us, Simon being one of them. Watching them say goodbye to their families made just how much I'm asking of them hit home, but it's too late to turn around now. At least I am not asking them anything that I am not willing to do myself.

Life or death, we all do it together now. No Lost, no Forgotten. Just one.

Huh, maybe we need a new name if we survive this, I think idly before shaking my head. I try to whistle, but fail, so I look over and Archel does it for me. All eyes turn to me, my mountain men stopping where they were beginning to climb into the trucks. It goes quiet and I take a deep breath, and with Jago's help, I hop up onto a jeep's bonnet to be seen easier.

"By tomorrow, we will reach the front line. The drive will be long and tiring with nothing to distract our minds, but the day after will be even longer. I'm asking for a big sacrifice, I know that. I know we won't all make it back, this is war. But know that anyone who fights with us, for us, you are fighting not just for me but for our people. For a future for the children still to come, so they can live in peace, so they can grow up in a free world, not one in chains. Yes, I'm asking a lot, but know that the outcome will be worth it. We are leaving now, so look around, say goodbye, memorise the faces you leave behind and take them with us. It could be the last time you do. For anyone who is scared, know that I am too, but it is not fear that makes us weak, it's the very fact that we keep going in spite of it that makes us strong. Keep fighting." I suck in a breath now, scanning the gathered crowd of men and women. In the middle I meet Trev's eyes and see the pride there and it strengthens me. "I want to thank you for taking me in, for giving me a home when I had none. I promise you, I won't stop fighting until our home is safe," I vow in front of everyone, and a cheer goes up as the trucks start. "We leave, so for anyone having second thoughts, know there is no shame in staying behind, but the time is now." I meet every eye I can. "For our home!" I call, and raise my crossbow as a chant goes up.

I turn around and take the hands of my assassin and doctor.

They help me down, pride and love shining in their eyes.

"Let's go, Princess." Archel grins. "Knew your mouth was good for something." He winks.

"Fuck, you're crazy, Pip, but I guess I am too." Evan laughs nervously.

"We got this, Team Piper for the win!" I tease, and they all groan as we head to the bikes at the front. Evan and Archel ride one, Clay is on another, and Jago and I are on the last...leading the way.

Leading my army.

We travel all day without stopping, only halting our journey when the moon is in the sky. We have massive numbers, so we don't try and hide, plus most people are heading to the front line now anyway. I do set up a perimeter though, because you can never be too careful. One of the perks of being a leader is that I don't have to take watch at least. Instead, we erect Worth's tent before joining my warriors outside.

They build fires and we all share a meal, someone starts to sing, another starts to play a guitar, and soon people are drinking and dancing. Some of The Lost even sing in a foreign language so beautiful that it brings tears to my eyes. Clay sits beside me, crooning in my ear in translation until I am panting with need from his proximity and voice alone.

The more I think of what's to come, the more fear takes over, and I have this need to be with my men. To touch them, kiss them, feel them in my body and prove to myself that they are here. That they are alive and with me. I don't want to think about it possibly being the last time or that I might lose one of them, or I might just chicken out and turn around to protect them.

I don't know how my men know, but they do, and their eyes turn to me filled with the same hunger and urgency, so I get to my feet, feeling powerful as they watch my every move, their bodies taut and ready to leap at me. With a wink, I turn and saunter back to our tent, feeling the flames of the fire dying away and the chill of the night taking over, sending a shiver down my back.

I am being hunted. I can feel it.

But this time, I want to be their prey.

I push through the tent and stand in the middle, my chest heaving from anticipation, my neck crawling with awareness as my fists clench together at my sides, waiting. Licking my lips, I tremble when a cool breeze brushes across my back before being replaced by a scorching heat, a body pressing against me. I don't know whose, I don't care. I'm a greedy bitch, I want them all tonight.

Tonight isn't the night for arguments or jealousy, it's the night to feel alive and human...to give into our desires. Our love.

Lips run along my neck, making me gasp at the heightened sensation of it. So sensual, maybe the fear and impending doom is making it all feel like...more. I fight the urge to turn my head and meet those exploring lips as I feel someone else stroke my side, then another set of hands joins to my right. All of their hands are on my body, caressing. Never stopping for long or touching where I need them.

I close my eyes and give in to their teasing, leaning back into the hard body behind me. I can tell now by the feel of him that it's Jago. His lips trail along the column of my throat, his hand coming around to squeeze my breast before he bites down on my neck and holds me there. I gasp, pain and pleasure shooting through me.

"Don't get lost in your mind, Brawler, eyes on us." How did he know?

I open them and he releases my neck, licking the bite mark lovingly, so achingly soft that I mewl, my own wetness coating my thighs in my trousers, longing for one of them to pay attention to my pussy.

Archel faces me now, his face hungry. Eyes alight. "You might be the pascha out there, but in here, tonight...you're ours, Princess," he whispers seductively. His eyes flick to my lips as he traces a hand down my front and cups my pussy through my trousers, making me groan and rub against his hand.

"I didn't hear her agree," comes Evan's teasing tone, and I look down to see him on his knees, his hands warming my ankles as he peers up at me with a cocky smirk. "Did you two?"

"I didn't, Doc, you are right." Archel grins, removing his hand from my pussy and tilting my chin up. "Princess, do you agree or do we need to prove it?"

"I agree," I murmur, ready to say anything to get his hand back where I need it.

"Good girl," Jago praises against my skin, pushing my head to the side to gain access to my neck where he leaves a path of stinging kisses.

"Yep, that's me. Now orgasms, please," I demand as dignified as I can, channelling my inner Worth.

"So needy," Archel teases, and cups my pussy again. "Do you promise to be a good girl?"

"No." I grin at him and he smirks.

"There's my girl." He laughs and then grabs my head and yanks me to him, covering my lips with his, swallowing my cry as Evan starts to pull down my trousers. I feel the air hit my bare pussy and ass, but Jago moves in behind me again, kissing my neck as Archel takes my mouth and Evan traces up my legs.

I have a moment to think of Clay, but it disappears when Evan parts my thighs and blows his warm breath across my pussy and Archel nips at my lips. Jago pulls me back, away from Archel who breaks our kiss and stares at me with dark eyes, lips parted.

My beast rips my shirt over my head and yanks off my bra, throwing them aside. I stand naked before them. They are still dressed, and it has the possibility of being overwhelming, but I have never been shy, and instead all I feel is powerful. These three men are ready to love me, worship me, and follow me into death itself...

I'm so lucky. I'm so loved.

But I'm not coming...not yet. "Mouth," I demand Evan, but he ignores me and my hands yanking on his hair, and teases me by running his nose along my wet center and then kissing each thigh as I grumble. I get it. I'm not in charge, so I relax and let them do what they want.

Only then does Evan lick along my pussy, tasting me and making me moan and reach for Archel. Jago's hands massage my ass, pushing me against Evan's mouth as he licks me like his favourite dessert, his tongue teasing as it dips into my pussy before circling my clit, again and again.

Archel kisses me once more, swallowing my moans of pleasure as I ride Evan's face. I am embarrassingly wet just from them taking charge, so when Evan finally flicks my clit, I scream. He sucks it into his mouth before lashing it with his tongue, his fingers plunging into my pussy but not moving, just stretching me as he throws me over the brink and I come, crying into Archel's mouth.

He pulls away, grinning even as I spot blood on his lip. I can't form a coherent thought, nevermind words, but he must see my gaze because he reaches up and dabs at the blood, his grin growing. "You bit my lip," he growls, but he doesn't seem hurt or upset...more proud. Men.

Before I can speak, I am spun to face Jago who kisses me hard, then pulls back and lifts me into the air. I wrap my legs around his waist and he drives into me, spearing my pussy with his hard cock, making me moan again. His hands grip my arse as he gives me no time to adjust, lifting and dropping me on his cock. He watches me, his eyes on fire, his hands rough, his cock hard and hitting that spot inside me that makes me moan and blurt things, and then suddenly, he's gone. He lifts me from his cock and tosses me to the bedspread where I bounce.

"Jago," I moan, spreading my legs wantonly. It's not like they haven't seen the goods before, and it was just getting interesting. He grins down at me, his cock wet and rock-hard.

My eyes flicker to Archel and Evan to see them playing rock-paper-scissors. Archel laughs when he wins and meets my eyes with a wink before starting to undress. "I wanted your mouth, Princess," he tells me.

I don't have time to think about what that means, because Jago gets to his knees next to me. "I'm going to take your ass, Brawler. I told you I would always have your back and I will tonight." A flash of desire shoots through me at his words and he leans closer, whispering against my lips. "I will keep my hand on your neck at all times so you know it's me. Tell me if you need us to stop. I will make them." He drops a soft kiss on my lips and rolls to his back, palming his cock and watching me.

Archel grabs me, holding me effortlessly, and lowers me until I'm straddling him and then he parts my ass cheeks. My heart slams against my chest as Archel strokes my face and Evan comes to my side, kissing my cheek. "Relax for us, Pip, you know we would never hurt you. We just want to make you feel good."

It's the fact that it's Evan saying those words, without jealousy in his eyes, that has me finally relaxing. He keeps eye contact with me as Jago slowly pushes into my ass, his cock wet from my pussy. He stops every inch or so, letting me stretch around him. I can feel his need, how much he wants to hammer into me, but he doesn't. He's gentle and loving, and when he finally bottoms out in my ass, I'm so full I can barely breathe, but also so turned on I can't help but squirm on his cock, making him grunt and slap my ass.

"Behave, Brawler," he commands. He drapes his arms around me and pulls me back until my spine is flush with his chest, his cock still in my ass, and this new position makes me cry out at how deep and hard I can feel him inside me.

He doesn't move, doesn't thrust, just keeps his promise by wrapping his hand around my neck, his thumb resting on my racing pulse as a reminder of who is behind me, then he stills altogether. If it wasn't for his heart beating and his cock jerking, I wouldn't even know he was there. But I can feel him, watching, waiting, protecting me always. My beast.

Evan crouches between our parted legs, his eyes flickering down my body hungrily and ending on my pussy before meeting my gaze. My eyes widen. Shit, is he going to fuck my pussy? Christ, will he even fit with Jago's cock in my ass? I know I said I had three holes, but I was being stupid...yet the idea has more cream leaking from my pussy.

Archel reaches down and swipes some up, licking it from his fingers and humming. "Better fuck her, Doc, before I get bored and do it for you."

Evan rolls his eyes but crawls up my body, sitting on his knees as he grips his cock and rubs it against my pussy, making my breath catch. Okay, I can see the appeal of the three holes thing.

"Evvie," I whisper, my voice cracked and pleading. He smirks at me and notches the head of his cock at my entrance, and only when I nod does he push inside. Not slow or steady, one smooth move. His long cock piercing me, filling me up. It's too much, I'm too full. They both hold still as I stretch and writhe around them, moaning at the feeling.

Then they start to move.

Evan pulls out and pushes back in, building up speed, fucking me slowly at first, but then it's like he can't help himself. He grunts, his thrusts coming harder...faster, and I close my eyes in bliss and then Jago. God, Jago.

When Evan pulls out, he pushes in, and they move in sync, working together to bring me pleasure. Their hands grip me, and Evan's mouth covers my nipple, sucking it in as Jago grips my neck. It's too much, too much...a tap comes at my lips and I turn my head and open my eyes to see Archel there. His hard cock waiting.

"Don't want to feel left out, Princess. Be a bad girl, won't you?" he teases, rubbing it along my lips as I gasp and moan, but touching him, feeling him, anchors me, so I grab his hard cock and suck him down, taking out my passion, my need, on him. He grunts, his cock jerking in my mouth, making my pussy clench down and the others cry out.

We are all one big ball of need, a circle of pleasure.

Archel fucks my mouth, not letting me take control as the others use my body. I'm theirs, they are mine. They know me better than anyone. Where to touch, where to lick. Their hands are everywhere, their cocks hard and branding me. Their noises of pleasure spurring me on.

Until it's too much.

Evan sucks my nipple, biting down hard.

Archel forces himself into my throat.

Jago squeezes my neck.

I come apart.

In their arms, I scream, sucking Archel down farther, my pussy tightening and milking Evan. With a groan, Archel explodes in my mouth and I swallow his release before he stumbles away. Evan yells and jerks between my thighs, his hot cum spurting in my pussy and filling me up before he falls away too, and then there is Jago.

He's fucking me so hard, so fast, I am just limp on top of him, letting him have his way. His heavy breathing brushes my ear, words of praise and love pouring out with each thrust until he reaches around and flicks my clit.

"Come," he orders...so I do.

I scream my pleasure into our tent as he drives into my ass once more and fills it with his cum.

My vision blackens from the pleasure, and when I come to, I am sprawled on Jago's chest. He pulls from my ass and we both groan, then Evan cleans me up as Jago moves away to wash himself, and then we all collapse on the bed, still breathing heavily but all smiling.

They wrap their arms around me, pulling me closer, and my heart...my damaged, tattered heart seals itself shut. Overflowing with their love. No matter what happens, we are together. What we have is beautiful and so different I know it's a once in a life- time type of love.

I love three men as a woman. As a leader.

Clay comes in and I smile sleepily. I was worried I wouldn't sleep tonight, and then I worried about where he was. I know we aren't at this point of our...relationship, or whatever we are, but I didn't want him sleeping out there either. He must see the ques- tions and thoughts in my mind that I don't even know how to begin to untangle, so he sneaks closer and dips his head, kissing me softly.

"Sleep, Pascha," he whispers, and curls up at my feet.

I lay my head back down, wearing a smile so full it might break my face.

"Goodnight," I whisper into the dark tent. With their bodies wrapped around me, I feel better, less lost...anchored by their pres- ence and whole now.

They fucked the worry right out of me, and my eyelids are heavy as I fall asleep in a cocoon of bodies. Tomorrow is a distant thought.

Chapter 26
Brought Some Friends

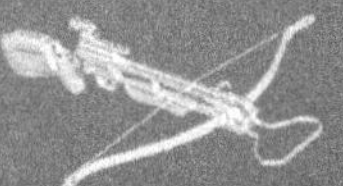

Even tangled up with my men, I wake early with energy and anxiety running through me. We have so much to do and the war is coming, I can feel it. So I wake my men with no chance of staying in bed. We pack up quickly, sharing teasing touches between us, and gather our people. Packing up takes little under an hour and then we are back on the road.

Soberer today, more serious, all of our people on edge. They can feel it too.

A change in the Wastes.

Today, I ride with Archel, and I squeeze him closer as we race through the sands. We only have a vague idea of where we are meeting the army Worth called together, so we travel for a long time. We stop for dinner, unlike before, because I want to make sure my men are okay and looked after. They have a fight coming up, after all. But today there are no laughter or songs, just a grim determination, and from The Lost...excitement and bloodlust.

Clay sneaks a kiss when no one else is looking, and I find myself smiling despite it all until I have to sigh and announce it's time to keep moving. Then I take to driving, Evan riding bitch as we head south. Passing a shanty city Archel described, it, too, seems sombre, serious, and almost empty.

We keep going past it, farther south than many have ever been, and I can feel my home growing distant, but I know I have to do this.

It takes two more hours before we see signs of life. There are men on patrol. They watch us but let us through. We slow down to show them we aren't threats and head straight until we see people up ahead.

There, in front of us, is Worth's amassed army. There are so many bodies spread across the sand they look like dots, and watching us arrive are three distinct figures. We pull up in front of them and I climb off to meet them—an older, plumper man, a skinny, creepy man, and an old woman who glares at me and points a shotgun.

"Who are ya?" she yells, and I grin as I hold up my hands. "Name's Piper, Worth sent me. Oh, and I brought a few

friends. Hope that's okay?" I wink.

The old woman laughs and drops her shotgun. "Well, why didn't ya say so, girlie? Come on, the more the fucking merrier. Hope ya brought some weapons 'cause it's going to get bloody."

"I was depending on it," I retort, and my men stream from the trucks behind me, forming a line as we face the other clan leaders. "Now, what's the plan? Because I have a few surprises I don't think the Cities people will be expecting."

Chapter 27
A War Line

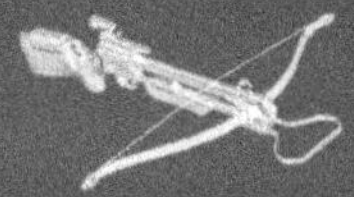

"She will be coming this way tomorrow morning if everything goes to plan," Nan tells me. We are gathered in the middle of their camp, my men mingling but staying close as I talk to the leaders to see where they need me and explain what I have planned.

"Okay, so we have until tomorrow morning to get everything ready. Split into teams. I want lookouts everywhere for tonight, we only sleep a few hours in case she comes early. Today, the others need to team up with a member of The Lost and help them set the explosives," I instruct, and only then do I realise I am almost questioning their judgement. I feel my men move closer as I wait for their anger, but they surprise me. A gleam enters the skinny man's eyes as he watches me, the man they introduced as Priest. The old man nods, Reeves, I was told, and Nan grins.

"Explosives?" Nan repeats with a twinkle in her eye.

I grin then. "Didn't think I wouldn't show up without some toys, did you? We set up fifty feet from our front line, and when they are close...boom!" I offer, and all the gathered leaders laugh.

"I like ya, I see why Worth invited ya." Nan grins, slapping my back and turning to the man next to her, Reeves. "Well, get on wit it, ya fat bastard, ya heard her! We got shit to do and hours to burn, let's show them fookers who they are messin wit!" she shouts, and everyone around us cheers.

It takes nearly all day but keeps my mind occupied. I help set the explosives. Clay shows me how and we assign each one to a member of The Lost who will be in charge of clicking the trigger tomorrow. The rest of the day is spent answering questions, and with the other leaders double and triple checking our war plans. We will stick to our people, each in charge of our own battalion to give the signal when we see Worth. The plan is simple, blow as many enemies to smithereens as we can, then we go in and clean up the rest with swords, guns, and bows. It keeps my mind busy, but my body is tense, wired up with anxiety of what is to come. There will be so much death.

I don't fear death, no, I fear the living more, but it doesn't mean I can face down an army without being scared. Responsibility is sitting heavily on my shoulders. If something goes wrong tomorrow, all these men I led here could die.

When it comes to sleeping in watches, I can't close my eyes. I sit on the line where we will stand tomorrow and stare out into the dark of the Wastelands. Far out on the horizon, I see the lights of the Cities, and I know tomorrow, ready or not, we will be at war. My men sit with me, all of us quiet for once, just holding each other, knowing it could be the very last time.

Before the sun rises, I kiss them all, looking deep into their eyes and telling them that I love them. Then, I wake the troops. There is no laughter or drinking today. No.

Today is a day for death, not happiness.

We stand as one army without division, not today. We stand in the scorching sun, in the sands that will soon run red with blood, and we wait. We wait for our queen.

A QUEEN
Epilogue

We wait for hours, not moving, not speaking. A waiting army. A trap.

Seeing Worth and the oncoming Cities trucks racing towards us, I step forward to lead my people, my fighters. My heart is racing from both fear and excitement, my hands tightening on my crossbow, my men framed behind me.

Turning, I stare them all down. I meet their eyes, my men...people of The Forgotten, Paradise, and The Lost united under one leader. One queen. One fight. "It's an honour to fight by your side today!" I yell, and they all cheer. "We fight for our future, our land, and our people! May we never be lost or forgotten again! Together, we are stronger than they! For our people! For our queen!" I shout, pointing my bow into the air as they scream their war cries with me.

It ripples through the thousands gathered in our line, everyone joining in the battle cry. Feet start to stomp and then a voice rises into the night. It's quiet at first, a lonely echo of one man singing the tale of our world. Then, another joins in, and another, until we all take up the song.

The lyrics are in our hearts, the beat the sounds of our weapons clashing.

This is our story, our world, not theirs. Not anymore.

We are warriors, rougher and tougher than they could imagine. Gathered from all over the Wastes, our only commonality is our determination to stay alive. To rebel in the face of danger, in death.

Voices climb, our cry going out to all four corners of the world, our song is our warning.

I hope they are ready, because they brought together the North, and now they will face our combined army with Worth as our leader.

Turning to face the front, I tilt my head back and let my voice join the others' cadence, pouring my heart, my very soul into it.

Heed our warning, Cities, for once where there was one woman...now lies an army.

I look to the men who are here with me, my men, my family. I started this journey alone, but I will never be alone again. Live or die, we do it together.

The assassin, the adventurer, the beast, the doctor, and the mountain man...

Always.

Acknowledgments

This book wouldn't have happened without Mal, the woman who encourages my crazy antics. Without Kaila and Jess eagerly awaiting chapters which meant I had to actually write them!
Of course, my readers. You are the reason I always write, why I always strive to be better. I hope I did Piper justice for you.

About K.A. Knight

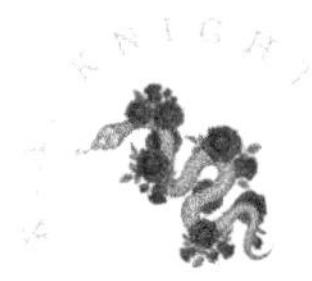

K.A Knight is an USA Today bestselling indie author trying to get all of the stories and characters out of her head, writing the monsters that you love to hate. She loves reading and devours every book she can get her hands on, and she also has a worrying caffeine addiction.

She leads her double life in a sleepy English town, where she spends her days writing like a crazy person.

Read more at K.A Knight's website or join her Facebook Reader Group.
Sign up for exclusive content and my newsletter here
http://eepurl.com/drLLoj

Other Books by K.A. Knight

CONTEMPORARY

LEGENDS AND LOVE *CONTEMPORARY RH*

Revolt

Rebel

Riot - coming soon..

PRETTY LIARS *CONTEMPORARY RH*

Unstoppable

Unbreakable

PINE VALLEY *CONTEMPORARY*

Racing Hearts

DEN OF VIPERS UNIVERSE STANDALONES

Scarlett Limerence *CONTEMPORARY*

Nadia's Salvation *CONTEMPORARY*

Alena's Revenge *CONTEMPORARY*

Den of Vipers *CONTEMPORARY RH*

Gangsters and Guns (Co-Write with Loxley Savage) *CONTEMPORARY RH*

FORBIDDEN READS *(STANDALONES)*

Daddy's Angel *CONTEMPORARY*

Stepbrothers' Darling *CONTEMPORARY RH*

STANDALONES

The Standby *CONTEMPORARY*

Diver's Heart *CONTEMPORARY RH*

DYSTOPIAN

THEIR CHAMPION SERIES *Dystopian RH*

The Wasteland

The Summit

The Cities

The Nations

Their Champion Coloring Book

Their Champion - the omnibus

The Forgotten

The Lost

The Damned

Their Champion Companion - the omnibus

PARANORMAL

THE LOST COVEN SERIES *PNR RH*

Aurora's Coven

Aurora's Betrayal

HER MONSTERS SERIES *PNR RH*

Rage

Hate

Book 3 - *coming soon..*

COURTS AND KINGS *PNR RH*

Court of Nightmares

Court of Death

Court of Beasts

Court of Heathens - coming soon..

THE FALLEN GODS SERIES *PNR*

Pretty Painful

Pretty Bloody

Pretty Stormy

Pretty Wild

Pretty Hot

Pretty Faces

Pretty Spelled

Fallen Gods - the omnibus 1

Fallen Gods - the omnibus 2

FORGOTTEN CITY *PNR*

Monstrous Lies

Monstrous Truths

Monstrous Ends

SCIENCE FICTION

DAWNBREAKER SERIES *SCI FI RH*

Voyage to Ayama

Dreaming of Ayama

STANDALONES

Crown of Stars *SCI FI RH*

***

SHARED WORLD PROJECTS

Blade of Iris - Mafia Wars *CONTEMPORARY RH*

***

CO-WRITES

CO-AUTHOR PROJECTS - *Erin O'Kane*

HER FREAKS SERIES *PNR Dystopian RH*

Circus Save Me

Taming The Ringmaster

Walking the Tightrope

Her Freaks Series - the omnibus

STANDALONES

The Hero Complex *PNR RH*

Dark Temptations *Collection of Short Stories, ft. One Night Only & Circus Saves Christmas*

THE WILD BOYS SERIES *CONTEMPORARY RH*

The Wild Interview

The Wild Tour

The Wild Finale

The Wild Boys - the omnibus

CO-AUTHOR PROJECTS - *Ivy Fox*

Deadly Love Series *CONTEMPORARY*

Deadly Affair

Deadly Match

Deadly Encounter

CO-AUTHOR PROJECTS - *Kendra Moreno*

STANDALONES

Stolen Trophy *CONTEMPORARY RH*

Fractured Shadows *PNR RH*

Shadowed Heart

Burn Me *PNR*

CO-AUTHOR PROJECTS - *Loxley Savage*

THE FORSAKEN SERIES *SCI FI RH*

Capturing Carmen

Stealing Shiloh

Harboring Harlow

STANDALONES

Gangsters and Guns *CONTEMPORARY*, IN DEN OF VIPERS' UNIVERSE

OTHER CO-WRITES

Shipwreck Souls (*with Kendra Moreno & Poppy Woods*)

The Horror Emporium (*with Kendra Moreno & Poppy Woods*)

AUDIOBOOKS

The Wasteland

The Summit

Rage

Hate

Den of Vipers (*From Podium Audio*)

Gangsters and Guns (*From Podium Audio*)

Daddy's Angel (*From Podium Audio*)

Stepbrothers' Darling (*From Podium Audio*)

Blade of Iris (*From Podium Audio*)

Deadly Affair (*From Podium Audio*)

Deadly Match (*From Podium Audio*)

Deadly Encounter (*From Podium Audio*)

Stolen Trophy (*From Podium Audio*)

Crown of Stars (*From Podium Audio*)

Monstrous Lies (*From Podium Audio*)

Monstrous Truth (*From Podium Audio*)

Monstrous Ends (*From Podium Audio*)

Court of Nightmares (*From Podium Audio*)

Unstoppable (*From Podium Audio*)

Unbreakable (*From Podium Audio*)

Fractured Shadows (*From Podium Audio*)

Revolt (*From Podium Audio*)

Rebel (*From Podium Audio*) - *coming soon*

Find an error?

Please email this information to thenuttyformatter1@gmail.com:

- *the author name*
- *title of the book*
- *screenshot of the error*
- *suggested correction*